Praise for *Quantum Santeria*

"Hernandez shows off his facility with a variety of concepts and genres, and each scene is realized to its full potential."

—*Publishers Weekly* (Starred Review)

"It's not every writer who can manage to be funny, terrifying, philosophical, metaphysical, and scientific at the same time, but narrative genre-blending is Carlos Hernandez's stock in trade. I start reading each story wondering what he's going to come up with next, and finish it having learned something about humanity and faith and also giant pandas or ghost jellyfish. A remarkable collection."

—Delia Sherman, author of *Young Woman in a Garden*

"Hernandez's *The Assimilated Cuban's Guide to Quantum Santeria* is fantastic and sincere, seamlessly blending science, magic and love. Whether rescuing trickster jellyfish frozen on Mount Everest, or reattaching legs to a lover's husband via superportation, Hernandez cuts to the human heart of each story and wraps an ebo around his readers."

—Eden Robinson, author of *Monkey Beach*

"In his debut collection, Carlos Hernandez explores the ways in which we conform our identities to fit into worlds that would otherwise break us. But all of his characters strive to reclaim the parts of themselves that could easily be thought of as lost. Funny, smart, and fierce, these stories are a breath of fresh air in a tightly constricted world."

—Christopher Barzak, author of *Wonders of the Invisible World*

"Irreverent, ebullient, dark, hopeful, sharply funny, and achingly sensitive, Hernandez brings us a rich tapestry of Latino experience. Absolutely not to be missed."

—Julia Rios

"*The Assimilated Cuban's Guide to Quantum Santeria* by Carlos Hernandez is an exceptional collection of imaginative stories that are as captivating as they are entertaining."

—Erin Underwood, editor *The Grimm Future*

"These delightful stories from Carlos Hernandez dance with a light step and a knowing wink, and yet that effervescent surface wraps jaw-dropping twists and mind-bending concepts within its boundaries. Science fiction and magical realism freely fraternize, quantum fluctuation and ritual incantations just two aspects of the same great mystery. In these intimate stories of families rent apart and repaired, that mystery is just as likely to be encountered in a humble kitchen or a lover's bed as it is in outer space or the deepest trenches of the ocean. Each story is a shimmering pond that once dived in proves bottomless. *The Assimilated Cuban's Guide to Quantum Santeria* is a remarkable debut, an intoxicating breath of fresh air."

—Mike Allen, editor of *Clockwork Phoenix*, author of *Unseaming*, Nebula and Shirley Jackson Award finalist

"*The Assimilated Guide to Quantum Santeria* is fiercely smart and entertaining; a polished collection of stories by one of speculative fiction's most distinctive and original voices.

"Hernandez's science fantasy transfixes as it explores technological paradoxes and inhuman intelligences in compellingly human (and humane) ways. And the Latino urban (and suburban) fantasy pieces sprinkled into the collection are like the best dark añejo rum: warm, smoky, exquisitely sharp and sweet. Hernandez's stories go down smooth and easy, and finish with a kick."

—Sabrina Vourvoulias, author of *Ink*

"Carlos Hernandez swindles you with a mixture of levity, authenticity, and sorrow that's too true to be unreal."

—Charles Tan

"Carlos Hernandez treats science, culture, and genre with a bracing irreverence. *The Assimilated Cuban's Guide to Quantum Santeria* is a zany, kaleidoscopic whirl of a book that delivers both tantalizing 'what ifs' and moments of true pathos."

—Sofia Samatar, author of *A Stranger in Olondria*

CARLOS HERNANDEZ

Earlier versions of stories from *The Assimilated Cuban's Guide to Quantum Santeria* appeared in the following publications:

"The Aphotic Ghost" in Bewere the *Night, Prime,* 2011; "Homeostasis" in Futurismic, 2009; "The International Studbook of the Giant Panda," in *Interzone,* 2013; "The Macrobe Conservation Project" in *Interzone,* January 2006; "Los Simpáticos" in *Hit List: The Latino Mystery Reader.* Arte Público Press, 2009; "More Than Pigs and Rosaries Can Give" in *Exotic Gothic V,* Volume 2, PS Publishing, 2013; "Bone of My Bone" in *Cosmopsis Quarterly,* Fall 2007; "American Moat" in *A Robot, A Cyborg & a Martian Walk into a Space Bar,* Nomadic Delirium, 2015; "Fantaisie Impromptu No. 4 in C#min, Op. 66" in *Crossed Genres Magazine,* Crossed Genres Press, 2014; "The Assimilated Cuban's Guide to Quantum Santeria" in *Interfictions II,* November 2009.

Rosarium Publishing
P.O. Box 544
Greenbelt, MD 20768-0544

ISBN: 978-1-4956-0739-4
LCCN: 2015937847

Cover Art by Bizhan Khodabandeh

Claire,

You're the most perfectly named person I've ever known.

THE ASSIMILATED CUBAN'S GUIDE TO QUANTUM SANTERIA

Table of Contents

Introduction

by Jeffrey Ford

The title of this collection, *The Assimilated Cuban's Guide to Quantum Santeria*, seemed wonderfully outlandish to me when I first encountered it. To the contrary, though, the book perfectly delivers on that title as if only that title could do it justice. Everything it suggests is here–Science, Faith, Assimilation, Particle Physics, Cuba, contemporary Latino culture in the U.S., and a sensibility that recognizes a vast world beyond. Not only do each of these elements appear within the book, but they appear, very often all at once, in each of the book's dozen stories. What with all these themes weaving together throughout, Hernandez's collection gives the effect of seeming greater than the sum of its parts. None of this becomes obtrusive in the reading. The stories are too strong–the narrative drive, the voice, the concision in writing, the smart dialogue, the slyly judicious application of research. They gracefully balance the book's thematic concerns. As a writer of short stories, I found much to admire in *The Guide* and as a reader, even more. Following are a few observations that struck my fancy and sparked my imagination.

There are "real" science fiction stories in this collection. What I mean by "real" is that the nature of the technology or the aspect of the physical universe that is central to the plot resonates metaphorically with the plight of the character or characters. This is a type of story-telling you don't encounter much in SF but which makes for the finest stories. Finding that metaphor to bridge the character and technology is often very difficult, so writers don't bother with it and what you wind up with is an adventure tale. I like a good adventure tale, but I'd rather find a "real" work of science fiction–the kind written by authors like Ted Chiang. Hernandez includes a number of such stories in *The Guide*, and the beauty of them is that they don't traffic in the technologies of past generations–rockets, ray guns, witty robots. The technologies at the core of these stories are extrapolated from cutting edge discoveries in a whole host of fields from neuroscience to the Aphotic Zone. As well, the characters' issues are contemporary ones we might witness or experience ourselves.

I mentioned earlier that there was a lot I admired about this book. The technique that makes these science fiction stories believable within the context of their fictional worlds is the author's research. Hernandez has obviously done his homework in that his explanations as to the nature of certain technologies or physical phenomena have a confident clarity to them. They are firmly based in science and so convincingly explained that it's difficult to tell where the science leaves off and the fiction begins. As a story writer, I love that sleight of hand. It takes a graceful touch to parse out research to the reader–not too much, not too little–so that the result is effective and yet not generally noticed. This goes for the stories in the collection that are also not science fiction. Aspects of history, culture, politics that appear throughout all seem right on, offering no reason to doubt their validity. This serves to draw the reader more fully into the story.

Although Latino characters appear in the early science fiction stories of the collection, you'll notice that Latino culture, and specifically Cuban and Cuban-American culture become more prevalently the focus of the fiction as you continue through the book. It's not that this is definitive, because some of the later stories deal with Science as well. These pieces range from the weird to the absurd to the fantastic. What's wonderful about all of the stories is that Hernandez very economically creates interesting characters, who, even though they don't always do the right thing for themselves or others, we root for them, we care about them. There's an emotional core to all of the stories here. Even in the midst of humor or horror, there's a human connection at play. There's something for the reader beyond the dazzling science and the enigmatic, beyond the clarity of the writing. These stories always return us to ourselves where we find the connection with a character's foibles, triumphs, mistakes, loneliness, fear, joy.

It's clear to see, through the writing, that this connection is at the core of the author's intent. There are very few instances of structural pyrotechnics. What you get is pretty much all story, all the time. Beginnings, middles, ends. The masterful economy of writing and the undeniable narrative drive pull the reader in and don't let go. With each of these pieces, it took no more than a paragraph, and often less, to hook me and make me want to find out what happens next. Nothing compares to a classic story structure with clear, descriptive writing. All of these stories, for whatever else is happening in them, no matter amazing scientific concepts or the mysteries of Santeria, concentrate their energy primarily on the character/characters and how they deal with their dilemma(s), their desire to connect, to understand themselves and where they belong. This is where the real power comes from in Hernandez's fiction.

Going back to the title of the book, which I mention in my opening paragraph, you might wonder where the "Quantum" aspect can be found. I counted a half dozen instances of the mention of or allusion to some concept from quantum physics (I'm betting there are more)– Schrodinger's Cat, the multiple universes theory, Heisenberg's Uncertainty Principle, etc. They lurk in the background of the stories and sometimes move forward to affect the outcome of the plot. It's fitting they should permeate the book in that they hint at probability instead of certainty. All of the stories here continue to give that sense of uncertainty, that impetus to make you read on, until at the very end when the wave collapses and the reader experiences the outcome of the drama. In other words, nothing is predictable to a certainty. How many times do you find fiction that you can say that about?

My last observation is one also involving the title. What better guide could an assimilated Cuban have than another assimilated Cuban. Hernandez's family is Cuban, and we get to see the world from a Latino perspective in these stories. The pieces where this is most obvious are some of my favorites in the book. Although I'm accessing these through the filter of a different culture, there is some magic there that allows me to find myself in them most readily. There is great humor and pathos in these stories. The descriptions of those things I'm unfamiliar with are succinct and illuminating, and I'm never confused as to what's going on. Perhaps the best of all is the final story of the book that carries the collection's title. Santeria, which is mentioned in the title and has an important part in the story, is the religion of African slaves brought to Cuba; a mix of Yoruban beliefs and practices blended with some Catholicism and native Caribbean faith. Because these slaves were not permitted to practice their religion outright, they had to veil their saints and holy figures behind those the Catholic Church approved of. In other words, they assimilated themselves and their religion into the new world. This assimilation was not a forsaking of their culture or religion but a way for it to survive and thrive against the horrors and iniquities of slavery. Hernandez's *Guide* is about how to survive contemporary culture with its incredible scientific advancements and mishaps, its sometimes tenuous relationships, its lack of certainty, its treacherous racial and cultural divides, and through all of it to be able to encompass your past and manage to hold on to who you really are.

An ingenious title for a wonderful collection. I hope you enjoy it as much as I did.

The Aphotic Ghost

Mountain

Sometimes when a body dies in Everest's Death Zone, it doesn't come down. Too difficult, too much risk for the living. Thing is, it's so cold up there, bodies don't rot. They get buried by snow periodically, but the terrific winds of the South Col reliably reveal them: blue, petrified, horned by icicles, still in their climbing gear, always forever ascending. They scandalize the Westerners who paid good money to climb Everest and who don't especially want to be reminded of how deadly the journey can be. But then their Sherpas usher them past the garden of corpses and, weather permitting, to the top of the world.

I am a Westerner, and I paid good money to climb Everest. But the summit wasn't my goal. I was going to get my son Lazaro off of that mountain, dead or alive.

Sea-Level

Lazaro's mother, Dolores Thomaston, taught twelfth-grade biology at the same school where I taught AP World History: Bush High, right on the Texas-Mexico border. Lazaro was born of a dalliance between us almost three decades ago.

Dolores had an Australian ebullience and a black sense of humor and a seeming immunity to neurosis that made her irresistible to me. She could have been 25 or 55, and I never found out which. She'd made a splash in the scientific world a few years before coming to Bush with a paper she co-authored on a deep-sea jellyfish that, interestingly, was immortal. After it reproduced, it returned to a pre-sexual polyp state through a process called cell transdifferentiation, and then become an adult again, and then a polyp, and so on. The layman's version is this: age meant nothing to that jelly. It only died if something killed it.

Dolores and I spent the summer together. I really believed we were on our way to getting married. That's why I wasn't worried when she started talking children. In fact, I was surprised to discover how much the idea of children tickled me. I had no idea how much I wanted to be a father until she put the prospect before me. I'd spent all of my adult life contemplating history, and now, suddenly, I was awash with dreams of the future.

She asked me what I would name the child, so I told her: "Brumhilda."

"Be serious," she said.

"I am!"

"Yeah? So what if it's a boy?"

I kissed her, the first of many that night. And then I said, "Lazaro."

Aphotic Zone

Dolores didn't just leave me. She vanished right after we consummated our relationship. She left a note on her pillow that I promptly set fire to in a skillet before reading, then spent the next two decades wishing I hadn't.

I didn't know she had died during childbirth, that she had opted for an ocean water-birth. Ocean-birthing. Of all the crazy trends. She never left the water.

I found all of this out from a young man named Lazaro Thomaston when he came to meet me. He was 21, already a man. By then I'd missed my chance to be his father.

Sea-Level

An hour since I'd learned I'd been a father for 21 years, Lazaro sat on the couch with me, showing me his portfolio. He worked as an underwater photographer and videographer. "It's second nature to me, being in the water," he said. "Really it's the ocean that raised me."

"Looks like the ocean did a pretty good job," I said.

He specialized in ultra-deep dives, descents into the bathyal region, which is the topmost stratum of the ocean's aphotic zone: lightless, crushing, utterly hostile. There he had recorded a score of species new to science; he'd made his reputation before he could take a legal drink. His images were haunting and minimalist, the engulfing darkness defied only by the weak bioluminescence of the sea life and, of course, him. Off-camera, he shined like a sun, illumining the depths like the first day of creation.

"These are incredible," I said. "You must he half fish."

"Got that from Mom," he said. And turned the page.

Mountain

Rather than take a leave of absence from work to climb Everest, I retired early. Lost some money that way, but I had more than enough money to get to the summit, get back, and bury my son. After that, the future would take care of itself. Or go fuck itself. Either way.

I was old to climb the world's tallest mountain, but not as old as some. The ascent from the Southeast ridge is by mountaineering standards fairly straightforward, especially with today's technology. If you died it was because you were reckless, or bad weather surprised you, or your body gave out and you probably should never have attempted it in the first place.

I was in reasonably good shape, but I needed work—strength-training, flexibility, cardio cardio cardio. And yoga: 60 years old, and I'd never learned to breathe. Guess it was time.

I learned to slow my heart. I learned efficiency, repose, elegance of movement. I learned to require less of everything: food, water, air, joy, meaning. I learned to sit.

I bought more gear than I could possibly use in ten ascents, watched every mountaineering video I could find, moved for a season to Colorado where I took a course on mountain climbing specifically geared toward seniors.

I finished top of the class. My instructor said he'd never seen anyone of any age so motivated. But he also said mountain climbing's supposed to be fun. Why so grim? Why was I going to climb Everest if not to have one of the greatest experiences of my life?

I told him my son was lost on Everest and that I was going to find him, but of course it'd been months and I hadn't heard any good news, so he was dead. But I'd be damned if I was going to let my son's body pose for eternity like a movie prop in Everest's death zone so that overprivileged jetsetters could get an extra thrill off of him. I was climbing to claim my son's body—if I could find him, if I could pick-axe his remains free from the mountainside—and bring him home.

But yeah, asshole, I'll try to have a grand old time all the way up.

Sea-Level

Lazaro and I had five good years together, during which time he told me almost nothing about his life prior to our reconnecting. I didn't take it personally. He wanted to sever himself from his childhood the way a lizard drops its tail to escape a predator. Whatever his past was, Lazaro wanted nothing to do with it.

I didn't pry. I figured he would tell me when he was ready.

But he never became ready. Instead, he anchored his life to the present, to me. And that happened to be more or less exactly what I wanted. I couldn't go back and be the father he'd never had growing up, but as consolation prizes go, this was the next best thing.

I'm a historian. I should have known better. Histories never stay severed. Like the tail of a lizard, they grow back.

Mountain

There was exactly one guide who would attempt something as stupid as trying to descend Everest with a dead body in tow. He had a Nepalese name but a British accent. To dumb-ass tourists like me he went by Roger.

His main suggestion was that we needed as many Sherpas as I could afford to help search for Lazaro. I could sell all of my extra mountaineering equipment at Base Camp to the rich and underprepared. There's where I'd get top dollar.

"I was hoping it'd just be you and me," I told him. "I don't really want a lot of people around."

He sighed. "Imagine a needle in a haystack," he said. "Now douse the haystack with water, and stick it in an industrial freezer until it's a solid hump of ice. Now remove all the oxygen from the freezer. Now put fifty kilos of equipment on your back. Now go get that needle."

Point taken. But what would I tell all those Sherpas? How could I instruct them what to look for without them thinking I was crazy?

But truly, what frightened me more was the prospect that they'd actually believe me. The Sherpa brand of Buddhism is animist enough that, when I told them what they were looking for, they might accept it as true. Accept it, and then get the fuck off Everest.

Aphotic Zone

I was leaving for Lukla in four days. My equipment had already left. It was too soon for adrenaline but too late to think of anything else. I sat in my living room and didn't read and didn't watch TV and didn't turn on the lights. My own little bathyal region.

Doorbell. I had ordered a pizza. I opened the door and it was Dolores.

She was 25 now, if that; there was nothing 55 about her. She was dressed for a Texas May: naked as the law allowed. Her body was muscled and sleek, like a gazelle's. Her hair was a corona. And that smile. That tilt of the head.

"Oh my," she said. "It's so good to see you, Enrique."

She was so composed. She was waiting for me to digest what I was seeing. But there was mischief there too, that evil sense of humor, even at a time like this. It really was her.

When I didn't speak, she said, "I told you I'd be back one day. So here I am, love. I'm back."

I didn't respond, and she watched me for a long time not responding. Her face drained of mirth. "In the note?" she said like a question. "You got my note, right?"

"I burned it on the stove," I said.

"Ah." Then she laughed. "Now was that any way to treat me, after what we shared? You wouldn't even read my explanation?"

"Treat you? You left me, Dolores."

"And I explained why in the note, love. It was quite necessary. That's why I left it—so you would understand."

"You're the one who needs to understand. Seeing that Dear John on the pillow, it ... it ruined me, Dolores. Until Lazaro came into my life I was in ruins."

She came close, then hooked her arms around my neck, and I

let her. Hers was not the body my body remembered. It fit foreignly against me.

"Have you been working out, love?" she asked, lips puckered puckishly.

"Apparently not as much as you," I said. And then: "Lazaro. I assume you know?"

"That's why I'm here, love. To help you. To save him."

Oh. Oh no. I suddenly felt tired and old. Whatever my own feelings about seeing her again were, I couldn't let her think her son was still alive, not after he'd been missing for months at the top of Everest. "Dolores, I'm not going to try to rescue Lazaro. I'm going to claim his body. Lazaro is dead."

"No, love."

"Dolores, listen—"

"He's not," she interrupted. But her expression was not that of a mother in denial; she looked at me pityingly, her mouth sagging with remorse. "There's so much I need to tell you."

She always could be a little condescending. And that helped me remember my anger. I broke our embrace. "What the hell makes you think I want to talk to you? You left me, Dolores. I thought we were going to get married. You left without a trace."

I could see she was about to remind me again that I had burned her note. But instead she metronomed her head to the other shoulder, smiling ruefully. "Do you hate me?"

"I think I do."

"I can tell you don't."

I sighed. "Maybe not yet. I'm still in shock. But I almost certainly will hate you. So let's talk before the hatred sets in and I refuse to ever speak to you again."

She came close again and hugged me to her and stood on her toes, allowing our breath to mix between our noses like a storm front. "Later, love," she said. "First, let's make up a little."

Sea-Level

Lazaro's most recent film, "The Aphotic Ghost," was nominated for an Oscar in short documentary a year ago. It chronicled a new species of jellyfish over 150 cm in diameter, a superpredator by bathepelagaic standards. As it fluttered about the lightless ocean depths, its body took on a vaguely pentangular shape, but with its five points rounded off. It looked almost like an undulating chalk outline, and its blue-white bioluminescence made it positively spectral: thus the name.

Lazaro's footage was gorgeous, unbelievably intimate. Jellyfish usually squirt away from lights and cameras as fast as they can, but the aphotic ghost—enormous, tremulous, poisonous, ethereal—let Lazaro swim along with it and gather images that were not only scientifically priceless but commercially lucrative.

It was me he took to the Academy Awards show. When he won the Oscar, the shot cut to me for three seconds. The caption read "Montenegro's Father." Not Thomaston, but Montenegro. By this point he'd taken my surname.

Mountain

"Why do you want to climb Everest?" I asked Lazaro.

"I'm always in the water," he said. He went over to the fish tank he'd convinced me to get. It was a saltwater tank two meters in diameter specially made for jellyfish: a Kreisel model with a constant flow of water whisking the jellies around like a washing machine. That's exactly what it looked like: a futuristic upright jellyfish washer.

I looked up from my book. "So now you want to go to the highest point on Earth because ... it's the farthest place from sea level?"

He smiled ruefully. "Something like that."

"Seems to me like the ocean's been good to you."

He turned back to the tank and watched the jellies spin. Sometimes the tank looked to me like a bird's-eye model of the galaxies. Other times it made me sad, these small, nearly mindless creatures being infinitely jetted around a tiny glass container for my viewing pleasure. They had no comprehension of the forces that governed them. They had no idea their lives were in my hands. And who was I to have dominion over anything?

"It has," he said finally. "The ocean has been my whole life. But it's also defined me." And then, a little softer, he added, "Limited me."

"Still, Lazaro, Everest is one of the most inhospitable places on Earth. You're an expert when it comes to deep-sea diving. But on a mountain you'll be—"

"—like a fish out of water?" he finished.

No mistaking his tone; he was dead-set. So I smiled and turned back to my book and simply said, "Something like that."

Aphotic Zone

Dolores stayed the night. We made love. Because I couldn't keep up with her, she kindly slowed for me.

After, she asked me to be patient. She said Lazaro was alive, but when she told me how she knew, I wouldn't believe her. But she'd find a way to explain so I would believe, and then I would save Lazaro. I didn't know what she was talking about, but my mind was aswim, awash, adrift. I let myself be overwhelmed by her. We entangled ourselves in each other and fell asleep.

When I woke I found she had disentangled herself. A note on the pillow said, "Read before burning." When I opened it, however, there was just a single word. "Bathroom."

One of Lazaro's video cameras was pointed at the bathtub. Taped to it was a note that read, "View before burning. Full explanation!"

The tub was full. Next to it was the freezer's icemaker bucket, emptied, and a box of Instant Ocean, which is what I used to salinate the jellytank water. It was empty too.

In the tub, its blue-white glow refracting through the ice, filling and emptying like a lung, was a fully mature aphotic ghost.

Mountain

I climbed Everest. More honest: Roger and the Sherpas climbed Everest and hoisted me behind them. They might as well have carried me up on a palanquin for all the effort I expended.

The search began the day after we arrived at the South Col. The weather was cooperating for now, and forecasts were good. If we were lucky we might get two days.

The cold had sunk an inch down into my body, anesthetizing me, preventing both hope and despair. It was the only reason I could function, this close to knowing. If I failed to find Lazaro, I could try again someday. But if I succeeded, he would be alive or dead. The wave would collapse. I would eject him from his superposition and either bring him back to life, or reify his death.

We searched half a day. I saw many bodies, none of them Lazaro. I wondered briefly if I shouldn't make it the work of the rest of my life to bring the dead down and present them back to their families. But let's see if I could succeed on my own mission first.

Roger, with a Rumpelstilskin-like prescience, knew not to pry, but the Sherpas couldn't comprehend that I couldn't care less about the stark and ominous wonders Everest offered. So, thinking I was like every other tourist, they kept trying to show me the sights. Two of them were dying to show me the most curious ice formation they'd ever seen.

I perked up. Ice formation? I followed.

It had appeared out of the ground last season, they said. They exhumed it out of the recent snow for me to see. It was the size of a sleeping dog and looked something like hand-blown Italian glass, impossibly whorling and curling into itself, a hyaline nautilus relentlessly tearing sunlight into rainbows. Deep in its center there seemed to be a dark nucleus, and strange, ciliated veins circuited throughout its interior. Climbing gear radiated from it like an explosion.

"Roger!" I yelled.

Roger came. "We need the cooler," I said.

He spoke to the Sherpas and they brought the coffin-sized cooler I had had specially made. It borrowed from ice-cream maker technology, had liquid nitrogen lining the metal interior. After I delicately placed the ice formation inside of it, I found I could just close the lid. "Tell them to help me pack it with snow," I said. Soon every Sherpa who could fit around the cooler was dumping snow and ice into it. When it was full I padlocked the lid.

I was weeping, but no one could tell because everyone's eyes cry this high up, and anyway tears freeze before they fall. I took several hits from my oxygen tank, then said, "Roger, this is futile. I'll have to reconcile myself to the fact that Everest will be my son's final resting place. We'll have to abandon the search. Gather the men."

I could see he knew there was more to the story. But all he said to me was, "Right." Then he told the Sherpas what I said. A few of them looked at me incredulously—the search had hardly begun, and now I was content to leave with just an ice-souvenir?—but the more experienced among them simply started packing up. Americans were generally regarded as the best tippers in the world, even when an Everest ascent failed. Tolerating their strange ways was a small price to pay.

Sea-Level

It was my fourth date with Imelda. She was a year older than me. She didn't dye her hair and was a retired librarian and said if I ever caught her playing Bingo I had her permission to kill her on the spot.

We had met through Back from Heaven, the nonprofit I founded to recover the bodies of those who died on Everest. She had joined me on our latest mission, our most successful to date: three deceased climbers retrieved, identified, and returned to their loved ones. One ascent and she was hooked; she joined the team as a full-time volunteer researcher.

And now we were seeing each other. And things were moving fast. Just four dates in and we were going back to my place.

I unlocked the door, reached around to flip the lights, then gestured gallantly for her to enter. She curtsied and strolled in.

And saw the tanks. I still had the smaller Kreisel with my original smack of jellyfish eternally smacking into each other, but what stopped her midstep was the new tank. It took up the wall, a tremendous bubbling cauldron of cornerless glass. In it, the two most enormous jellyfish she'd ever seen pulsed with slow dignity through the water, their blue-white auras commingling. A third one, still just a polyp, trailed behind them.

"Jesus!" she said. "Wow. Just wow."

"Do you like it?" I asked, moving behind her, wrapping my arms around her waist.

She leaned against me. "They're so beautiful." And then, searching for a more precise description, "So unearthly."

"My son's an underwater filmmaker. He discovered this species of jellyfish."

She turned to face me, rested her hands on my shoulders. "No!"

"Really. You'll meet him someday. And I'll have to show you his masterwork: 'The Aphotic Ghost.' He won an Oscar for it." I directed her attention to the mantle.

She looked, then turned back to me and smiled. "You are just endlessly surprising, Enrique." Then, turning herself back to the tank, but belting my arms to her body, she said, "So when do I get to meet the Academy-Award-winning filmmaker?"

"It's going to be awhile, I'm afraid. He's spending time with his mother right now."

"Ah. I see. Let me guess. You and she can't be in the same room together?"

"Not at all. We're in the same room all the time. And she'll always have a special place in my heart. It's just that ... well, let's just say we come from two different worlds."

"Say no more," she said, squeezing my arm. She turned back to the larger tank and, after a moment's contemplation, she pointed at the polyp and said, "The tiny one's cute. Does it have a name?"

"She does," I said, pulling Imelda a little closer. "Brumhilda."

Homeostasis

Eight seconds of footage, from a security camera so old it surrounds every object in the picture with rainbows. Man at a gas station robbing the attendant. Pantyhose flattening his nose. Waving a small, mean knife like a snakecharmer's pungi.

Customer walks in. Good-looking guy, California hair, white as a country club. Has no idea; walks in texting. The robber runs over and slams the knife through the top of his head. In to the hilt.

Someone with the username "venividivicibitches" tries to troll /r/ funny with an animated gif from the security camera that infinitely loops the last few seconds of the attack and ends with the subtitle "lol." Unsurprisingly, redditors downvote it into obscurity.

~

Angela in the waiting room with her kids. Greg Jr. is painstakingly choosing his playlist. Lucy is asleep, her Hello Kitty purse wobbling treacherously on the precipice of her knees. Chase is unknotting his shoelaces. He's only learned to tie them, likes to practice.

This is the end of everything, thinks Angela. It's her only thought; it repeats like that animated gif she saw of Greg on Reddit. She has luminous wet patches beneath her eyes, remnants of the tears she obliterated before her children could spot them. Thank God for no-run mascara.

An IC nurse is jogging toward them. It's Bonnie. She is 270 pounds, wears pediatric scrubs covered in cartwheeling pandas. Still a full first down away from the waiting room, she yells, "Ms. Justice!"

Greg Jr. yanks out his earbuds; Chase stops playing with his laces; Lucy opens her eyes instantly. She had been fake-sleeping.

"Greg?" asks Angela.

Bonnie reaches the waiting room. Stops, stoops, grips her thighs for support. Huffs and swallows. "He's awake," she manages. "He just opened his eyes."

Angela forgets she has children. She runs.

~

"What's wrong with Daddy's head?" asks Lucy.

"Shut up, Lucy," says Greg Jr. He hits her, she starts crying, there is a scene. But it's Bonnie who must broker a truce. Angela is bedside, watching Greg. Chase, dead-faced, watches Angela.

Angela is so close to Greg's face she can see his vacant eyes saccade. He smells like he smells when he comes home from work, before his evening shower, after all the colognes and deodorants have died away. His own animal self.

The robber's knife went all the way through his head; its point poked out from his palate like a shark tooth. It's a miracle he didn't die instantly. It's a miracle he didn't die during the operation to remove it. It's a miracle his eyes are open and saccading.

The arc of skull they removed during the operation is 110 mm long by 40 mm wide by 25 mm deep. Where once was skull there is now a cream-colored computer. It bulges like a Mohawk from his head.

An eneural, it's called. Angela has heard of them, passingly. There was a report on *60 Minutes* a few months back: on the one hand, real people, who would otherwise be heads of cauliflower, leading normal lives thanks to eneurals; on the other, reports that crooked governments—including, allegedly, the U.S.!—are using them to control people's minds. So are eneurals good or bad? You decide.

The eneural is now Greg's corpus callosum. It will perform thalamic functions, will take over for damaged parts of his diencephalon. Without the eneural, he will never fall asleep again. Were it removed while he was asleep, he would not wake.

Everyone loves Chase because he has big eyes. Those eyes are locked onto his mother. He says "Mommy?" every once in a while, yanks on Angela's sleeve. To no avail. After today, he will trust the word "Mommy" a little less.

~

Greg's eyes had locked onto Angela's an hour ago. She put her hand on his cheek in response and nodded and raised her eyebrows as if to say, "Go ahead, Greg. Tell me." Then, twenty minutes ago, his bottom jaw started moving, like a dummy's. She watched him and cried as quietly as she could. She cried so quietly Lucy could hear her tears strike the bedsheet.

And now Greg, hoarse and dehydrated, blinks and says, "Hey you."

"Hey," says Angela.

~

Greg's knees and elbows don't work. He has to kick his whole leg forward when he walks. He can operate his fingers only in unison. Physical therapy is helping, but it's slow going. The other day the staff applauded him for picking up a pencil.

One night at dinner—he must eat with a bib now—he pushes himself free of the table and moans and stands and sticks out his arms and starts making his stumbling way toward Chase.

He and Chase used to love to play Frankenstein. Greg thinks it's one thing he can still do. Hell, maybe his condition will even improve his impersonation.

Greg Jr. instantly understands what his dad is doing and feels humiliated. He hates that bib more than anything. Lucy, who'd been stirring her food rather than eating it, starts barking out fake, forced laughter. Angela launches herself out of the chair and follows Greg with mincing steps. "Are you okay?" she subvocalizes in his ear. She doesn't know what is happening. She has read all the conspiracy theories surrounding eneurals she could Google and is only 99% convinced there's nothing to them.

Chase used to run howling from the table and hide, giggling loudly, behind the sofa. But now, with big, inscrutable eyes, he just licks mashed potatoes off his spoon and watches Greg approach. Greg pauses in front of him, arms outstretched. Chase's eyes don't meet his. Instead, they are looking at his head. At the eneural.

~

Four months, and Greg completes physical therapy. Everyone is amazed by his progress.

A month more, and he is back to work. Real estate, a profession he loves like a lover: a rich lover who is scared Greg will leave it, so it showers him with money and expensive delights. His manager tells him as long as he can smile and look handsome, he'll always have a job with them. Greg tells him about the new casing for his eneural: it's covered with a wig made from his own hair, fits his skull seamlessly. Clients won't even know it's there.

Two months later, Greg is employee of the month. Not only is he among the office's top three performers, but the new improved Greg can spool out thirty years of amortization in his head, figure continuously-compounded interest over a decade without a calculator. Uses those tricks to impress buyers.

Three months after that, Greg slides into third during a company softball game. It's a close call. They give it to him because nobody can believe he can play softball at all. But it is a legitimate close call. Even if he hadn't been stabbed in the head and now needed a computer to keep him alive, it could have gone either way.

~

Now Greg always eats with a bib. He doesn't have to anymore. He just likes to.

"It makes sense," he says to Angela. "Remember what my ties used to look like?"

He found a good deal online for wholesale lobster bibs. The bibs have a picture of a lobster in a chef hat holding up a platter with a cooked lobster on it. "Aren't they funny?" says Greg. "Though in truth, the bib-makers are playing off of a lobster stereotype. Lobsters probably don't go out of their way to eat other lobsters in the wild. It's just when they're jammed together in tanks and traps that they start cannibalizing each other."

Angela squints at him. It's not a nice squint. "How do you know that?"

Greg doesn't know what he's done wrong. "I don't know. I read it somewhere."

Somehow she squints even more. "That's not the sort of thing you used to know."

Best to make a joke of it. "That was then, my dear. Now"—and he taps the eneural for emphasis—"I remember everything. Did you know lobsters don't have a centralized brain? And lobsters can be right- or left-handed. The dominant claw is called a 'crusher.' And do you know how to tell a male lobster from a female? Males have these things called gonopeds ... hey! Where are you going?"

~

Greg Jr. is doing worse in school; Lucy's about even; Chase draws nothing but mummies now. But Bobby Entin draws pictures with headlines like "I like to kill Mommy" so nobody at preschool is worried about Chase.

After reviewing the report cards, Greg says "Let me talk to Junior."

It is the last thing Angela wants. But the best she can do is ask "Are you sure?"

"You know he only opens up when he's pitching. And no offense, honey, but you can't catch." He kisses her on the head—she flinches, he ignores it—then heads out the screen door to the back yard.

Junior's arm is shockingly better since Greg last caught for him. Every time the ball lands in Greg's mitt it buzzes like an alarm clock. Sometime during his absence, someone taught Junior to throw a split-finger.

"D in math?" asks Greg.

"So?" says Junior.

"So Ds are for stupid people. And you're not stupid."

The ball thuds into Greg's meaty mitt. "I don't need math."

Greg throws a grounder; Junior fields it gracefully. "I do math every day at my job."

"No you don't."

"What?"

"You don't. Your eneural does it for you."

"Ah," says Greg. "So what does that mean? Instead of learning algebra, you're going to get an eneural like your old man?"

"Beats studying." A little too much action on that split-finger, but

Greg backhands it, saves the wild pitch. "Nice one, Dad."

"Thanks. Well, we'd better get an eneural in your head soon, or you'll never pass math. Angela!" Greg yells. "Bring out the big chef knife. I'm going to stab Junior in the head."

Junior cracks up. "Nuh-uh!"

"Uh-huh!"

"Mom won't let you."

"Yeah," Greg concedes, "you're probably right. Tell you what. Why don't I help you with math tonight? It was always my favorite subject."

"Can't."

"Why?"

Greg Jr. taps his head right where an eneural would sit. "Mr. Lopez says we're not allowed to use calculators."

Greg stands up, flips up the catcher's mask. Junior is laughing the honest, merciless laugh of a fifth-grader.

Just a joke thinks Greg. He pulls down the mask, crouches, punches his mitt. "You just tell Mr. Lopez that your dad *is* a calculator, and if he has a problem with me helping you with your homework, he can come talk to me. One more pitch, then we go inside to do some math, okay?"

"Okay," says Junior, still laughing. Then he gets suddenly serious, sets, checks first base.

Greg keeps calling for heat, but Junior keeps shaking him off. He likes his new split-finger better.

Angela reads online that, while some fundamentalist religions accuse eneural developers of playing God, the International Theological Commission of the Catholic Church has come out in support of eneurals. The Commission finds that "As the brain is no more the soul of a person than any other of the body's organs, prolonging or enhancing its function does no more to 'create life' than any other prosthetic."

At the press conference announcing the Commission's findings, Cardinal Secretary of State Salvador Bianchi says, "The matter is simple, really: a man who has lost his soul cannot get a new one by means of an eneural." The always-colorful cardinal adds: "Science can make the legs of a dead frog dance by running electricity through them. But that doesn't mean dead frogs *like* to dance."

~

Angela's parents are dead. She is an only child. Before she had kids she used to have a lot of friends, but now she has her family. But she can't talk to her family about this. She can't talk to Greg.

She turns to Nurse Bonnie. Bonnie works the night shift, so most nights she has plenty of time to talk.

Everyone else is asleep in the Justice house. Angela in the amber darkness of the kitchen, her hand cupped around the phone's receiver. "Bonnie, I feel like ... I feel like I don't know him anymore."

"Oh, honey," says Bonnie. "Of course you know him. He's still the same Greg."

"See, that's just it, Bonnie. I don't know if he is the same Greg. Some things are the same. Most things. But not everything."

"Okay," says Bonnie. "But you're not the same person you were before the attack either, right?"

"No," says Angela. She pauses to mourn the person she once was. "No I am not."

"It's natural for people to change, Sweetie. That's just part of life."

"Yeah, okay, but it's more than that. It's not that he's changed. It's that ... what if Greg died the night of the attack?"

The living silence of the phone connection buzzes in Angela's ear. "I don't think I follow you," says Bonnie.

Angela takes a deep breath. "I mean, what if Greg died that night and now the eneural is just pretending to be him? What if it's just reading Greg's memories and using his body to impersonate him, but really Greg died almost a year ago, and now I'm living my life and raising my kids with a ... a fake Greg? What if he's all body and no soul?"

There, thinks Angela. Breathing feels suddenly more satisfying. *I said it.*

Bonnie says nothing for a long time. The kitchen is still monotone brown. Aren't eyes supposed to adjust to darkness? "Well, honey," Bonnie finally begins, "let me ask you something. Before the accident, how did you know Greg had a soul?"

Angela wakes up a little. "What do you mean how did I know Greg had a soul?"

"Just what I said. How did you know?"

Angela laughs. "Everybody has a soul, Bonnie."

"But how did you know? How could you tell there was a soul inside of him?"

Angela switches the phone to her other ear to buy some time. "I don't know. I could tell, is all. I could feel it."

"What, exactly? What could you feel?"

Angela shuts her eyes. "When we were in bed and I lay my head on his chest, I could feel the life there. Okay? I could feel his life shooting up my ear canal." She laughs at herself. "I know that sounds crazy."

"It doesn't. Keep going."

A smile rises from the depths of her body up to her face. "Sometimes when he came home from work I'd be in the kitchen prepping dinner, and he'd sneak up behind me and wrap his arms around my waist and scare the crap out of me. I scare really easy, so it worked every time. And when he would do that, I could feel his soul. I could feel the ... mischief inside him. And then it would jump from his body into mine, like electricity, and his mischievous mood would become my mood, so instead of getting mad I'd just start laughing. We stand like that and laugh together, and then I would call him a sonofabitch and tell him to go get cleaned up for dinner. His soul used to make mine laugh, Bonnie. That's how I knew."

"And now when you touch him, you don't feel his soul?"

Angela opens her eyes. Then her mouth falls open. Then she says, "To tell the truth, I don't really know."

"You don't know, Sweetie? Either you can feel his soul inside him or you can't, right?"

Angela puts the receiver in her lap for a moment. She raises and drops it two, three times. Finally she presses it to her ear and mouth and, in the smallest voice she has, says: "Bonnie, we don't really touch anymore." And instead of sobbing she adds quickly, "I don't want to touch him."

The line goes quiet. The kitchen crowds her from all sides. Then Bonnie says, "Angela, hang up the phone. Go hold your husband."

~

When Angela gets back to her bedroom she sees Lucy asleep on Greg's chest. Greg smiles at Angela through the darkness and mouths, "Nightmares."

"Bullshit," Angela mouths back. She is smiling patiently.

Greg mouths a sentence too complex to decode without sound. Angela holds up her hands and says, "Wait." She walks over to his side of the bed and kneels. In her ear Greg whispers: "Do you want me to go put her in her bed?"

Angela shakes her head. This is getting to be a habit with Lucy—they will have to have a talk with her in the morning—but no need to cause a scene now, disturb the whole house. In Greg's ear, she whispers, "But can you make a little room for me?"

Greg looks at her. Every other time Lucy has come to their room claiming nightmares, she slept between Angela and Greg. Angela liked her there; she found that, with their daughter separating them, she slept better.

So Greg is surprised she wants to be next to him. "Really?" he whispers.

Angela nods. Greg gently scoops up Lucy and moves her to Angela's side of the bed, then cautiously scoots himself over. Lucy licks her lips but does not wake; her head finds its way back to Greg's chest and settles in. Angela snuggles up next to Greg; she must lie on her side to keep from falling off the bed.

Angela places her head on Greg's belly. She is looking at Lucy. Her daughter looks so much like her. Lucy's mouth is slack; her arm is thrown over Greg's stomach; she could not be more asleep.

Angela listens to Greg's chest. She hears blood and breath and even a little digestion. And, from a little higher up, she feels the high-pitched thrum of the eneural. It is an alien presence in Greg's body. But it is just that, a presence—one voice in the choir of his homeostasis.

Angela takes Greg's hand and places it on the back of her neck. She can feel the caution in his palm—he is excited, eager, but plays it cool so that she doesn't get spooked. So like him: caring and boyish and endearing and gentle. *It's good,* she thinks, her forehead just touching her daughter's. Sleep is coming quickly now; Angela has time for just one more idea. She sighs and settles in and thinks, *It's enough.*

Entanglements

I didn't know Karen was married until her husband Chase was wounded in action—an IED took both his legs at the knee—and was coming home. She couldn't leave him, not now. She had to break it off with me.

I should have been angry, but all I felt was a vacuous shock. I had no idea how to act, so I tried to imagine what a decent person would say in this situation, and parroted that. "What do you need?"

She didn't answer for a while. Her kitchen smelled like a Pennsylvania July. The mason jars lining the high shelf broke the morning sunlight into rainbows. Through the window I watched the corn swaying like the crowd at a revival. I was leaning against her counter sipping orange juice; she sat at the table double-clutching her mug and letting her tears fall where they may.

"Chase can't have children anymore," she finally told her coffee. "I will never be a mother."

I thought terrible things. Among the least savage was, *We were planning a family together. You and me. Remember?* But out loud I said, "Right now you need to focus on Chase."

She looked at me, her smile full of self-loathing. "Do you hate me, Jesús?"

"No," I said automatically. "You're human. You made a mistake."

She cocked her head at me like a confused bloodhound, then laughed through her nose; no sound, just bitter air. "I don't get you. I don't get you one bit."

I swirled my juice. "You want me to yell and scream?"

"I want you to feel something! Jesus Jesús. Do you know what Chase would do to me if he found out I'd been cheating on him all this time?" She was about to sip more coffee, but she stopped suddenly and yelled, "Aren't Spanish guys supposed to be fiery?"

I stopped leaning, stood straight. I dumped out the rest of my juice in the sink, washed the glass, dried it with the rag, set it oh so carefully in the rack.

"What are you doing?" Karen asked.

I stepped away to admire my work, made a box of my fingers like a cinematographer framing a shot. That glass was perfectly clean. Still looking at it, I said, "Spanish guys come from Spain. I'm Puerto Rican." And without another word I left.

~

As I drove to the lab where I work—I'm a physicist with the BES— my thoughts turned to Chase. I felt for him the kind of barrenness only fields of burgeoning corn can inspire.

His service to his country had left him mutilated. He'd suffer for the rest of his life, physically. But worse, there was the secret pain of his wife's betrayal waiting to reveal itself to him. Maybe someday when he was feeling stronger, maybe when he was starting to feel like he'd gotten a bit of his life back, Karen would unburden herself and tell him about us. Or maybe one day when she just felt like hurting him.

I had to pull over for a minute to collect myself.

Like everywhere in Pennsylvania this time of year, a cornfield abutted the road. I got out of the car and walked up to the six-foot-high wall of stalks. Took deep breaths.

These fields always remind me of my research. If there are Many Worlds, that means that there are many versions of me out there: an infinite number, maybe. Uniqueness is our most pervasive illusion. I'm just one of many cornstalks in the field.

I pushed a stalk gently, set it swaying. Flexible, but solid. Vibrantly alive. Indistinguishable, yes, from the thousands of others in this field: until you get up close. Then it becomes uniquely itself. The stalk was an embodied history of the little sufferings and triumphs that have allowed it to be here now, mature enough to yield corn. It had goals for the future: surviving, reproducing. And Fate had given it a farmer who has done everything possible to help it flourish.

For now. I started getting lost in the metaphor. That same farmer would soon mow it down, it and all its buddies. This whole field of slightly different stalks would be razed to the dirt. Where was the lesson in that?

There was none; it was just a field of corn. But even if the universe has no use for right and wrong, humans do. My affair with Karen had left me feeling very, very wrong. I needed to make amends.

So, with the stalks of corn as witnesses, I said aloud, "I'm going to help you, Chase."

~

I met Chase in person for the first time three months after he'd come home. I invited him and Karen—she pushed his wheelchair—to the BES superportation lab late on a Sunday afternoon, when I was sure I could be alone with them. After I met them at the door and we introduced ourselves, they followed me to our experiment chamber. Karen rolled Chase carefully behind me; she was terrified of crashing into some multi-million dollar piece of government equipment.

The first time I heard Chase speak, he said to Karen, "Why the fuck are you going so slow?"

"There's no rush," she replied.

"Fuck you there's no rush. The game starts at 7:30."

Karen stopped moving; though I was studiously pretending not to hear any of this, I paused too. "You said you'd hear him out."

Chase craned to glare at her. Then, low and angry: "You owe me."

When he turned back to me, he was smiling: but like a hyena sizing me up. I sized him up right back. His hair was bristly and straw-colored, like he'd picked up a handful of hay and stuck it on his head. Harley Davidson muscle shirt, cargo shorts, nothing to cover the puckered, scarred ends of his legs. The tan he must've developed overseas had largely faded and his skin was returning to its default papier-mâché color, though freckle-speckled. His solid build was starting to slacken and fatten; he was starting to melt into his wheelchair.

And he had good hyena-teeth. He was smiling when he said, "Before we go any farther, Doc, why don't you explain to me what I'm doing here? See, that way, once Karen hears how full of shit you are, we can go home and I don't have to miss the opening pitch."

I put my hands in my pockets and paced toward him. "You're not talking about the All-Star Game, are you? You actually watch that?"

He said nothing. He was shocked that a scientist could know anything about baseball.

"Look, Chase," I said, "I get it. You think this is just a waste of time. You think I'm some clueless egghead, or worse, some fraud who's out to rip you off. You're only here because of Karen. She's the only person in the world right now who could've gotten you here on a Sunday."

He folded his arms. "So?"

I closed the distance between us and took a knee in front of him. "You're here because you love her. Because you want to make her happy, even when you know she's wrong. Because now she makes your life possible. What would you do without her, Chase? If she got sick of your foul mouth and your bad attitude and the burden of caring for you, and left you?"

I glanced up at Karen. She was stone-faced. It had taken me this many months to convince her I wasn't plotting some kind of secret revenge on her, like some morning talk-show revelation/confrontation/conflagration. She kept telling me she still loved me, that she only wanted the best for me, and why would I ruin the wonderful memories we had shared together by destroying her life: or Chase's, who, I should remember, was a war-hero and deserved better?

Only after weeks of repeating that I only wanted to help Chase did she finally halfway believe me. Now, though, her strained face told me she thought I was indeed about to betray her. She was stoically preparing herself for the ugliest moment of her life.

Chase, meanwhile, reacted just like I thought he would. A guy like him is a tea-kettle; his shame at being disabled always boiled just under his skin, looking for any weak point through which it could escape, whistling. He bowed his head and, with a voice thick with self-pity, said, "Karen is the one good thing I have left in my life. I would do anything for her."

I smiled and nodded. Karen cocked her head. Then she squeezed Chase's shoulders and, looking at me with a face somewhere between relief and wariness, said, "I'd do anything for you too, baby."

I stood up. "What you're feeling right now, Chase—that's what I need you to hold onto. And Karen, you too: hold onto every bit of love and loyalty you feel for Chase. Love is entangled across universes. We're going to use the love you feel to find good matches for you."

"The fuck you talking about?" said Chase, staring at me, hard. I'd exposed his vulnerability, and now he needed to assert himself. He was used to making people look away whenever he wanted these days. A legless man glares at you, you avert your eyes; that's the rule.

I didn't look away. I even smiled a little. One hyena to another.

"I'm part of a team that's researching a process called superportation. That over there," I said, pointing to the 320 sq. ft. gray-concrete cube in the center of the room, "is the heart of what we call our Classical Information Aggregator. ClassAgg for short. It's where we conduct our experiments."

Chase, like any good Pennsylvania farmer, scowled at all that mumbo-jumbo. But to my face he said, "Well, don't stop now, Egghead. Tell me how it works."

"I'd have to lecture you for a year on current entanglement theory to even scratch the surface," I said. I opened the door to the ClassAgg and flourished like a New York City doorman. "Why don't I show you instead?"

~

I love watching the faces of people when they first get a look inside the ClassAgg. It looked like a homey Pennsylvania efficiency apartment, featuring a 12-point stag-head presiding over the faux fireplace and framed, embroidered psalms hanging on the walls. The quilt on the full-sized bed was a gorgeous example of the local art. On the gingham futon sat an oversized Raggedy Ann. Coffee and whoopie pies—Karen loved whoopie pies—waited for us on the Amish kitchen table.

"This room is so darling!" said Karen. I'd showed it to her several times back when we were lovers, but she had to sound surprised for Chase. "I want to move in!" she flourished.

Chase didn't seem able to see through her lies. Glad I wasn't the only one. "This is science?" he asked, not without humor. "How is this science?"

"Let's eat and talk," I said.

So we dipped our fingers in cream filling and spooned sugar in our coffee while I did my best to explain uncertainty and entanglement in layman's terms.

"The room's a little goofy by design," I said. "To a lot of Pennsylvanians, it looks like Grandma and Grandpa's house, and if not, it's still campy and funny. Either way works for us. For our experiments, we need people to be as relaxed as they can be."

"That sounds like something a shrink would say," said Chase, suddenly suspicious. "Is this all a trick? Are you a fucking shrink? I ain't going to no shrink!"

Karen pinched his arm. He turned to her and dared her with a "What?"

I just kept talking. "We're not trying to help you get in touch with your inner child here. For superportation to work, we need to get you in touch with the other Chases out there, ones that are similar enough to you so that we can copy information from them."

Chase stopped mid-chew. "What do you mean, 'the other Chases?'"

"Like that one," I said, gesturing with my chin.

I'd gotten lucky; the timing was perfect. I had started the ClassAgg before I entered the chamber, and now, as if on-cue, Chase and Karen looked across the table and saw a silvery, liquidy form sitting across from them. It looked exactly like Chase. It was speaking to someone we couldn't see. A second later it started laughing like a silent movie. It was standing on two perfectly healthy legs.

"That's me?" said Chase. Then: "That's not me. That's some trick. Is this a movie set? Is this reality T.V.?"

"Science is full of tricks," I said. "This trick allows us to translate information of Chases from other universes and bring it here, into the ClassAgg. We call it superportation."

~

Some Chases joined the army but were never deployed. Some Chases were, but were never hit by the IED. Some were hit by the IED but made a full recovery. Some died in action. Some Chases never joined the army at all; they became poets and classical violinists and waiters and civil engineers and started businesses that failed and businesses that succeeded and were arrested for tax-evasion and became congressmen. Some Chases died when they were kids; some became the richest men in the world. Some married Karen, but most didn't: they died virgins, or married other women, or were gay and moved to other states to marry men or stayed here and lived with men out of wedlock, or lived in universes where Pennsylvania allowed gay marriage at this point in the local history.

But the most important thing I explained to Chase is that, out in the cosmos there were innumerable, luckier Chases who had perfectly functioning lower halves. I could sneak him into the ClassAgg a couple of Sundays a month and—using his love for Karen and Karen's love for him—find other Chases. Then I could superport information from those other universes onto his own body.

The upshot was, through an enormous expenditure of energy, and only while he remained in the ClassAgg, for a couple of hours every month I could give him mercurial legs. For as long as it lasted, Chase would be whole again.

~

If you want to know what happiness is, give someone his legs back. Even if it's temporary or incomplete. Even if it helps heal the marriage you wished every second of every day would fail, because you want Karen for yourself, even after everything that's happened. Tell the love you feel for her to go fuck itself. Bring happiness back to a body the world has ravaged, and some of it will vicariously trickle down to you. You will rediscover what agency feels like. Agency, you will suddenly remember, feels good.

If, on the other hand, you want to feel like a lovelorn teenager, drive into a cornfield and lie on the hood of your car next to someone who: 1. has already betrayed you once, but; 2. you want more than anyone else in the world, yet; 3. is utterly forbidden to you, and thus; 4. is even sexier because of it. Just lean back on the windshield with your hands pillowing your head and listen to the rustling stalks and look up at the stars. Try to be honorable. Try to be a good friend.

"Thanks for dessert," I said to Karen. She and Chase were constantly finding ways to thank me for sneaking him into the ClassAgg for the past four months. That night's thank-you had taken the form of a homemade four-berry pie. It sat on the back seat now, untouched, tepid.

"It was the only excuse I could think of to see you tonight," said Karen, her eyes locked on the moon. "I have to tell you something."

"You couldn't text me?"

"No."

"Okay. What?"

She swallowed. "Chase wants a baby."

I thought this through for several seconds before I responded. Then: "He figures there are some universes where you are pregnant right now. He thinks I can superport that information to our universe, the same way I've been superporting legs."

She laughed joylessly. "Our very own immaculate conception."

I waited a few seconds to make sure what I said next I could say completely without affect. I said, "Is that what you want?"

"First I want to know if you can do it."

The last thing I wanted to do in any universe, ever, was to help Chase and Karen have a baby together. Because that would be it. Karen would be gone forever.

Only thing is, the scientist in me wouldn't stand for it. I'd betrayed my professional ethics more than enough for the sake of my stupid, stupid heart. Being good at my job was one thing over which I still had control. So I thought through the idea dispassionately, scientifically. And I can honestly say the best answer I could give was, "No. It's impossible. It'd be just like Chase's legs: the information vanishes as soon as you turn off the ClassAgg's power."

There was relief in her voice. "That's what I thought."

"There are other options." This was me still being professional and self-sabotaging. "I could show you what your child or children look like in other universes. I could superport them a while into the ClassAgg. Maybe Chase would like to see them. Maybe you would, too."

She shook her head. Her voice was raw and tender when she said, "It'd be like seeing ghosts. That would break poor Chase's heart."

At least she sounded raw and tender. I realized then I had no longer had any idea how to interpret her words. She had become a cypher to me, a placeholder zero of herself. Her words were dialogue from an audition-script: a good actor could play them a million different ways.

Yet I still wanted her. What the fuck was wrong with me?

I was awoken from my reverie by a touch. Karen's hand had cautiously crawled over to mine, like a crab seeking a mate. I lay very still. She interlaced her fingers with mine. Neither of us said anything for a time.

Eventually, her eyes jumping from star to star, she said, "Chase is coming back to himself. Those months when he first came home, there was nothing left of the man I'd fallen in love with. He was pure rage."

"He'd lost both his legs."

"Yeah. Who wouldn't be angry?" She squeezed my hand a little tighter. "And I thought, 'Karen, you slutty bitch, this is exactly what you deserve. You deserve a hateful husband you will treat you like shit for the rest of your life.'"

"No one deserves that."

She looked at me for a second. Then she turned back to the sky and, rueful, said, "*You* should think that. You have every right to think I deserve every bad thing that could happen to me. What I did do you, Jesús—unforgivable.

"Yet here we are. Not only did you forgive me, but you've given Chase his hope back. He feels like he's living a miracle, thanks to you. You know what he says? He says, 'I feel like every Chase in the universe is coming together to help me get through this.'"

It was the longest we'd held hands since Chase had returned. "That's a nice thought," I said.

"He's not nearly as angry anymore. He can envision a future. He wants kids now."

"I can't give him kids."

"But you made it possible for him to dream about the future again. You gave him his *vision* back. It's the greatest gift anyone can give."

"Glad to help."

She laughed. "'Glad to help.' Really, that's it? That's all you want to say?"

"What else should I say?"

She shook her head and smiled. "Always so practical. So understated. You know why I fell for you, Jesús?"

"Yep. Because I'm 'Spanish.'"

She squeezed my hand, hard, as punishment; I giggled evilly. "Never going to let me live that down, are you?"

"It was pretty racist, m'dear."

"I know. I mean, now I know. I didn't realize I was being racist. I'm sorry."

"It's okay. If I'm being really honest," I said, letting go of her hand so I could roll on my side to face her, "I'm not really all that Puerto Rican. Really, I'm white."

Now *that* cracked her up. "Jesús, honey, have you looked in a mirror? You are *not* white."

"I know I look brown. But I've forgotten all my Spanish. I have a Ph.D. in Physics from an American university. I have money, a white ex-wife, a white ex-lover, and a Pennsylvania split-level I bought seventeen years ago. I don't live the life of someone who has to struggle against racism every day. It's not fair for me to call myself Latino."

I looked up. The moon pulled a curtain of clouds around itself like a magician, and the field grew a little darker. "Can I be really honest, too?" Karen asked.

"Sure."

"I *did* fall for you because you're Spanish. Latino. Whatever. I mean, your name *sounds* super-Latino—Jesús Camacho!—and you have brown skin and kinky hair. But you're right. I mean, you speak perfect English. Better than me."

"Better than 'I.'"

Her laugh ascended to the stars. "See? So yeah, fine, you're white.

But off-white. I was lonely without Chase, and you were different enough to be exciting. But not *too* different. Just enough."

Maybe some people in my shoes would've been offended by Karen's words. I wasn't. Because—again, being totally honest—I thought of myself in exactly the same way: Latino enough to be interesting, but white enough to fit in. Before Karen, I had no idea how much racism I'd internalized.

"You know why I fell for you, Karen?" I asked her.

"Seriously, no idea. I'm an administrative assistant with a high school diploma who eats too many whoopie pies and goes to church mostly for the gossip. You could do a lot better."

"I fell for you because you're so honest. Even when it makes you look bad. Everyone else keeps their evil parts hidden. Not you. You share everything you're thinking: good, bad, ugly, whatever. It's so refreshing."

Her face became mannequin hard. She told the moon, "You mean, except for the part where I was lying to you about my husband, and lying to my husband about you."

What could I say? "Yeah. Except for that."

I thought I had ruined the moment, but I saw her squint a little; she was thinking, and the thought seemed to amuse her. "You know what I want, Jesús? I want to know how the other Karens did it."

"Did what?"

She rolled over and got make-out close to my face. "How they managed not to fuck up our relationship. In some universes right now, there are Karens and Jesúses who are perfectly happy together, even after Chase came back. Every possibility can happen, right? Somehow, some brilliant Karens out there figured out a way to keep seeing you."

As gently as I could I said, "That sounds impossible."

"With all the gagillions of universes out there, you're telling me there isn't a single Karen in the entire cosmos who figured out how she could keep you *and* Chase?"

"I don't know. Maybe. But we still only get to live in this universe. And in the here and now, I don't see how to make that happen."

"But we have a ClassAgg! Don't you see? That thing is a fucking crystal ball! We can search for those universes. Find out how they made it work." She took my hands. "Jesús, there's a way! A way we can be together again!"

She was almost crying she was so happy. She wanted so much to be right. And she was, kind of. But when physicists use the word "information," they mean mass, particles, position in space and time. They don't mean philosophy and morality. It's true that we could spy on all the Karens and Chases and Jesúses living their lives across realities, but we couldn't talk to them or ask them how we should fix our broken lives. The ClassAgg only let us spy on others. It had no opinion on what anything meant.

~

It was Chase who called me. "Jesús, it's time, man, it's time! Her water broke!"

"I'm on my way. What do you need?"

"Nothing man, just get your ass to the hospital! Wahoo!"

I wasn't family, so they wouldn't let me in the delivery room, even though Karen and Chase told everyone in the hospital I was more than family. But rules are rules, so Chase came out regularly to update me, and every time he reported, he thanked me for the miracle I'd given Karen and him. He called me his angel. Twice he summoned me into a hug, and each time I locked his wheels so I wouldn't lose my balance, then stooped over and embraced him until he had finished crying.

At 4:40 AM, Karen and Chase became the proud parents of a healthy 8 lb., 11 oz. boy with ten fingers and ten toes and his whole life ahead of him.

It was hours more before they would let me in to see the baby and the proud parents. When I did finally enter the room, Chase was cradling the sleeping newborn in his lap, while Karen lay on the bed with her eyes closed, looking like a vampire's most recent meal, black-eyed and enervated.

I whispered from the door, "Hey, happy parents!"

Chase gestured me over; I tiptoed so as not to wake the newborn. "He's just the most beautiful thing I've ever seen," Chase whispered. Only surface tension held the tears against his eyes; they would fall the next time he blinked. "It's like he's made of 'perfect information,' right Jesús? Like you gathered all the best ideas from every universe and put it into our child. That's what you did. There in the ClassAgg, you made all this possible. It's a miracle. You gave Karen and me a child of our own."

"Yeah," said Karen, "a child of our own." I looked at her and found she was staring at me. Through her exhausted rictus I could see that same infuriating look of hers. Once again she was waiting for me to betray her.

I knelt next to Chase's wheelchair and brought my face close to the child's. The sleeping baby took easy, sonorous breaths. "My God," I said, and I meant it. It was hard to imagine the universe had any problems at all when it had babies in it breathing so peacefully.

But the truth is, babies are born into a universe of problems. My son's skin was as brown as mine.

The International Studbook
of the Giant Panda

Part 1

It's a cool Pacific-coast morning when I pull up to the gate of the American Panda Mission's campus. Security is tight: two guards cradling M-16s and girdled in kevlar ask me what I am doing here.

"Gabrielle Reál, *San Francisco Squint*?" I say, giving them my best can-you-big-strong-men-help-me? eyes. "I have an appointment with Ken Cooper?"

One guard walkie-talkies in my press credentials. The other stares at me behind reflective sunglasses. Nothing inspires silence quite like a machine gun.

Finally: "O.K., Ms. Reál, just head straight, then take the first right you see. Mr. Cooper will be waiting for you."

I follow the almost-road to a nondescript warehouse. Outside, park ranger and chief robot-panda operator Kenneth Cooper is waiting for me. Full disclosure: Cooper and I used to date. Which is why you're stuck with me on this story instead of some boring, legitimate journalist.

Cooper's been Californiaized. Back when I knew him he was a hypercaffeinated East-coaster working on a Biology M.S. Now he's California blond, California easy, eternally 26 (he'a actually 37). Flip-flops, bermudas, a white, barely-buttoned shirt that's just dying to fall off his body. Not exactly the Ranger Rick ensemble I was hoping to tease him about.

I park and get out; I'm barely on terra firma before Cooper's bag-piping the air out of me. "So good to see you, Gabby!" he says.

I break off the embrace, but keep ahold of his hands and look him up and down. "Looking good, Mr. Cooper. Remind me: why did we break up again?"

"You were still at Amherst. And I left for California. This job."

I let go, put a hand on my hip. "Biggest mistake of your life, right?"

He holds out his hand again—wedding ring—and I take it, and we fall into a familiar gait as we stroll to the warehouse, as if we'd been walking hand in hand all these years without the interruptions of time and space and broken hearts.

"Don't be jealous," he says. "There's room enough in my heart for you and pandas."

~

The warehouse isn't as big as it looks from the outside. Straight ahead and against the back wall is mission control, where a half-dozen science-types wear headsets and sit behind terminals, busily prepping for the mission of the day. From this distance it looks like a NASA diorama.

To the left are cubicles, a meeting area, and the supercomputer that does most of the computational heavy lifting for APM. On the right is a makeshift workshop—benches, spare parts, soldering irons, and a 3D printer big enough to spit out a zamboni. Maybe that's where they print all their science-types.

And in the center of it all, a gigantic pair of headless panda suits hang from wires in the middle of the room.

I move in for a closer look. The suits are suspended like marionettes from wires that connect to a rig in the ceiling. They're pretty realistic, both to eye and touch, except that each is about the size of a well-fed triceratops.

"Gabby," Cooper says, "I'd like you to meet the greatest advancement in panda procreation since sperm meets egg: Avalon and Funicello."

"Cute names."

But I can barely speak. Their panda-musk fills the entire warehouse; I can smell them from here. It's greasy and rancid; it smells like I'm eating it. And here's the recipe: buy the grossest musk-scented antiperspirant you can find and melt it in a pan. Then use it as the binder for a bearmeat tartare.

But why douse the suits in funky pheromones at all? It's not like any real pandas are here to smell them. Right, Ken?

"In a few minutes," he replies, "you will become a genuine panda. If every bit of our work weren't 100% real, it would be useless."

By "real," Cooper means that he and I will be donning these panda suits to remotely operate the most realistic robot animals the world has ever known. Those two robots are miles away from the warehouse, where they live among and regularly interact with APM's real giant pandas. Whatever we do in the suits, the field robots will mimic exactly.

And usually what APM does is sex. Sometimes they use Funicello to collect semen from one of the "boars," or male pandas. Other times they'll use Avalon to inseminate a sow, using semen collected earlier.

And sometimes it's just robots fucking. Avalon and Funicello simulate coition in front of a live panda audience so that the reproductively-challenged bears can learn where babies come from. That's our mission today, in fact: to demonstrate for APM's male pandas the proper way to impregnate a female. And playing the female lead in today's performance is yours truly.

~

Cooper and I remained close even after he left for California. He knew I'd come to Cali for the job at *The Squint*, and he knew getting the scoop on APM's secret operations could have made my career as a science correspondent. But he rejected my every request, just like APM rejected every other journalist. The nonprofit has been secretive from the moment it was founded. If you engage in virtual bestiality, no matter how noble your scientific goals, you're going to make some enemies—and in APM's case that includes paramilitary terrorists. They've learned to keep a lid on things.

So why am I here, now? Because—speaking of paramilitary terrorists—APM's still reeling from the fallout of their worst-case scenario: five months ago, Constance Ritter, a 22:19 saboteur, was killed on-premises. The means of execution was robot panda.

After the PR fiasco that ensued, APM now sees the need for more transparency in their operations. Step one of damage-control is, apparently, me. I can hear Cooper pitching me now: "Let's suit her up so she can tell the world just how effective our methods are. Sure, she's a Media Studies major who I had to tutor night and day to get her to pass Biology for Non-Majors, but all she'll be doing is operating a multi-million dollar robot in order to seduce and sexually satisfy a giant panda boar. How hard can it be?"

And somehow, impossibly, APM said yes.

I've never had a more terrifying assignment, and I've been in warzones. I have no idea how to have panda sex. What if I'm terrible? Wait, what do I mean "if"? *Of course* I will be terrible at panda sex. The real question, Ken Cooper, is what if the pandas imitate my terrible panda sex and never reproduce again?

"You'll do fine," says Cooper. "You're going to be the sow. Our all-male audience will be imitating me, not you. All you do is lie there and take what I give you."

I raise an eyebrow. "Isn't that the line you used on me when we first met?"

"Works on pandas too."

Oh, that smile. Mama warned me about robot panda jockeys like you, Ken Cooper.

To help ensure I don't ruin the reproductive chances of an entire species, Cooper takes me to the office of Dr. Mei Xiadon, 59, project lead for the American Panda Mission. Dr. Xiadon's going to teach me how to use the panda suit to operate the field robots.

We enter her office. From ceiling to floor, electronics spill from every surface, a cascade of circuitry and servos and screws. A wall of gray-grim lockers stand against the far wall, making the room even more claustrophobic. The desk is buried in half-finished robotics and paperwork fingerprinted with grease-stains. It looks like it came from a film-school sci-fi movie set.

Seated behind the desk is the woman herself. One of the foremost giant panda experts in the world, Xiadon spent a decade directing the celebrated Wolong Panda Center in China. That was something of a coup, seeing as she is not Chinese, but Chinese-American. APM was able to lure her back to the States with the promise of putting her at the helm of the most cutting-edge panda conservancy in the world.

"Mei?" says Cooper.

Dr. Xiadon, startled, looks up from her work. She's about five-foot-nothing. Veins of silver run through her black hair, which is coiffed into a Chinese schoolgirl's bowlcut. Her button-down APM-branded denim shirt is baggy enough for shoplifting. She has small features, except for her mouth. Her big, round, harmless teeth seem only good for smiling. But, as her expression changes from surprise to pleasure, I can see they're very good at that.

"Oh! You're Gabby!" she says, suddenly coming alive. She throws herself halfway over her desk to shake my hand. "Ken's told me all about you."

"It's an honor and a pleasure to meet you, Dr. Xiadon. I'm so happy to have a chance to oh my God are those panda thumbs on your wrists?!"

"Yes they are!" says Xiadon, showing off her prosthetics. She makes them wiggle, which makes my stomach flip. "Aren't they great?"

One thing that makes pandas unique is their "thumb," a sixth digit that is actually a wristbone free-floating in the tendons of their forelimbs. They use those thumbs primarily to cut open bamboo—a neat little adaptation that, coupled with their unique throats and the special mix of enzymes in their guts, make the pandas' weird choice in cuisine viable.

"Why did you get those?" I ask her. "So you could understand pandas better?"

Ask a stupid question. But she lets me down easy. "Naw," she says, and grabs a mailer tube lying like a fallen log on her desk. She jabs a panda-thumb into one end, sinking it all the way through the thick cardboard, and slices the tube all the way to the other, in one clean stroke. The papers inside the mailer flower open and waft onto her desk. "I just use them to cut packages open."

"You must get a lot of packages," I say dryly.

"Tons," she says dryly.

It's Xiadon's job to teach me everything there is to know about operating a robot panda. Well, everything I can learn from her in an hour.

But first, Xiadon heads over to the lockers to try to find me a "superdermal," the form-fitting special suit one wears to operate a robot panda. They look like dive skins, except that they are studded head to toe with chrome-colored rivets.

After some searching, she turns around and holds up a rubbery, doll-sized unitard. Peeking around it, she smiles and says, "Why are you still dressed, babycakes? Strip and put this on."

In no time I'm down to bra and thong. I stop and look at her. "This naked?"

"Ken, get the hell out of here!" she says, laughing.

"What?" shrugs Ken. "It's nothing I haven't seen before."

"Out." And Ken sulks off.

Then, back to me, smiling. "Nakeder."

I get nakedest. Xiadon tosses me a superdermal.

It looks too small for me. It looks too small for a spider monkey. But as I put it on it stretches in surprisingly accommodating ways. One foot, then the next, then the arms, then the good doctor zips me up in back. I'm in.

Nothing's pinching, nothing's too tight—being an A-cup is a bonus today. I am starting to sweat a little. "Good," says Xiadon. "Sweat helps the connections."

She brandishes the helmet I'll be wearing. It looks like a bear skull made from machined aluminum, with rubbery black patches holding it together. The eyes are covered with what reminds me of the metal weave of a microphone. In all, it looks like the lovechild of a panda and a fly.

Inside the helmet—it's a two-piece affair that's assembled around the head—I see a jutting plastic sleeve for my tongue, and a pair of tubes that will go disturbingly far up my nostrils. Xiadon turns the mask so I can get a good look at it from every terrifying angle. I think she's enjoying my horror.

"You've been taking the pills we've sent you?" she asks.

I have. Since receiving this assignment, I began a regimen of capsules that delivered a cocktail of chemicals and nanotechnology. In conjunction with this helmet, they presumably will help my brain process the sensory experiences the field robot will receive. My sense of smell will be as good as a panda's, Cooper told me. I haven't noticed any improvements leading up to today.

"You wouldn't," says Xiadon. "It only works when you're in the suit."

But that begs the question I've been dying to ask. "This is all so complicated, Dr. Xiadon. Brain-altering chemicals, nanotech, virtual reality suits, robot pandas—it's like one of those overly elaborate schemes supervillains concoct in B-movies. There must be an easier way to save the pandas."

"Actually, there isn't," she says. She places the helmet-halves on her desk, then leans against it and crosses her legs at the ankles. "I've been doing this a long time. We've tried mating pandas in captivity. Terrible track record. We've tried artificial insemination. Not much better. We've tried releasing them back into the wild. Abysmal. We have decades of brilliant scientists with excellent funding and the goodwill of the entire world failing to increase panda numbers. So you've got to ask, why?

"The problem," she says, grabbing the faceplate of the helmet and studying it as she speaks, "is us. Humans. We pollute animal behavior. We ruin instinct. So we need to stay as far away from pandas as possible, while still using everything we know to help them help themselves.

"So how do we do that? By building a surrogate bear, one so realistic they will accept as one of their own, but imbued with humans smarts. Through them, we can collect semen in literally the most natural way possible. Same goes for delivering that semen. And best of all, we can use the robots to show pandas how to mate, so that one day, when there are enough of them, not only will they not need us anymore, they won't want us anywhere near them."

"But the robots are controlled by humans. Isn't that pretty much the same thing? Won't that pollute panda behavior too?"

She hands me the faceplate face-down, so that I'm looking at the tubes and tongue-sleeve. "That's what this is for. There's a giant panda inside you, Gabby. All we have to do is bring it to the surface."

~

Cooper is already inside of and operating Avalon when Xiadon and I head out to the main room. Specifically, he's running in place, thanks to the wires that keep the panda suit suspended so that its paws only just scrape the floor.

It's mesmerizing, watching him run in the suit. It's nothing like the goofy loping you usually see on nature shows or at the zoo. This is cheetah-fast, the back legs long-jumping forward, lunging as far as Avalon's shoulder, while the forepaws push powerfully off the ground. Then, for a split second, the forelegs reach forward and the hindlegs stretch back, and the panda suit flies.

"Isn't that a little speedy for a panda?" I ask Dr. Xiadon.

Her eyes are locked on the panoramic bank of view screens above the two panda suits. It looks like we're getting an Avalon-eye view on-screen, since all I see is a bear snout and a nonstop rush of bamboo.

"Ken's not acting like a panda right now," Xiadon says. And I can see instantly that she's pulled a Yoda on me. Before she was funny, friendly, even silly: not the Jedi Master I'd flown halfway across the galaxy to speak to. But this Xiadon is hard, shrewd, all-business. This is the Xiadon who runs APM when nosy journalists aren't around. "There must be a problem."

And when I don't seem to get it, she adds, "Terrorists."

We hustle to mission control, where everyone is anxious and moving fast. Dr. Anita Deeprashad, APM's mission manager, fills us in. "Avalon has been shot," she says.

"Damage?" asks Xiadon.

None: the robot pandas have withstood a shotgun slug at 20 yards, and this joker had apparently shot at the robot using some "Oscar Meyer rifle" that, according to Deeprashad, "didn't even muss Avalon's hair."

Deeprashad is late-sixties, with long braided hair as bright as sea salt. She's wearing a glorious gold and purple sari, and sports an onyx-and-pearl panda bindi on her forehead. Yet she talks like a Hollywood action hero. California infects absolutely everyone.

"Any real pandas hurt or killed?" Xiadon asks. No and no, says Dee-prashad.

Now Xiadon can relax a little. "And the terrorists?"

"Chasing one of them down." Their eyes meet. They don't say a word, but I can break their eyebrow Morse code. They're both suddenly worried that another PR debacle could occur if Ken mutilates another 22:19er with me in the room. They're silently debating whether to have me escorted away.

"Nope," I say. "I'm staying right here."

They both sigh, resigned.

"Ken's the best there is," says Xiadon. I think she means it, but it sounds like she's trying to convince herself.

By contrast, there's no doubt what Deeprashad means. "You're about to see the professionalism and restraint we exercise when arresting these criminals," says Deeprashad, taking my hand and patting it in an endearingly un-American way. "Ken has a light touch when dealing with these 22:19 scum. Not like me. I'd pop the bastards' heads off like I was thumbing open champagne."

Deeprashad is killing me! I want to talk like a Hollywood producer to her. "And ... scene. You were beautiful Anita, beautiful! You're going to be a big star, baby! Huge!"

~

APM's archenemy is 22:19, a group that takes its name from that chapter and verse from Exodus: "Whosoever lieth down with an animal shall be put to death." They formed about a decade ago in objection to any animal husbandry practice where humans harvest sperm from an animal. It doesn't matter that you're getting off an animal for science, says 22:19. Bestiality is bestiality in the eyes of the Lord.

22:19 started by attacking turkey farms and horse-breeding facilities, becoming increasingly more aggressive as time went on. But they gained their greatest notoriety once they declared war against the American Panda Mission. They capitalized on the perceived twin abominations of modern technology and the erosion of Christian values in American politics to appeal to radical Christian denominations. It wasn't long before some of them saw 22:19ers as God-touched heroes waging a holy crusade against the evils of science.

With an influx of capital and new members, 22:19's salvos became progressively more audacious, especially against APM. They claimed responsibility for the arson two years ago that caused more than $16 million in damage to APM equipment and prompted the move to this new facility. Their growing infamy and belligerence caused the United States to classify them as a terrorist organization.

Predictably, that label initially bolstered their numbers. But it also meant, under the most recent iteration of the Patriot Act, these "enemy combatants" could be captured or even killed by any citizen or legal alien of the United States without fear of prosecution.

Not too many enemy combatants have been killed or captured on U.S. soil by U.S. citizens. In fact, all combatants so captured have been from 22:19 by APM. To accomplish this feat, APM has employed the most unlikely anti-terrorism technology ever conceived: the robot giant panda.

It sounds funny, I know. But make no mistake: the robot giant pandas are shockingly effective. Their metal skeletons shrug off bullets like snowflakes, they can run through bamboo-dense terrain at 50 kph, and we have evidence of just how easily they can end human life. Two 22:19ers trespassed onto the APM campus on November 5, 2027. One of them filmed the other's death.

Constance Ritter, the 22:19 member who was killed, had a head that was just as firmly attached to her neck as anyone else's when the day began. But as the footage shows, a second later the robot Greg Furce was jockeying took a swipe at her, and tick, her head flies out of frame in a split-second. Her body takes a comparatively long time to kneel, then topple over. The male 22:19er, never identified, runs through the dense bamboo whisper-crying "Oh shit oh shit oh shit oh shit" for the rest of the clip.

APM has the legal authority to kill 22:19 trespassers, and given how much stronger a robot panda is than a human, it's something of a miracle more people haven't died. But as APM found out the hard way, in terms of public perception, even one death is one too many.

~

Back on the monitors, the bamboo forest has given way to an open field. We can now make out, faintly in the distance, a man is running away from the robot as if his life depended on it. Behind him, the robot's closing, fast.

It's extraordinary, watching the panda-mime Cooper is performing for us live while, above him, the silent viewscreens show us the field robot rising and falling as it runs in exact synchronicity. The two are precisely linked—if there is any lag, my eye can't detect it.

With each galumph, the robot closes the gap between itself and the suspect. Terrorist or no, part of me can't help but root for the running, terrified human. This looks like the kind of villain-cam you get in horror movie chase-scenes.

We can see the terrorist clearly now: dressed in Eddie Bauer camouflage and toting a rifle that looks plenty dangerous to me. But according to Deeprashad, against robot pandas you might as well be throwing raw hotdogs.

Cooper leaps one last time—the Avalon-suit extends into a full Superman stretch—and when the onscreen robot lands, his quarry vanishes beneath it.

"Got him," Cooper reports seconds later, his voice throaty with adrenaline. The control room cheers.

In person, Cooper has bellyflopped onto the floor and lies there, splayed like a rug. The field robot, following suit, has bellyflopped onto its quarry.

The robot panda will lounge upon the flattened suspect until backup arrives. Said suspect will be charged with a long list of offenses, both state and federal. He'll have the full weight of the Patriot Act thrown at him. That means life imprisonment is on the table in California. At the federal level, so is execution.

But his first journey will be to the hospital. Cooper reports he heard "a loud crack" when he landed. The suspect is now "mooing like a sick cow."

Deeprashad moans a little. Xiadon is hard, expressionless. They're both wondering if they made a grave mistake allowing me to witness this.

"How badly is he hurt, Ken?" asks Deeprashad.

Seconds pass. Xiadon and Deeprashad exchange looks. Then: "No worries, Anita." Cooper replies. "This jerk will have his day in court. He'll probably just be wearing a cast on his gun arm that day."

~

Cooper has joined us at mission control, catching his breath after the chase. He sits barechested, the top half of the unitard hanging limply in front of him, his metal, bug-eyed panda helmet on his lap.

He's smiling like an MVP and, like an MVP, can't wait to tell the press about his game-winning play.

"The hardest part is getting back enough of your humanity before things go bad," he says, pouring water alternately in his mouth or over his head. "That's what happened to poor Greg. He just couldn't become human again in time."

"So people lose control of themselves when they operate the pandas?" I ask. "Is that what happened to Furst?"

"No," says Xiadon.

"Yes," says Deeprashad.

They have an eyebrow duel for a few minutes. Then Xiadon says, "Kind of. We train our jockeys relentlessly, and we have kill-switches and overrides here at mission control to take over if the jockey loses control. But we all blew it that day: Furst, me, Anita, everyone at mission control. It just happened too fast. Really, it was just like any other animal attack. You know when you hear how an animal trainer who's been working with the same tiger or killer whale for years is suddenly mauled, out of nowhere? That's what happened. Furst surprised us all, most of all himself."

"But Furst isn't a tiger or an orca," I say. "He's a highly-trained human being doing highly-specialized work."

Cooper is shaking his head. "Gabby, I said it before and I'll say it again. We're not acting like pandas out there. Acting doesn't work; the pandas see right through us. We go to great lengths to *become* pandas."

Talk like this makes me wince, especially from Cooper, who I knew in a former incarnation. It's a little too crunchy for a girl who had to spend decades purging her Latina, magical-realist childhood out of her reason. "Look, I understand the importance of your work here. Really. You use robots so that they can look and smell right. You do everything you can to put yourselves in the right mindset. But at the end of the day it's still acting. There's no way to forget you're just a human being playing the role of panda bear."

Xiadon and Deeprashad interrupt each other explaining how wrong I am. All the technology both inside (the nanotech, the chemicals) and out (the unitard, the helmet, the panda suit) give jockeys a near-perfect panda perspective of the world. Thanks to a process called "migraineal suppression," the left brain's ability to process language, reason causally, and in short think like a human will be reduced to be more in-line with ursine IQ; via "cerebellar promotion," the mammalian brain will take over the lion's share of the decision-making process; through "synesthetic olfactory emulation," the operator's sense of smell will become the primary way of getting information about the world, borrowing some processing power from the brain's occipital lobe. And so on—they release a cataract of jargon, each doctor trying to out-science the other. They might as well be reciting from *Finnegan's Wake*.

Finally Cooper gets a word in edgewise. "With all due respect, Doctors, talking's exactly the wrong way to go about this. Let's get Gabby inside a bear. Then she'll get it."

Part 2

I'm crawling into the suspended suit that will give me control of Funicello. The entrance to the suit is, of course, the ass. I have to goatse my way in. Lovely.

It's dark in there, but there's a light at the end of the tunnel: the neck-hole through which I'll stick my head.

The suit, still suspended on wires—couldn't they have lowered it to make getting in easier?—sways gently as I earthworm forward. On the way, I feel metal rivets, like the ones studding my unitard, embedded in the suit. "Am I supposed to line up the studs on my outfit with the ones in the suit or something?" I yell.

No answer. Cooper had told me that no one would speak to me once I entered the suit, but I thought I'd try. How am I supposed to figure out what to do if no one tells me?

I slip my arms into the forelegs and my legs into the hindlegs. I was sure I was going to be too slight to be able to operate this monster, but actually I fit pretty well; it conforms surprisingly snugly to my petite person.

I thrust my head through the neck. Cooper is there waiting for me, austere and erect, holding aloft the panda helmet, one half in each hand. He looks like Joan of Arc's squire standing at the ready to help her don her armor. Of course, that makes me Joan of Arc in this conceit, which is kind of how I feel: heroic, but a little looney too.

If the idea of being fastened into a metal helmet à la The Man in the Iron Mask sounds claustrophobic to you, let me make it worse. The tongue sleeve makes me feel like I'm being intubated. The nose tubes, that I have to snort like a coke-fiend as Cooper feeds them up each nostril, feel like they're touching my frontal lobes by the time they're all the way in.

Cooper fastens the helmet around my head, screw by screw; slowly my world fades to black. Even after several minutes in the helmet I can't see a thing. My eyes must have adjusted by now, but there is just no light in here to strike my retinas. It's vacuum-of-space quiet in here too. All I can do is breathe and wait.

The panda musk.

I smell it now (with my human nose). It's still got a sharp, umami tang, but it's not as overwhelming as it was before. I take it in breath by breath, and it modulates from being obnoxious, to being interesting, to just being. Soon it's the new normal.

They activate the suit. No vision yet, no sound, no cybernetically enhanced smell or taste: just feeling. The suit merges with my body, becomes one with my idea of myself. I am huge now, heavy, and much, much stronger. I can sense a great reserve of strength in my limbs and jaws, just waiting for me to order it around. My head is gigantic. My hands are monstrous paws, and they have panda thumbs, which I know exactly how to use.

They must be activating the suit in stages, I realize. The first stage was just for me to get a feel for this body, grow accustomed to its power, its gravitas. The second stage is to synchronize the suit with the field robot I'll be controlling, so that I begin to operate it from the same position it is in now.

The suit starts to move. I'm just along for the ride. I try to stop the suit's movements just to see if I can, strain against the moving limbs. I fail.

I'm now curled up on the ground. I can feel grass tickling my belly. My head is resting on my arms. It seems that my first job as a bear will be to wake up.

My ears come online. I hear birdsong and wind, the rustle of bamboo gently swaying like wooden windchimes.

Now my virtual eyes open, slowly, sleepily. The first thing I see is my nose: white fur, black tip. Beyond it I see my foreleg, where my nose is tucked. The fur feels coarse against my snout.

I experiment with lifting my head; it is exactly as easy as lifting my human head. I didn't feel or hear any actuators or servos helping me. It's all just me. I'm a bear, I'm in a clearing, and I see a bamboo forest before me.

My stomach itches. Before I know what I am doing, I get up on all fours, then lean back and fall on my well-padded bear-fanny. I don't have to think about balance; my body knows what to do. And so, still scanning the area, I lazily scratch my belly.

There is no difference between satisfying a virtual itch and a real one. Both feel wonderful.

This whole experience feels wonderful. This is amazing. I think I understand now how all-encompassing this virtual reality can be. I sit scratching and taking in my surroundings and marveling at how uncanny this all is. It really feels like I'm a panda.

But I'm wrong. I have no idea what it means to be a panda. Not yet. Not until they activate the nose.

~

Early humans had a much better sense of smell and taste than we do today. Studies have shown that, depending on the individual, somewhere between 40% to 70% of the genes devoted to those senses are inactive in modern homo sapiens.

While those with a mere 40% of their olfactory genes deactivated might make excellent sommeliers, those with 70% get along just fine. "We don't need acute olfaction and gustation to detect traces of poison or putrefaction the way our ancestors did," says Dr. Natalie Borelli, a Cal Tech professor of biocybernetics and director of Good Taste, a federally-funded program trying to create a prosthetic human tongue that allows users to both taste and speak. "We don't need to sniff out our food, or detect camouflaged predators. For us, there are very few situations in which smell is a matter of life and death."

But for the panda, smell serves as the organizing principle for life. Sight just tells the bears what's in front of them at the moment—and for the panda, it doesn't even do that very well. Pandas have relatively weak eyesight, and even if they could see better, most of the time they'd be staring at the same informationless wall of bamboo just inches from their snouts. Hearing gives them more range than sight, but is similarly limited to the here and now.

Smell, however, tells the history of their territory reaching back months. Sometimes you will see a panda approach a tree or a large rock and seem to snarl at it. But that lip-curling, called the "flehmen response," actually exposes its vomeronasal organ, which allows it to detect the pheromones of other pandas. Those pheromones tell it what pandas have been in the area, how recently, their genders, how big they are—vitally important if you're weighing your chances in a fight for a mate—and how close females are to estrus.

That last bit is especially important. Sows are in estrus for a bedevilingly short time, sometime for only a single day of the year. But thanks to his vomeronasal organ, a panda boar knows when that all-important day will be. A boar will enjoy most of mating season not by mating, but by mellowing out to estrogen-drenched sow-pee, growing accustomed to the pleasures of its one-of-a-kind bouquet, recognizing it as friendly and desirable, and having their testicles triple in size through a process called "spermatogenesis."

This is a key aspect to how pandas mate in the wild, a lesson humans were slow to learn when they tried to mate captive bears. Without this long, leisurely process of familiarization, a boar is more likely to maul a sow than mate with her: which, unfortunately, has led to the maiming or death of more than a few eligible she-bears in captivity, sometimes in front of a horrified zoo-going crowd.

For the most part, pandas are solitary creatures. There is no term of venery for a group of pandas. We could default to the generic terms for groups of bears: a "sleuth" or a "sloth." We could take one of the ad-hoc suggestions from the Internet: a "cuddle," an "ascension," a "contrast," or my favorite, a "monium" of pandas. But the fact is there isn't much need to speak of pandas in groups, since they spend almost all of their time alone.

There are two exceptions. One is when a mother is tending to a newborn cub. Even then, however, you wouldn't speak of a group of pandas, since the mother usually gives birth to a pair of cubs but tends to only one, leaving the other to die. Mother and cub will go their separate ways once the cub can fend for itself.

The other exception, however, is that fateful day when a sow is ready to mate. Then it can truly be said that pandas gather. Boars will contend with each other—usually through demonstrations of strength rather than battles to the death—for the right to conceive.

This is a panda behavior that has become increasingly rare in the wild, since panda numbers have dwindled so dangerously low. But its resurrection may hold the key to a true resurgence of the population.

For you see, while the victor gets the sow, the losers get the consolation prize of watching the winner's happy ending play out before them. It is in this fashion that younger, less-experienced boars are taught the ins and outs (ahem) of mating.

Biologists have tried to use videos of pandas having sex to mimic this effect for captive pandas. But humans found panda porn much more interesting than pandas ever did. There's no substitute for the live show. A panda can't trust anything it can't smell.

But if the scents are right and the sounds are right, would-be suitors will find themselves a nice vantage point and spy on the mating couple. Yet another distinction between humans and the rest of the animal kingdom collapses: we are not the only animals who voyeur.

Perhaps the best term for a group of pandas is an "exhibition."

~

I inhale the world in a way no human ever could. Scarves of scent, of all aromatic "colors," ride the wind, wending their way from all over the bamboo forest into my nose. When I open my mouth, even more smells rush in. I respire, and in comes all Creation.

But this is my first minute as a panda; I don't know how to differentiate between particular odors. I can tell flora from fauna, I can smell the sweet rot of dead plants, the thiol-thick stench of animals decomposing. But I lack the lexicon of fragrances to link each hyper-distinct scent with the real-world object that generates it.

All I know is I smell a lot of death. I'm stunned at how pervasive it is, how relentless. Pandas are often portrayed as peaceful and contemplative, but with all the decay that must unstoppably flood their noses every waking second of their lives, it would be impossible for a panda to be a Buddhist. It inhales suffering every second of its life. Were I a panda full-time, I'd spend my days raging against heaven for its indefatigable cruelty.

The strongest non-rot odor is the musk of other pandas. That I find, to my surprise, I quite enjoy. Now I know why, back at APM headquarters, they go to the trouble of dousing the suits with that noxious, bestial cologne. That musk is my lighthouse, my Rosetta Stone. That's how I will know Ken Cooper.

Or rather, that's how I will know Avalon, the robot-bear he's jockeying. There are at least four boars in the area, but only one musk smells like his. All I have to do is wait. Cooper will find me.

But so will the other bears. And that frightens me. I don't trust other bears. I don't trust anything. All this death. What I want to do is head into the forest of bamboo and sit quietly and hide, and maybe eat.

Oh God, yes, please, I need food. I'm starving.

Basically, I'm paranoid and famished. If you want to know what it's like to be a panda on the cheap, get high by yourself, and fill your fridge with nothing but bamboo shoots to snack on. Oh, and kill some mice and leave them to rot in their traps.

~

Eat or fuck? Eat or fuck?

Fuck.

I might be killed. Go fuck. I'm so hungry. Go fuck. No, no, not out in the open. Anything can see me. I want to go deep into the bamboo and hide and eat quietly.

No, Gabby. Go fuck.

I go fuck.

My head is raised and calling out. I am making noise. This is insanity. I want to shut my mouth, stop announcing my presence, but I can't. (I literally can't. Mission control—i.e. Xiadon and Deeprashad—partially operates the bear, making it call out and urinate as I walk. I can feel liquid trickling down my legs, but I can't stop it.)

Bears. They're coming. They're converging on me. I know them by their odors.

I stop, sit. I'm still peeing uncontrollably; my bear-ass is getting wet.

This isn't much of a clearing, but it'll do. And if I need to run away, the bamboo forest is right here, ready to envelop me, hide me.

I can hear one of the boars now. I don't see him. He's sliding through the bamboo, slow and deliberate. I can hear the shape of his body as he pushes stalks aside and comes for me.

He's grunting, low and repetitive. Each grunt sends a thrill racing over my skin. I can barely remember I am me.

There's another boar. He's farther away, but his smell is more intense. Something deep within me groans. My need flowers.

A third approaches, but I don't care. The second bear, his smell. I'm intoxicated. I want him.

That's not Avalon, human me, barely audible, thinks. *Where is Cooper?*

On-cue, Deeprashad's voice enters my head. "Sorry about this, Gabby, but we're going to have to pull the plug. We located the second terrorist. Ken's en-route to help capture him. So we won't be able to continue. We're going to move the robot to a safe space and shut you down."

I know she said this to me, because I heard the recorded transcript earlier. But here, now, inside Funicello, I have no idea. All I know is that's a big, glorious, scary-ass bear coming for me. I can hear his massive ursine body parting the forest.

The first suitor moves to intercept the big bear. I hear them meet. There are growls and yelps, and what sounds like a brief chase. Then the first suitor runs off, yelping and crying.

Apparently Deeprashad's been trying to talk to me all this time. "Can you hear me, Gabby? Gabrielle Reál, are you there?"

Something in my voice gives both of them pause.

"She's there," says Xiadon. "But she's a bear."

"I need to override Funicello and extract Gabby ASAP. Just waiting for your order, Mei."

I'm not following this conversation very well, but I know they're about to separate me from the bear that is juggernauting through the bamboo forest to find me. I don't think this in words, but in whatever way a languageless mammalian brain constructs thoughts, I think to myself, over and over, *I want to stay. Please don't take me.*

"Gui Gui is moving in quickly," Xiadon says. "He subdued Wei Wei. He might be ready, Anita."

"Oh Jesus. Not now."

I'm punchy and dizzy and scared and happy and I don't have a clue what I'm saying or hearing. All I know is that big bear is trudging toward me again. And every step makes my flesh horripilate.

"All Gabby has to do," says Xiadon, "is stick her ass in the air and present. If Gui Gui does nothing, no harm, no foul. But if he's interested—"

"You can't be serious," says Deeprashad.

I face the direction of the incoming boar. He's still just a jumble of rustling sounds and a pheromone bouquet, but both are getting stronger. I call out to him, this time because I want to. Inside the helmet I call out; I sound congested and tongue-tied thanks to the tongue-sleeve and the tubes up my nose. But at the same time I call, I hear the robot bleat like a panda sow at the height of estrus. I might burst before he gets here.

But here he is, his moon-sized head peaking through the bamboo. My god he's massive. His mouth is open; he is flehmening me like a heavy-breather. I have never been so scared, so ready. He is so beautiful.

"We've got to stop this, Mei," says Deeprashad.

"Too late," says Xiadon, not the least bit unhappy. "Gabby, can you hear me? Gabby, you're going to have to go through with this. Don't worry. We'll help control you from here. Just relax, no sudden moves."

It takes all of my intellectual power, but I am able to produce two words: "Okay. Yes. Yes. Okay. Yes. Okay."

Gui Gui comes into the clearing, approaching neither slow nor fast. I rise. We touch noses; his lip rises, and he takes my odor in his mouth, eats it. He licks my face a few times. I lick his, my human tongue sliding back and forth in the helmet's sleeve.

"Jesus," says Deeprashad. "You sure you haven't done this before, Gabby?"

The boar moves behind me, smells me from behind. He jams in his nose, machine-gun sniffs my most sensitive parts. He nuzzles and licks. I turn to sniff him. We make a yin-yang of ourselves, inhaling each other's backsides. This is his musk at full strength. I'm drunk, terrified, ready.

Somewhere off in the distance I hear Xiadon saying over and over, "Now, Gabby! Present! Face on the ground, butt in the air!"

The front of me drops to the ground; I raise my rear up. I briefly wonder if the other bears can see us. But to be honest, I don't really care. This is for me.

Gui Gui mounts me. He mostly supports his own weight. I adjust to make us fit together better, then press my backside into him. And he presses forward.

The suit doesn't stimulate my human genitals, or any part of my brain in charge of sexual satisfaction. I don't orgasm, not even close. What I receive instead is communion. The event horizon that constitutes my sense of self grows outward. I breathe in the ground beneath me through my nose, and it becomes me; I inhale the stalks of bamboo that surround us, and I am they; I am the boar who mates with me, and I am all the death in the forest. But I am the life, too. Two other boars are in trees nearby—yes, I've smelled them out—watching, learning. I snort them into me, snort up more and more of the forest, the world, until it's no longer useful or desirable to think of myself as a me.

~

The last thing APM wanted was to put an amateur like me in a real mating situation. But as accidents go, this was a very happy one for APM. My mate, Gui Gui, was seen by APM as the next in line as a possible panda suitor, as APM's other boars were still a little young and uneducated in matters of love. Gui Gui had been observing Avalon mounting sows for two seasons. It seems he learned all he needed, since he successfully deposited a healthy payload of sperm into Funicello.

Gui Gui will now join that elite group of boars whose sexual exploits are recorded in *The International Studbook of the Giant Panda*, a registry of every boar whose sperm has been used in procreation attempts. His sample will be divided into test tubes of 100,000 cells and sent to breeding facilities all over the world.

Moreover, three of APM's five sows will enter estrus within the next few weeks. This could be the beginning of a wonderful career for him as a professional stud.

~

My helmet is unfastened screw by screw. I'm still panting, dazed. Suddenly my panda-head is halved, removed, and all that's left of my mind is my own mind. In front of my face is Cooper, smiling like a dumbass.

"You did great," he says. "You were perfect."

"Always am," I say sleepily. I'm not ready to lose my dream of being a panda yet. I'm resisting returning to the world. "And you missed it."

"I was busy," he says. And then, with mock modesty: "I got her."

"Who?" I ask, blinking.

"The second terrorist. I caught her. And I didn't even break anything on this one."

"Good for you," I say. But I don't give two shits. Talking to Cooper is shrinking me. Sentence by sentence, noun by noun, he's turning me back into Gabrielle Reál. But I don't want to be Reál. Not yet. I want my body to be as large as my imagination for a while longer.

And now Deeprashad is kneeling next to me. "You were glorious!" she says. But then she takes a paw in her hand. "But we need to talk seriously about your security. Unfortunately, you will now be on 22:19's list. Since in their eyes you've ... had relations with a real bear, that makes you a sinner. And therefore a target. But APM will—"

"Anita?" says Xiadon. Cooper and Deeprashad part a little so I can see her behind them. "We can discuss that later, maybe?"

Anita wrangles the words back into her mouth. Then, tight-lipped, she says, "Sure thing, Mei," pats my paw, backs off.

"You too, Ken."

"What'd I do?" asks Cooper. He was trying to be funny, but it comes off a little strained. I notice his finger is ringless now. Does he take it off to jockey bears? Probably. God, I hope so.

When he delays, Xiadon gives him the take-a-hike thumb. Reluctantly, he winks at me and leaves my side. That just leaves me and the good doctor looking at each other.

"It's beautiful, right?" Xiadon asks. "It's hard to come back, I know. But it's okay. Take all the time you need."

And I'm giggling. Out of nowhere. And then crying, too: my patented giggle-cry, confusing and disturbing to watch, I've been told since I was a kid. But I can't help it. I wasn't just alive when I was a panda; I was in life, indistinguishable from life. Now I feel manacled by thought, self-awareness, words. Especially words. Language is the knothole in the fence: you're grateful to be able to see through to the other side, sure, but wouldn't it be better just to jump the fence?

Xiadon raises a hand as if she is going to wave hello, but instead she wiggles her panda thumb at me.

That little gesture snaps my crying jag. Now I'm just laughing. I lift the suit's right paw and wiggle my own sesamoid bone at her. At least I'm still that much a panda.

The Macrobe Conservation Project

1.

My asiMom was okay. She was like a pillow, a walking talking pillow. But she gave good hugs and smelled right. They did a good job with her: sometimes when she hugged me and I closed my eyes it felt like it's supposed to feel and I forgot that she's not my real mom.

I saw her in the shower a few times. She didn't care. She took showers every day exactly at 5:45 PM, even if I messed up every clock in the house, because her inside clock was always right. She didn't even need to shower because she was just a robot, but she did anyway. My dad said that that made her more realistic. But if they cared about that, why didn't they give her nipples? Or any hair, except on her head? She didn't even have a butt crack. Sometimes, just when I was forgetting that she wasn't my real mom, I'd remember that she didn't have a butt crack and I'd get a little freaked out.

My dad's one of the head honchos on the station. He's the lead scientist on the Macrobe Conservation Project. He said that he was the one who wrote all the grants and traveled all the way back to Earth to shake hands with all the jerks in Washington, and so now he was the one in charge, and if Malloy or Grisget or any of those other pieces of skrak thought they were going to hone in on his dream, they had another thing coming. He went to work at 6:00 and got home at 6:00, but they always called him back at night with some big macrobe problem. Sometimes on the speaker I'd hear Dr. Malloy or Dr. Grisget or one of those other pieces of skrat saying, "Don't worry, Lance, this is no big deal. We just wanted you to know. You just have a good time with your kid tonight. We'll handle this." That drove my dad nuts. He waited until they hung up, and then he cussed like crazy at them while he tied his tie back on, and told my asiMom to clean up dinner and make up a plate for him to eat later. Mostly he didn't come back though. Just stayed in the lab all night.

He said that we could cuss all we wanted while we were on the space station, just me and him, but only in Macrolog. Macrolog is the pretend language Dad and I made up for the macrobes. It's what the macrobes are thinking whenever scientists are probing them or taking tissue samples or whatever. The whole language is just swear words: skrat and fragbag and kikface and dunkaballs and a bunch of others. Almost all of them have the letter k in them. I think my dad thinks the letter k is dirty.

Skrat is my favorite. Dad's too. It sounds the dirtiest. Sometimes I told my asiMom to go skrat herself, to see if she'd do anything. But she just kinda looked at me like she didn't get it, and smiled, and then went back to whatever she was doing. Didn't matter, you can't skrat without a buttcrack anyway.

2.

I had an asiBro too who was supposed to be like my brother, but he wasn't like my brother very much. For one thing, they made him a younger brother, and Lance Jr. is my big brother. But they only make younger asiBros. My dad told me that they tried making older asiBros for a while, but that all these little kids were following them around and burning themselves or getting their fingers cut off or getting themselves killed in the dishwasher, because the asiBros didn't know what they were doing and couldn't protect all those dumb little kids from all the dumb stuff they do. I asked Dad why they make asiMoms then, since they're supposed to be substitute moms, but my dad got really serious, the way he always does before he tells a really stupid joke, and said, "Randy, you of all people should know that kids never listen to their parents." Ha ha ha.

The Lance Jr. asiBro was really annoying. He was smaller than me and dumber than me and he followed me around all the time. He was boring, and there was no way to get rid of him. I told my brother about him, and he said "He sounds just like you!" I called him a skrat-clown and I didn't tell him what it meant, so he asked my dad and my dad just laughed at him.

3.

Summer on the space station was okay, but not as knife as I thought it'd be. I thought it was going to be like space camp, only real. But it wasn't like space camp. It was just real.

The space station was pretty small. And it wasn't set up for kids. There were places to work and places to eat and rooms to sleep in and places I wasn't allowed to go by myself, like Engineering or the Macrobe Lab. Mostly I just stayed in my room and played video games with my asiBro. And that was kinda dunkaballs, because he was way too good. I can never beat the real Lance Jr., and the Lance Jr. asiBro was a stupid robot with reflexes like you wouldn't believe. And plus, whenever he beat me, he would say, "Good game, Randy! If you would like, I can lower my challenge setting. Would you like me to lower it now?" And yes I would like, but I felt like a kikface asking my pretend little robot brother to go easy on me, so I never did. Instead I switched to single-player games and made him watch. He didn't mind. He just sat there and cheered me on.

4.

I went to the lab sometimes with my dad. Not a lot, but sometimes. There wasn't a lot for me to do there anyway. All I could do is look but don't touch.

It was still pretty knife. It looked like a morgue, probably because of all the dead people. The center of the lab had sixteen incubators with sixteen dead people lying in them. You couldn't actually see the dead people, because the incubators weren't see-through, I guess so the scientists didn't have to stand there looking at dead people all day.

The incubators weren't for the dead people, because if you're dead, there's nothing to incubate. The incubators were really for the macrobes. The cadavers—that's what my dad liked me to call the dead people—were the hosts for the macrobes. So really they had two incubators: the real incubators, and then the dead people.

It seemed like a lot of work to keep those things from going extinct. I didn't get it at first. I mean, why would you want to protect animals—if you can even call them animals, since they look like blobs of Jell-O that were made with toilet water—that will also take over your brain the first chance they get? So I asked my dad one day. Actually, I told him maybe New Hope would be better off without macrobes. "I mean, the less things that will eat your brain, the better, right?" I said.

He got real serious. I could tell because he stopped eating. The skrat on his fork started dripping through the tines, but he just held it in the air, because he had turned into Professor Dad and it was time for a really long science lesson: "Randy, we're the outsiders. We're the guests to New Hope. We came here because we did a really good job of ruining our own planet and are going to need to move everybody off of it in the very near future. And now that we're getting a second chance, you think the first thing we should do is just start killing off species left and right?"

"No," I said. I was staring at the skrat on his fork. It kind of looked like a macrobe.

"We've only been here a very short while, and already we know that the macrobes are an essential part of the planet's ecosystem. There's a certain type of tree on the planet called a 'brain tree' that needs the macrobes in order to live. Maybe other trees do too, we don't know. But trees give us the oxygen we need to breathe on New Hope, just like they did on Earth. It wouldn't be smart to start killing off all the trees, would it?"

"No."

I said no twice already, but once you get my dad going on macrobes, there's no stopping him. "And anyway, macrobes are one of the most interesting life forms we've ever discovered, Randy. Certainly the most advanced parasites we've ever seen."

And then I saw a way to ask him about the knifest thing about macrobes: the dead people. "Yeah, I don't get that. How can they be parasites? Doesn't the host of a parasite have to be alive? I think they're more like scavengers."

He looked at me liked I had dunkaballs coming out of my nose. He finally ate his forkful of macrobe and said, "That is a very perceptive thing to say, Randy. Did you think of that yourself?"

And I said, "Yeah, dad. I'm not stupid."

And he said, "Hey kiddo, that's not what I meant! But no, technically, the macrobes are parasites. See, they're not just eating up the bodies they inhabit, like a scavenger would. They're actually preserving it! They get inside a dead body and spread throughout the nervous system, and they get everything working again, almost like the body has come back to life! That's hardly the behavior of a scavenger, right?"

And I said "Yeah. But then it's like they're not really parasites either. They're symbiotic. They help their host, so they're not just mooching off of it like a leech."

I could tell he was impressed that I knew what symbiotic meant. And then he said, "Well, they don't really help out their host, because the host is dead, and it stays dead. And, if you put a macrobe in a live human, well, believe me, you'd know it was a parasite! Eventually it would spread through your entire nervous system, go up your spine, and take over your brain, just like you said. But with a cadaver, it doesn't matter if a macrobe takes over the brain, because the cadaver isn't using it anyway."

"What happens when the macrobe takes over the brain?"

"In a cadaver, not much, because we sever a lot of the neuromuscular connections to avoid complications." He gave me a weird look before he kept going. "In theory, though, a macrobe could take over enough to … move a human body around, maybe."

"And make it walk and talk again? Like the living dead?"

My dad was laughing. "No, not like the 'living dead.' Where do you come up with this stuff? You think this space station is going to turn into a zombie movie?"

"That'd be so knife."

"Yes, very knife. But to answer your question … I can't answer your question. We don't know exactly what happens. That's exactly what we're trying to find out here."

I scooped up some of my macrobe-skrat with my fork and let it hang in the air for a minute and stared at it and watched it drip through the fork-teeth. And then I asked my dad, "Dad, why did we have to come to this space station?"

"What do you mean?"

"I mean, why couldn't you do your experiments with the macrobes on New Hope? Why'd we have to go all the way to outer space?"

My dad got a big, crooked smile on his face and leaned back in his chair and put his hands behind his head. "I'll tell you, Randy. But this has to be a secret between us."

"Okay."

"The reason we're on this space station is because none of the brand-new nations on New Hope have the dunkaballs to say that they are letting me stick macrobes into cadavers on their soil. Sure, they want me to save the ecosystem and bring the macrobes back from the brink of extinction, just as long as I shoot myself into orbit to do it!"

And just when things were getting good, those fragbags Malloy and Grisget called with another skratty problem they were having. So my dad left and I helped my asiMom clear dinner. After we finished, she said "You are a good son." And then she added, "If you would like me to increase the amount of praise I give you, please say 'Increase praise' at any time."

5.

I don't even know why I have to be here. With you. I'm not crazy. I know my dad thinks I'm crazy, but I think he's crazy, so we're even. I'm not a "danger to myself and others." I got that off of my chart. I don't know who wrote that, but it's not true. If you wrote that you're wrong, and I know you wrote that.

When I was on the space station I only got in trouble twice in the whole summer. And the first one wasn't even that big a deal. I just used a nailgun without permission. On my asiBro.

Why did they have a nailgun in a space station if it's so dangerous?

They shouldn't have just left it lying around either. How was I supposed to know? It was just there, in Engineering, and okay, I wasn't supposed to be in there, but it's not like they locked the door or anything, and the nailgun was just there. And I didn't take it for that long either. I just wanted to see what it could do.

But you can't use a nailgun on anything in a space station. Everything's so breakable. It's not like there was any wood or anything I could've used.

So I took it back to my apartment. I didn't need my asiMom for anything, so I told her to go recharge, and she did. And then I told my asiBro to come over.

He came over and said: "That is a nailgun." He was always identifying things, like I was some sort of kikface.

And I said to him, "Hold out your hand." And he did, and I shot him between the knuckles with the nailgun. The nail went in maybe a centimeter before it hit metal. The asiBro said "Ow that hurt," but I could tell it didn't. He still had the same happy idiot look on his face, and he didn't even try to pull it out.

So I shot him a few more times. Okay, a lot more times. It was funny. He just kept saying "Ow that hurt Ow that hurt Ow that hurt Ow that hurt" in the same normal voice over and over. It didn't matter where I shot him: face, stomach, foot, chest, knee, or right in the dunkaballs.

That was the day I discovered that when an asiBot is getting damaged, it calls its owner's phone to let them know what's happening.

My dad busted into the apartment out of breath and looking really scared. I know he was really worried about me, but I wasn't doing it for attention. I didn't know my fragbag pretend brother was going to call him and narc me out. Well anyway, my dad didn't stay scared long. He was too busy getting really really angry.

6.

My dad said I was lucky he didn't send me back planetside. I told him he couldn't, because no ships were coming from New Hope for another five weeks. He told me that I was wrong, mister, and that I was a kid and I didn't know everything, so I should listen to him, because there was a whole ship-full of post-docs coming from New Hope that very day, and he was sure the captain would be willing to take me back. I said fine, I'll go spend the rest of the summer with Mom and Lance Jr. At least Lance Jr. wasn't stupid enough to just stand there while I shot him with a nailgun.

And then my dad got quiet. It was weird. He just sat there and looked at me. It was so weird that when he finally said, "Go to your room," I did without even yelling or throwing stuff or anything. A little while later I heard him leave, and I didn't hear him come back that night.

He told me the next night at dinner that he'd been busy all day with the new post-docs. He said he wasn't mad any more, and that he'd had my asiBro checked out, and that it was fine, no harm done. So, if I wanted, I could have him back. But only if I promised not to shoot him any more.

7.

Besides getting my asiBro back, my dad took me to meet all the new post-docs to show me he wasn't mad. They were all eating together in the mess when I came in. When I saw they were human, I was really relieved: I thought a "post-doc" was some kind of new alien creature they had discovered. Turns out they're just Ph.D.s.

But they were pretty knife. A lot younger than my dad and Grisget and Malloy and all the other scientists on the space station. And funny. They were always fragbagging around. My dad said they have skrat for brains. I said they do not, they just like to have fun. He said you don't go on a scientific space station to have fun. I said you can say that again and he said what? and I said never mind.

I hung out with them pretty much all the time. I knew the space station, so I showed them around, and they said I could be their mascot. They gave me a Ph.D. in Space Station Knowledge and Etiquette and called me Doctor Randy and took me with them everywhere, even into the Macrobe Lab without my dad.

Their first real day in the lab was a week after they came, and I went with them. Dr. Grisget was conducting an orientation for them in the lab. He kept congratulating them and telling them what a great honor it was to have been selected for this post-doc. Maria Centas, who was the same height as me and was always laughing about something, said to me, "This guy is really full of himself, isn't he?" And I nodded yes, but I didn't say anything because I didn't want Dr. Grisget to notice me and tell me I wasn't allowed to be there.

But then he did something really knife; he opened one of the incubators. All the post-docs huddled around it, so I couldn't really see. He said, "Ladies and gentleman, this is the reason you are here. The Macrobe Conservation Project is dedicated to saving macrobes from extinction, thereby helping us to preserve the ecosystem we discovered when we first landed on New Hope." And then he said the whole history of the whole project, how when settlers first came to New Hope they cut down a lot of trees, only they didn't know the difference between the different kinds of trees, and they didn't know that they were cutting down brain trees because they didn't have that name back then. They didn't know that brain trees were basically trees with brains, and that they had a symbiotic relationship with macrobes, and with the trees getting cut down the macrobes started dying off. Plus a few people had been infected by macrobes, and the macrobes started taking over their brains, and that scared a lot of people, so they started killing macrobes like crazy. And since a macrobe is basically just a big squishy gray-and-green blob of toilet-water, it was really easy to kill them. Dr. Grisget said, "Now they are almost extinct. We are all that's left to protect them from total annihilation."

I finally squirmed through the post-docs so I could see inside the incubator. I'd seen glimpses inside them before. Mostly they shaved the cadavers' heads and had them in those green paper outfits they give you in hospitals that don't close in the back. But this one was a woman, and you could tell because she had long curly woman's hair, and an earring in the ear I could see, and she had a dress on with flowers. Earth flowers.

I wasn't tall enough to see her face, but I knew the dress was my mom's. She had the same hair as my mom too. I couldn't figure out why my dad would take one of my mom's dresses and put it on a dead lady. My mom would be so mad if she found out.

8.

I wasn't supposed to call New Hope by myself, because calls from the space station were very expensive. But I didn't like that my dad had put one of my mom's dresses on one of the cadavers.

Lance Jr.'s big kikface appeared on the monitor. "You're in trouble, Randy," he said. "You're not supposed to call."

"You're in trouble too," I said back. "You're not supposed to answer."

"There's no one else around to answer. Aunt Lois went out for groceries."

"Where's Mom?"

Lance Jr. looked at me totally dunkaballs. "She's with you, stupid."

"No she's not, fragbag. She's with you."

"Since when? Is she coming home?"

"She's always been home. You're not funny."

"I'm not trying to be funny, dickhead." And then he kind of squinted and said, "You haven't seen Mom?"

And then I saw my mom walk right behind him on the monitor. I pointed behind him and shouted, "See, skratbreath, she's right there! Liar!"

Lance Jr. turned around, then turned back to the phone. "Man are you dumb. That's just an asiMom." He turned around again and said "Come here," to my mom and my mom walked over in the exact same way an asiMom walks. Then Lance Jr. said "Increase praise." And my mom put a hand on his head and said, "Sorry, but praise level is already set to maximum." Lance Jr. kind of shrugged at me and said, "I learn best from positive reinforcement."

9.

That night during dinner, Dad got a call from Dr. Malloy. "We're having a little bit of a problem here," he said, "but it's nothing we can't handle, Lance." My dad said, "I'll be right over," and then, when the speaker was off, he said, "This place would fall apart without me." And then he headed out of the door.

My asiMom cleared the dishes, and my asiBro asked me if I wanted to play a game. I told him to go fragbag himself. He said, "I don't know what 'fragbag' means. Would you like to add the word to my dictionary?" So I told him to go recharge himself instead. And then I watched the clock for exactly five minutes. Then I got up and followed my dad.

You need an I.D. to swipe to get into the Macrobe Lab, so I stopped at Maria Centas' room and took hers. She was having dinner with the other post-docs in the mess and she never locked her door.

I swiped her card and went in the lab. I crawled on the floor and peeked around incubators to find my dad. The floor was cold and really clean.

Dad was shaking hands with Dr. Malloy. "I know I say this every night," my dad said, "but thanks."

Dr. Malloy just gave him a few pats on the back and said, "You take care of yourself, okay? For your sake, and your sons'." And then he started walking toward me, so I had to duck behind a different incubator and hide there until he left the lab.

Once Dr. Malloy was gone, I peeked around the incubator to watch my dad again. He had opened one of the incubators, the one with the cadaver that had on my mom's dress. He just looked at that dead lady for a long time. Then he put his arm under her and kind of propped her up until she almost looked like she was sitting. He moved the hair out of the dead lady's face and he said, "Hi, Cathy." My mom's name is Catherine.

And then he took out the biggest syringe with the longest needle I've ever seen in my life and stuck it in the dead lady's ear. All the way. I almost screamed. It took a long time to push all of the medicine into the dead lady's brain. When he was done, he put the syringe on the tray and then held the dead lady with both arms, just looking at her and waiting for something to happen.

The dead lady's head sat up like only her neck had come back to life. Then she opened her eyes, then closed them, then practiced opening and closing them. She opened and closed her mouth next, in exactly the same way. She stuck out her tongue then sucked it back into her face and moved her eyebrows every crazy way they would go.

My dad took out his pocket recorder. He turned it on and said, "6:44 PM, stimulant administered. Macrobe 'Catherine' exhibiting advanced facial movement ability. Cadaver has recovered doll-eye movement, but lacks a blink reflex and is not yet breathing. Macrobe 'Catherine' seems on-schedule to fully permeate the medulla in three to five weeks." Then he turned the recorder off and put it back in his pocket.

And then he hugged the dead lady again. And he kind of rocked her back and forth and he said, "Cathy. Oh Cathy. Why did you leave me Cathy?" And all the while, the dead lady never stopped making all those insane faces.

10.

I snuck out of the Lab and went back to the apartment. I told the asiMom and the asiBro to follow me. The stupid asiBro said "I am not fully recharged yet. Do you want me to stop recharging now?" And I said, "Yes, fragbag!" And so he stopped recharging and followed me.

The three of us went to Engineering. Now the door was locked because of the nailgun thing, but I used Maria Centas' I.D. and the door opened. "Follow me," I said, and they followed.

We walked to the space station's trash compactor. It was huge; it looked like it could crush a planet. I walked them over to it and said, "Get in."

They climbed in. I couldn't believe how stupid they were. What did they think was going to happen?

I told them to kneel, and they did, both of them looking up at me like I was the dad. Then I said "Pray," and they both bowed their heads and folded their hands, and the asiMom asked, "What prayer would you like us to say?" And I said, "Just pray quietly," so they just pretended to pray quietly. Then the asiBro said "This is a fun game!" and the asiMom said, "Honey, you have to be quiet. We're praying now."

I walked over to the compactor's command console—that's exactly what it said on the front of it, "Command Console," like you could control the whole world with it—and hit the big red button. I'd always wanted to.

The compactor came to life and this big slab of steel started to slowly push down on the heads of the asiBots. It kept pushing until I couldn't see their heads anymore. "Keep praying!" I yelled. Then I heard metal getting smashed and glass breaking and small electric pops and plastic splintering. And then the compactor hit bottom. It stopped there for a moment, and then started to slowly come back up.

I turned to face the door. I'm sure both asiBots had called my dad to tell them they were being destroyed. I was sure he would come running, just like last time. And when he got there I would ask him if that dead lady was really my mom.

Los Simpáticos

You don't know my name, but if you are Latino, live next to a Latino, or have watched television within the last year, you know my work. My name is Desideria Belén Ayute, and I am the sixty-one-year-old executive producer for *¿A Quién Quieres Matar?*, the reality-TV show where we find fulanos who want to hire a hit man and get them to admit on hidden camera all the filthy details. Oh, it's a good show. Three years on the air in every Spanish-speaking country on the planet, and still on top—even today, even after all this ugliness. Wait, who am I kidding? Even more now. The show's reruns are doing better than this season's crop of telenovelas and variety shows. If only, somehow, Xavier could enjoy all this success with us, life would be perfect. But that's not life, mi vida. Life and limes are delicious, but sour.

Theoretically, *¿A Quién Quieres Matar?* could run forever. You wouldn't believe how many people out there are willing to pay tens of thousands of dollars to kill a friend or family member. I'm an old woman, so I can remember a time when, if you wanted to kill someone, you'd go grab your machete and do the job yourself. But this new generation, with their American ways and their American dollars, they don't want to get their machetes dirty. They'd much rather hire some poor guajiro fresh off the boat and hungry for money to do it for them. And there's never any shortage of hungry guajiros.

Xavier Morales was the actor who played the hit man on our show.

We pixilated his face and slowed his voice in post-production so people wouldn't recognize him on the street. But we were fools to think we could keep his identity a secret. Some Internet idiots with too much time on their hands revealed his identity before the first season was over.

We thought the show was done. But it wasn't—because even though millions watch our show, billions do not: they watch something else, or don't watch TV, or whatever. In fact, once his cover was blown, ratings went up, especially with women viewers ages 18 to 30. You know why? Because Xavier was gorgeous. What a guapetón that man was! Beautiful and manly and gentle and powerful and funny and, my God, what a dancer! And though he was Cuban through and through, he was born in the States, which meant that most of the nasty parts of machismo—like the part that thinks it's perfectly okay to backhand a woman—had been shrunk to nothing, like successfully-treated tumors. But the good parts of machismo—the valor, the tenacity, that almost savage cheeriness that is impervious to neurosis—remained perfectly intact. I had sexual fantasies about that man six days a week at least.

So you can imagine how upset I was when the police called me that morning to tell me he'd committed suicide.

Earlier the previous evening, we had wrapped up shooting our special New York City edition of *¿A Quién Quieres Matar?* It was the weirdest shoot we'd ever had. We were all set up in our rented third-floor apartment in the Bronx to receive our mark of the week, a lanky

Dominican named Tito Angelobronca. Seventeen years old, going on twelve: he slumped in his chair and only spoke to adults when spoken to, and even then only with sullen one-word replies. He wanted Xavier to kill another high school boy named Miguel Fernández for, as far as I could tell, no good reason: he gave half-reasons like girls and neighborhood slights and "that puto's a punk-ass bitch! He's got to go, yo!"

So Tito was coming to the apartment to finalize all the details with Xavier, to give him all the information a real hitman might need for the job. And Tito had a special request: he wanted Xavier to make it look like a suicide, and wanted Xavier to leave a note behind that read: "Soy simpático," which means "I'm likable" and/or "I'm sympathetic." It was a damned weird thing to write on a forged suicide note. Xavier was going to ask him what that meant when he showed up.

Besides Xavier and the hidden cameras and my crew, in the apartment were a half-dozen of New York's Finest who, once they had all the evidence they needed, would burst from their hiding places and wrestle Tito's chicken-bone frame into a chair. Then, if he waived his rights—and they almost always did—Xavier would interview him. And then the police would haul the suspect off, and we'd start breaking down the equipment and heading to our next location: Miami, our bread-and-butter city. There's never been a hitman in Miami who's been unemployed for more than twenty minutes.

So there we were, waiting, ready to get the whole dirty business on-camera. Only it wasn't Tito we saw, courtesy of our hidden cameras, walk into the apartment building. It was an old woman, dressed in the humiliating motleys of some chain restaurant: Hawaiian bowling shirt, red slacks, black visor, disintegrating sneakers. Her eyes looked as big and black as a horse's. She was stooped but sure-footed; she climbed the stairs like someone who had ascended Machu Picchu every day of her life. In one hand she carried a brown bag that said "Large Brown Bag" on the side.

We weren't ready for her, but in the reality-TV biz you learn to adjust fast. While the rest of us hid, Xavier slipped into character: a laconic, efficient sociopath. He dragged a chair in front of the apartment door and sat facing it, waiting for her to knock.

She didn't. She turned the knob and walked in and didn't close the door. Her huge eyes were shut into slits; her mouth was pursed; her hands were fists. She looked at Xavier with the combination of derision and fear that we Latinos usually reserve for the Antichrist.

Xavier, smiling like the Antichrist, said, "I think you have the wrong apartment, abuelita."

She replied in Spanish, but I'll translate: "This is the right place. One look at you, and I know this is the right place. You're the assassin. You're the man Tito wants to hire to kill Miguelito. Well, you won't be killing anyone today. Tito is not going to hire you. I found out about his plan. I know everything. That's how I knew to come here. And I have put a stop to it." She dropped the bag on the floor. "Ten thousand dollars. Consider yourself paid. All I ask is that you leave Tito alone. He will never say anything to anyone about this, and neither will I, may God split me in two with a lightning bolt."

All of us were stunned. But Xavier could handle anything. After a short pause, he stood and went over to the bag, took out a rubber-banded brick of bills, rifled through them appreciatively. Then he smiled and in Spanish said to the old woman, "Okay, abuela. Paid in full. So it's over."

The old woman squinted her horse-eyes. "Don't try to find Tito. Don't try to hurt him. You'll never find him."

"I kill for money, woman, not for pleasure. I have been paid, and I didn't have to lift a finger. Why would I want to kill him?"

"Because he has seen your face. He can report you to the police."

"But you won't let him. You told him he could never say anything to anyone, because if he did, I would kill him."

"Yes. Just as you say."

"But abuela, now you have seen my face, too. Maybe you think I am going to kill you?"

"Yes," she said. Sudden tears fell like ballasts from her eyes. "I do."

I saw Xavier's character waiver—the hitman persona shimmered, almost dissipated. But he collected himself. "I understand. I see it all clearly now. You think I won't let either of you live. You have done everything you can, but you think I will kill you both anyway. But listen, abuela. Killing clients is bad for business. I have a reputation to maintain. So long as you and Tito keep quiet, it's better for me to take the money and be on my way. We can all win."

She was still crying, but she didn't let that get in the way of scrutinizing Xavier. "Don't lie to me. God is watching you. You are going to let Tito live?"

"Yes, abuelita. And you, too."

"I am an old woman. If you don't kill me, soon enough something else will. But Tito is just a boy. Swear to God you will not kill him."

"I swear in the name of God that I will not kill Tito Angelobronca."

She narrowed her horse-eyes. "How can I trust an assassin?"

Xavier laughed and replied, "I don't know, abuela. All I can offer is my word."

She studied him for a moment. Then she said, "You are going to hell. Unless you change your ways, God will punish you for your terrible sins. You should pray every night to Jesus Christ, and confess your sins, and change your evil ways."

"I know, abuela. I know."

"If you keep your word, I will pray for you. One rosary every day." She turned to leave. "Perhaps the Virgin Mary will hear me and intercede on your behalf. Perhaps your heart will open up to God's love. You can still be saved from eternal damnation. Pray every night, and in the end you may spend eternity in God's loving presence." She pulled the door shut and was gone.

We watched the monitors, jumping from one to the next as she left the range of one staircase camera and entered that of another. It wasn't until she left the building that we started breathing again.

The crew and cops erupted in an astonished disputation: "What the hell was that?" we asked each other, laughing and scratching our heads. Could we still make an episode out of this weird twist of an ending? And then there was the money, all that money: of course we had to return it to the abuela. It was her money, not Tito's, we were sure—scrimped and scoured from who-knows-where to save the life of her unworthy grandson.

Well, that could be our ending right there! We could have Xavier return the money to her, tell her it was all pretend, all just for TV, and that she didn't have to live in fear. We'd just have to make sure she was ready, so that she wouldn't do anything rash—like have a heart attack—when she saw Xavier again.

Xavier. He sat with his elbows on his thighs, hands covering his face. I went over to him, put a hand on his shoulder. He knew it was me by touch. "Oh man, Mámi," he said. He always called me 'Mámi,' which I kind of hated and kind of adored. "That was hard. I shouldn't have done it that way. I should've told her it was all an act."

"Are you kidding?" I said, and moved around to the front to give him a hug. The first rule of being a good producer is hug first, talk money later. "You were perfect. Thanks to you, we'll still be able to salvage a show out of this. And she'll get her money back. Everyone's going to benefit from this, thanks to you."

He groaned. "I tortured her, Mámi. I made her suffer. I could've been so much kinder. Why didn't I just tell her the truth? Why did I stay in character?"

"Because you're a good actor, and you had a job to do. We're going to fix everything. We're going to make everything right."

Into his hands he said, "I have to make it right, mámi. I have to."

"You will," I said. "Don't worry. We'll fix everything. First thing tomorrow."

As I entered Xavier's hotel room the next morning, tears dragging clots of mascara down my face, I thought to myself, *I told you we were going to fix everything, Xavier. Why didn't you believe me?*

~

This part is a little sick. I know it is. I am ashamed, but not as ashamed as I should be, and that makes me even more ashamed. I brought a camera crew with me to Xavier's hotel room.

Look, I'm a TV producer. This was a legitimate international news story. I had a responsibility to the public. Plus, I didn't want to go there alone. So I brought Eugenio, the oldest cameraman in the industry, and Constancia, the show's viper-tongued director, to whom I would trust my eternal soul.

The only reason I got into that hotel room in the first place was because, after many shoots in New York of *¿A Quién Quieres Matar?*, I'd made friends with a lot of NYPD detectives and, in a small but real way, helped them arrest some dangerous people before they could do any real harm. And everyone wants to be on TV, even detectives.

Enter Detective Dan Burdock. I always think of him when Billy Joel sings the line: "He's quick with a joke/ or a light of your smoke,/ but there's someplace that he'd rather be." Yes, poor Danny always dreamed of being a star, but since he had a complexion like a post-poisoned Viktor Yushchenko, he was better off as a detective, where he could use his looks to intimidate low-lifes.

He was the one who had called me, who was now leading me and my crew through the room. The detectives, crime scene investigators, and the coroner had all done everything they needed to do. At Dan's request they had left a few key items in place so that I could film them. But not Xavier. They had, of course, removed his body. They had even remade the bed. He was utterly disappeared from the room.

Once my crew was parked, plugged in, and rolling, Dan, overacting, looked into the camera and set the scene for us. "Here is where the apparent suicide took place. I say apparent, because the official report won't have been filed yet, but it's pretty cut and dry. The victim, Xavier Enamorado, was found this morning at seven-thirty a.m. by Alonzo Guiterrez, his personal assistant. Xavier was on that bed, seemingly asleep, but Alonzo couldn't wake him, checked his pulse and found none, and immediately called the front desk for an ambulance. There were no signs of struggle, forced entry, or robbery in the room."

He smiled at the camera like an idiot. Didn't he realize how much more he had to explain? In a voice that displayed not a hint of irritation, I asked, "Detective Burdock, how did Xavier do it?"

"Oh, right," said Dan. His face grew appropriately grave, and he said, "Cyanide."

I could literally hear Constancia making a face. "Cyanide?"

"And how do you know it was cyanide?" I followed up.

Detective Dan looked into the air philosophically. "You see, as a New York City detective, you become an expert in identifying poisons just by using this," he said, tapping his nose. "Cyanide has a unique smell. A little like almonds, but bitter. Furthermore, the victim often changes color, because what cyanide does is it causes cells to suffocate. Mr. Enamorado was pretty blue when we found him." I could see him trying to formulate a bad pun, but luckily he restrained himself and continued. "We're waiting for a toxicology report to verify this hypothesis, of course, but really, that's only a formality. I'd bet my shield it was cyanide."

Before I could follow up, Constancia asked, "Potassium cyanide?"

"Toxicology will tell us for sure. But yes, probably."

"So where'd he get it? Where's the container? How'd he get it into his system?"

Dan didn't like Constancia's tone—she had a way of making everybody sound incompetent—but he didn't break character. "We believe we've successfully reconstructed Xavier's last hours. Basically, the answers to all those questions can be found right there," he said, pointing to the nightstand. Besides all the other typical nightstand-y stuff, there stood a large milkshake cup with the word "GruuvyJuuce" written in a groovy, juicy typeface on the side.

"The way we figure it," Dan continued, "Xavier was feeling depressed about the shoot yesterday. Yes, we know he was upset; Alonzo told us. So he goes out, picks up some cyanide on the street, then stops at a GruuvyJuuce, takes the cyanide on the way home, washing it down with the shake, gets back to his hotel room, and goes to sleep. Forever," he said grimly, looking straight at the camera. You can always pick out the reality shows on TV; they're the ones with all the bad actors.

"Picked up cyanide on the street?!" screamed Constancia. "That is the absolute stupidest theory—"

I covered her mouth. She mumbled for a second in my palm, but then finally shut up. I removed my hand, but gave her an admonishing look. "What's GruuvyJuuce?" I asked Dan.

"It's from one of those new powershake places that're popping up all over the place. Can't see the appeal myself. They're really expensive, and they have all these weird fruit flavors I've never heard of. Like this one: It's got this neon-peach-orange color, and it smells like nothing I've ever seen before."

"You see smells?" asked Constancia.

I shot her a look, then went over to the nightstand, leaned over the cup and took a long whiff. "It's mamey," I said.

"What?" asked Dan.

"Mamey," said Constancia. "Tropical fruit. Cubans love it."

Something was bugging me. I turned to our cameraman and asked him in Spanish, "Eugenio, mamey. Don't people use them for home remedies?"

Like any good cameraman, Eugenio was loathe to talk while we were still rolling. But he was also too polite not to respond, so after a moment's hesitation he said, "Of course. They use it to cure everything: good for headaches, stomach problems, VD, warts, malaria, everything. They make a hair tonic with it in El Salvador to keep you from going bald. I should get me some, eh?" he said, patting his bald head.

We all laughed, even Dan, whose Spanish was so bad he can't even order at Taco Bell. But I could tell Eugenio wasn't done. It took a minute of staring at him expectantly, but finally he continued: "And you can use the seed to make a drink that will induce an abortion. I had a cousin from Pilar del Río. You know the type: one of those bobas de la yuca who can't keep her legs shut. Well, she got herself into trouble, and there was only one way to fix trouble like that. That mamey potion almost killed her, but she lived, and it worked. It got rid of the baby all right." Eugenio's mouth clapped shut. He hid behind his camera so I wouldn't see him getting choked up. "Poor little baby. Never got to be born. My poor little nephew."

"What'd he say, Desi?" Detective Dan asked.

I was about to answer Dan when Constancia's cell phone/computer/surrogate brain went off. "It's Alonzo," she said, handing that overcomplicated gizmo to me.

I took it, struggled to figure out how to work the stupid thing, let Constancia press the right button for me, and then, finally, said "Ai, Alonzo. How are you doing, niño?"

"I'm okay," he said. "You know, rough day." A beat. Then, "I shouldn't have left him alone."

"No sea estúpido. What were you going to do, crawl into bed with him? There was nothing you could do. This isn't your fault."

He wasn't convinced. But like a niño bueno, he said, "Okay."

"Hey, you're not alone, right? You keeping busy?"

"Yes, Mámi," he sighed, just like Xavier would've. He imitated Xavier in everything.

"Don't lie to me. What are you doing right now?"

"Ai, my job, Mámi, okay? In fact, I have good news. I found the abuelita. We can return the money to her."

"That was fast. Good work."

"She works at this place called GruuvyJuuce. Mámi, it's perfect. I was thinking we could give her back the money right there, right at the store while she's working. Man, what a great moment that's going to be." And then he added sadly, "Xavier would've loved it."

I pulled the phone away from my ear. For a few seconds I thought I could hear the roar of the ocean. But it was the sound of my own blood surging into my head.

"What is it?" asked Detective Dan.

"It's a homicide," I said to him. "Xavier was murdered. And I know exactly where to find your prime suspect."

~

Latinos don't like mysteries. The Brits, they're a mystery-crazy people. Americans too. But us? All that confusion and ambiguity at the beginning, all those subtle clues to make you feel stupid when you see the solution at the end, all those red herrings purposefully put there to trip you up. No, what the New World mind likes is *intrigue*. Just lay it all out: this person wants this, that person wants that, and here's everyone's sordid past, and here are all the evil things everyone is planning to do. Now, sit back and watch it all play out. And *judge* them. Oh, that woman, she's the biggest puta I've ever seen in my life. Oh, that man, he's a salvaje; he'd eat his own father down to the skeleton if he thought it would help him get ahead. That's the reason why the telenovela has become the art form of choice for us. Look, just let us know everything up front, so that for once in our lives we can make a full and fair judgment about something. To hell with mystery. Real life is all too full of them.

Like the one I had on my hands now, concerning our seemingly courageous, self-sacrificing abuelita. More and more, she was looking like a monster.

Detective Dan had discovered through a little research that there had been a strange upswing in cyanide poisonings in New York. The victims were almost exclusively boys and young men, African-Americans, Latinos, Asians—no Caucasians—ages fifteen to twenty-five. Almost all the victims had some gang affiliation, so the first thought was some kind of gang rivalry. But how would a gang get ahold of enough cyanide to carry out more than a dozen poisonings? So that's when the focus switched. Investigators started looking for a chemist, exterminator, someone who worked at a job, probably at a large corporation, where he might have special access to deadly poisons.

Yes, he. They were looking for a serial killer now, one with a score to settle with young men of color, and serial killers were almost always male. *Almost* always.

You with me? Here's what they had been looking for: a male, middle-aged, science nerd of color—probably African-American or Latino—who was picked on all through school and who now wanted to punish his former, or current, persecutors. The police didn't once imagine that an old woman, who was probably illegal and probably had next to no education, would know how to extract cyanide from the seed of a mamey. Almost any abuela of a certain age remembers the old ways so well, they can never learn the new ways of this country. I'm sure our abuelita never learned to work the computer cash register at GruuvyJuuce. But making poison out of a mamey seed? What could be simpler?

So now a new profile was forming: Abuelita was worried about her little Tito. She was willing to do anything for him. But he was reckless, dangerous. Getting involved with gangs. She had to remove the bad influences from his life. Keep him safe, no matter the cost, the risk to herself. So she takes a job at a GruuvyJuuce so she will have a ready supply of free mamey seeds, and she uses her campesino knowledge to kill the men she thinks are corrupting her Tito.

But why kill Xavier? Sure, she thought he was a hit man, but she had paid him off, had collected that huge amount of money to do so. Why go to all that trouble just to kill Xavier a few hours later?

Dan's theory was that she had "buyer's remorse" and wanted her money back. Constancia thought that her plan all along was to find out where the hit man lived, used the money as an excuse to get through the door, and then poison him when he wasn't looking. Eugenio thought she was arrebatada and that you can't figure out crazy people's motivations. That's what "crazy" means, right?

All three of them were wrong. The money was found in the hotel room; if that's why she did it, why didn't she take it back before the police confiscated it? And unless she was an idiot, she wouldn't have poisoned him using a cup that came from the place where she worked—and one look into her horse-eyes told you that woman was no idiot. And as for Eugenio: sorry, viejo, but even crazy people have motivations. They may be crazy motivations—they may think they are being chased by wolves or are covered in ants or were José Martí in a past life—but they're still motivations. We just hadn't figured out what motivated our Mamey Murderess to poison poor Xavier.

But we didn't need to figure it out. We just needed her to tell us. There were several ways you could do that. You could haul her ass into the station, stick her in a room with Bad Cop and Worse Cop and let them throttle it out of her. Or ...

"Or," suggested Detective Dan, in a low, conspiratorial voice. We were going over the evidence in the police station, and he didn't want anyone else overhearing us. "Or, we can go to her apartment, set up a few cameras, get some nice incriminating footage, *then* bust her. That way, we get our killer, and you get your ending. Everybody wins."

"What's in it for you?" asked Constancia. That girl has all the finesse of a blind rhino, but I was wondering that too.

"I've been a detective a long time," said Dan. "I'm actually overdue for retirement. Maybe it's time I tried a new career."

Uh-oh. I knew this day would come: the day Dan Burdock would ask me for a job. How do you tell someone whose help you desperately need that he's too ugly—way, way, way, *way* too ugly—for television? Well, if you're Constancia, you blurt it out, consequences be damned, and then you don't get what you want. If you're Eugenio, you're embarrassed, you don't say anything, and you fill your network with ugly people and you go bankrupt, and all those ugly people have to go out and find new jobs anyway.

Me? I am a producer. Managing talent is what I do best. I hugged him. "Oh, Dan, I can't believe how lucky I am! We've been wanting to hire a police consultant forever for *¿A Quién Quieres Matar?*, but we just haven't found the right fit. But who could be better than you? Oh, I'm so happy!"

I kept on hugging him; it was the best way to monitor his reaction. I could feel his whole body processing what I had said. "Consultant?" he asked, bewildered.

"Oh, you'll love it!" I said, hugging him even harder. "Easy work, great pay, and you're there on the set of the hottest show in Central and South America."

"And the Caribbean," Constancia added.

"Consultant," Dan repeated. But this time it wasn't a question; it was an answer. "Well, I guess that does sound pretty good."

He hugged me back to seal the deal. Constancia came around so I could see her and soundlessly mouthed, "You are my hero."

Making sure my chin didn't touch Dan's shoulder, I mouthed back,

"Watch and learn, baby."

~

There are two kinds of justice: fairness and revenge. Fairness is infinitely better, but most of the time, it's impossible. For instance, absolutely nothing about Xavier's murder was fair. So what could we do? The only thing left was to get revenge.

But you have to be strong. You have to have the stomach for it. Take Alonzo, for instance. He was so shook up, he might not do anything, or worse, he might even harm himself, stupidly feeling guilty for something that wasn't his fault, while the person who's actually guilty suffers no consequences. Me? No way was I going to let that hija de la gran puta get away with killing Xavier. I was going to get justice. Let the state stick her in jail for the rest of her life. Better yet, strap her to a chair and fill her veins with poison. That'd be nice. I'd be in the front row to watch her die.

Yes, I believe in the death penalty, and no, I don't give tres pepinos if those comemierda criminals suffer like hell on the way out. Look, I couldn't work in this business if I didn't love liberals, but on the death penalty you people are dead wrong. You and I can fight about it after I finish my story.

I set Alonzo to tail the Mamey Murderess (code name: MM). He sat in that GruuvyJuuce all day, sucking on tropical shakes infused with Hoodia gordonii and ginseng and all sorts of expensive, worthless crap. He was suffering so much about Xavier, the worst thing I could've done was give him time off; instead, I gave him a job that he had to do in public. That would keep him safe, and it would help us nab his murderer.

So Alonzo was watching the MM while we set up hidden cameras in her apartment. It was a dingy little place in the Bronx almost as big as a Rubik's Cube, minus all the happy colors. Dan was the only person from the NYPD with us, both because we weren't exactly going by the book on this one and because the place was so small, we wouldn't have had any place to put more cops. As it was, I had to give most of my crew the day off. It was me and Constancia and Eugenio and our two skinniest audio/video interns. We paid off the landlord, set up our control room in his apartment (which was two floors down from MM's), and armed every stairway and every room of her apartment with all-seeing cameras no bigger than the eye of a rat. Dan dragged himself under her futon frame. It was even money whether he would be able to pack his beer-gut under there, but somehow he managed. Everything was in place. We were ready. All we could do now was wait.

So we waited. And waited. Apparently abuela was working a double shift. Great.

We were half drunk with boredom—Dan had fallen asleep under the futon—when the front door opened. There in the control room, with the landlord peering over our shoulders, we scrambled to our battle stations, scanning the monitors.

Into the apartment walked two teenagers. One I didn't know, but he wore the GruuvyJuuce work uniform: It was just like abuela's, save he wore a yellow button that read "Employee of the Month." The other teen was Tito.

As they walked through the door, Tito said, "She's not going to be home until late tonight. You know, you work there. Jesus, stop being such a pussy."

"I'm not a pussy," said the Employee of the Month. "Didn't I prove I'm not a pussy?"

Tito turned to him and, with a tenderness I didn't think he was capable of, hugged him. "Yeah, you proved it," Tito said into his ear. "You're a Simpático now. No one's going to fuck with you ever again."

Employee of the Month hugged Tito back. And started to cry. "Tito, I'm scared. I guess I am a pussy. I'm sorry. I don't want to be. But I'm scared."

Tito broke the hug, but held his shoulders and shook him encouragingly. "It's okay. This was your first time. The first time is always the hardest. You hear me? It gets easier from now on. You know why? Because now you're a stone-cold killer. You proved you got it in you. You proved you're worthy of being a Simpático. And nobody messes with the Simpáticos, Miguel."

"Miguel?!" the entire control room asked in one voice.

That name was all Detective Dan needed to hear. While they had their little moment, Dan scurried out of his hiding place and, with a viciousness you'd expect from a man twenty years younger, proceeded to beat the will to live out of them. It was the most savage attack I've ever witnessed. All of us in the control room were wincing and oohing like a professional-wrestling audience as Dan landed blow after merciless blow. It made me a little afraid of Dan, knowing he had that kind of sociopathy available to him. I mean, those two were crying and begging for mercy, and they got none. I felt bad for them.

I mean, I would've felt bad for them, if they hadn't killed Xavier.

~

Little Tito, eight years old, has a toothache. Bad. Mom and Dad can't afford a dentist, so abuela whips up a home remedy, a poultice made mostly of mamey seeds. It's worked for generations. He'll be better in no time.

Instead, Tito gets cyanide poisoning. The emergency room doctors save his life, but always after that he has a little trouble breathing. His life has barely begun, and his abuela had already fucked it up.

That's what his abuela thinks, anyway. She blames herself for all the misfortunes that have befallen the family: Her son died, then her daughter-in-law died, and then it was just her and Tito.

When you're a chicken-boned asthmatic going to high school in some Bronx neighborhoods, the pursuit of learning can be danger- ous. The good news is that, no matter how chicken-boned you are, you can fire a gun. As long as you're crazy enough to bring one to school, you get the kind of rep that will keep you safe.

And the kind of rep that will draw people to you. Tito finds himself surrounded by friends even more desperate for protection than he is. So long as he'd shove his piece in the face of anyone who messed with them, they would do anything he told them to. Almost accidentally, Tito starts a gang.

Tito calls it "Los Simpáticos." Like *Goodfellas*, Tito's favorite movie. The gang grows fast. He names some lieutenants, whips up a completely clichéd and plagiarized loyalty oath. As for initiations, well, there are plenty of putos he wants dead. But when the Simpáticos kill some puto, he wants all the other gangs to know who did it. And he's been fascinated by cyanide since he was eight years old. He knows an old family recipe that will give him all he needs.

One day, some Simpáticos and initiates are sitting around Tito's abuela's place—she lets him do whatever he wants, so guilt-ridden is she—watching *¿A Quién Quieres Matar?* Everyone loves the show, except Tito.

"Xavier Enamorado is bullshit," he says. "He's a poser. *We're* the real deal. We kill people. That puto is bullshit."

Miguel makes the mistake of saying, "He's got money and women, and he's on TV. That ain't bad."

By the time the show's over, the only way Miguel's ever going to be a Simpático is if he kills Xavier. And if he doesn't join now, he's dead.

But Tito likes the idea of killing Xavier so much, he's going to help Miguel. "I'll pretend like I want to hire him to kill you. I'll get him to come see you at work. You get him to buy some GruuvyJuuce. And that's when you poison him."

It takes over a year to arrange everything. The hardest part was getting our attention, making us think Tito wanted to kill Miguel. Tito trolls the same chat rooms we troll when we're looking for marks. He starts posting comments, making it clear he wants to hire a hit man. We saw his posts and thought we had an easy mark. We were so used to being right, we hardly even checked out his story. We were so proud and stupid a punk like him fooled us.

Once we make the first contact with him, Tito assumes we're going to tail him so we can get film footage on him before the hit. So he and Miguel have to start playing their parts. He fakes a big fight with Miguel at his abuela's apartment in front of his friends and abuela, whom he sometimes forgets is in the room. She, however, sees everything with her big horse eyes and doesn't know the fight is fake. Later that month, she hears Tito on the phone, talking to Xavier, arranging the hit on Miguel. Though her English is rocky, she catches the drift of the conversation. She is terrified.

For the first time since she poisoned him with her toothache remedy, she comes alive. She confronts him. And since he thinks we've bugged the place, he confirms her worst fears—he is paying someone ten thousand dollars to kill Miguel. She pleads with him. Threatens him with eternal damnation. He laughs and says, "Look around, old woman! You're already damned!" He thinks that's a good line for television and hopes we will use it.

Tito and Xavier arrange a meeting. He leaves the address on the kitchen table for his abuela to see—that is how impotent he thinks she is. But she has resolved to save Tito from himself. She steals ten thousand dollars from the GruuvyJuuce safe, where she is a shift manager, and, on her lunch break, takes it to Xavier before Tito's meeting is to occur.

Remember Xavier after his meeting with Abuela? He couldn't wait until morning to try and make everything right. He has to find her, set everything straight. But he doesn't know where to find Tito or his abuela. The only person he has any information on is Miguel. So he goes to see Miguel at his job. GruuvyJuuce.

Miguel had trouble telling us about the conversation he had with Xavier at GruuvyJuuce. He kept saying, "He was a good man. He just wanted to fix everything."

But in spite of all the new wrinkles, Miguel, who'd been carrying cyanide with him since Tito's first conversation with Xavier, stuck to the plan. He told Xavier that he would call Tito's abuela and have her come to his hotel to collect the money. Xavier was frazzled, febrile with guilt. He wouldn't have been hard to convince.

Miguel even gave him a mamey shake. On the house.

~

I am not heartless. But I believe in justice. And this time, that meant revenge.

But you have to know how to work it. Otherwise you make too many sacrifices. I wasn't going to shoot those two little comemierdas myself, and I wasn't, in some made-for-television act of supreme stupidity, going to hire a hit man to kill them either. Why would I have to, when the government is more than happy to take care of the details for me? I have plenty of money. All I do is hire a pack of bloodthirsty lawyers to go to court and prove that Tito and Miguel should be tried as adults, and poof!, they're tried as adults.

I hear you saying: "Okay, but there's no death penalty in New York." That's true, but that just means the government won't go through the hassle of killing them itself. Instead, they're going to be incarcerated with hundreds of hardened criminals who know what those two skinny little putos have done. You know how many fan letters a week we get from American jails? If I were Tito or Miguel, right now I would be praying to God for a heart attack before I set foot in prison.

But here's how you know I'm not heartless. I've hired lawyers for abuelita. Right now, they're negotiating with GruuvyJuuce, trying to convince them of what a PR coup it would be for them to drop the charges, especially since we returned the money she stole. I think it's going to work. My lawyers are good.

So everything's about as right as I can make it. But it's not right in any objective sense. Poor Xavier is forever dead.

But usually good enough is all there is. You work with the money, talent, and time you have to make everything the best it can be. That's all you can do.

Well, and develop a taste for limes.

More Than Pigs and Rosaries Can Give

"I'm opening your mail, Pedrito!" Sophie yelled from the kitchen.

"That's nice," I mumbled back. I was sitting shirtless in my white-leather baseball-watching recliner, witnessing the Marlins getting Hemingwayed by the Yanks 10-3. It was like one of those mobster movies where you watch the only wiseguy who deep down is a decent person get shot 54 times in slo-mo. Not exactly the time to respond to Sophie's provocations.

But when a commercial break finally euthanized the inning, I did respond. "¿What are you doing opening my mail, vieja entrometia?" I yelled back to her. Her Spanish wasn't the greatest, but I'd called her a nosy old lady plenty of times before. She knew that phrase all too well.

I smiled and turned back to the beer commercials, but I guess I had the TV turned up too loud. I never heard her pad up behind me. Then she sprung: she reached over the chair and pulled my nipples so hard she turned them into dunce caps.

I yelped, begged for mercy. Mercy was slow in coming, but finally she tucked her mouth into my neck, tender as can be, and said, "That's for calling me 'vieja.'" Only then did she release them.

I pressed a kiss into her cheek. "You started it. And anyway, I like viejas. You're only 54. You think we fuck now, wait 'til you're 77. You're going to have to join the hip-replacement-of-the-month club."

She produced the pages of a handwritten letter, shook them under my nose. "Do you want your mail or not?"

"¿Who's it from?"

"Gustavito."

"¿Who else?" Gustavito—the craziest of all my Cuban cousins. "¿What's he scheming now?"

"He says he found Milhuevos."

Sophie didn't move a millimeter. She was waiting to see how I'd react. Maybe I'd be austere, reverential, in keeping with the seriousness of the news she'd given me. Maybe I'd be pissed at her for making light of some of the most serious news we'd ever received. But that's the Cuban way: mix a few shit-jokes and pranks in with the heartbreak, or you won't make it through another day. Our marriage never would have lasted if we stayed mad every time we fucked with each other. 80% of our communication was mindfucks.

But 20% was pure tenderness. "Mámi," I said. "¿He really found Mámi? ¿What'd he find, exactly? ¿Her remains?"

"I'm not sure. Look here," she said, pointing to a word in the letter. "He said he found her 'paredón.' What's that?"

I laughed. "Mi vida, I love you so much I forget sometimes you're not Cuban. So okay, if a 'pared' is a wall, a 'paredón' is a big motherfucking wall. Kids could play handball against it, you could stick a full-sized billboard advertisement on it, Diego Rivera could paint the entire epic history of a lost civilization on it, that big." And then, gently, I added, "Also, it's a great place to line up people and shoot them."

"Like Che did to your mom," she completed. She curled up a little more in my lap and shuddered. Then, thoughtfully, she added, "Gustavito's sure they found the right place, but I thought that town had been abandoned." I nodded. "How can he be sure?"

Ever the journalist, mi vida. But I had skimmed the second half of the letter. "He found a historian. Someone who works at one of the museums of the Revolution. He's been doing research. It looks like ... oh Christ. Oh Christ on a cracker."

"What?"

I laughed. "It seems our good historian Jesús has a side-business. He finds suckers—sorry, I mean Americans—like me and offers to find where their loved ones had been executed by the Cuban Revolution and recovers the soul for them. Gustavito thinks Jesús can help us communicate with my long-dead mother."

"Get the fuck to Carthage," said Sophie, snatching the letter from me. As she read, joy and wonder beamed behind her eyes. "I knew something crazy was going on. But my Spanish wasn't up to deciphering how crazy. I love your family!"

"Me too, mi vida," I said, a little more melancholy than I'd intended. "It's total bullshit, you know."

"I *don't* know. You're the cynic of the family. I'm open to new possibilities."

"¿So, what? ¿You think we should go?"

I could feel the incredulity radiating from her head. "Are you kidding? Of course we're going! What's wrong with you?"

Sitting on the plane waiting for take-off, I reread Gustavito's letter. Not much to go on: Gustavito's way better in person than on the page. So I closed my eyes and tried to remember everything I could about Mámi.

It wasn't much. She was executed before I was two. Most of what I knew about her was how she died.

Cuba, 1959: Castro's coup had, against all odds, succeeded. Che had just won a decisive battle at Santa Clara. As he headed for Havana to join Fidel and the other revolutionary generals, he stopped at places along the way, holding "trials" to punish Batista loyalists. Now don't get me wrong: Batista was an hijo de la gran puta, and plenty of people who worked for him were his corrupt little putos, building their fortunes off the misery of others. But there were also the decent government functionaries who simply did the necessary bureaucratic work of keeping Cuba going. It was hard to tell who was a bastard and who was just trying to keep society afloat. So you held trials to separate the guilty from the innocent, ¿right?

Wrong. This was a revolution. There needed to be executions. So Che would accuse you of sympathizing with Batista, then you'd offer your defense, then you were found guilty, then he'd stand you in front of a paredón, then a firing squad ripped you apart. Most of those executions took place in La Cabaña prison in Havana, but Che perfected his "pedagogy of the paredón" on the way there. The secret was to get the crowd to demand blood. Then the deaths aren't on you; it's the will of the people. "¡Pa-re-dón!" the people yelled. Their new government simply obliged them.

Mámi had worked as secretary to the mayor in the little town of Brota Flor. According to Pápi, the mayor was a likable, handsome sleazebag, all pomaded hair and New York suits. None too bright, and a zángano to boot: always looking for an angle instead of an honest day's work. So it fell to young Mámi to keep the town running behind the scenes.

This she did for almost a decade. But then when Che came rolling through, the townspeople, caught up in revolutionary fervor, told him that it wasn't enough just to fusillade the mayor. Mámi was the real bureaucratic brains of the town. If anyone in town had served Batista's interests, it was she.

The trials were over in minutes. Guilty. Now, the fun part. ¡Pa-re-dón!

When the mayor was brought forth to be executed, he fell to his knees. He wept and coughed and begged for his life. When they went to tie and blindfold him, he tucked himself into a ball and refused to rise. The crowd jeered. "¿What kind of a maricón are you? ¡Stand up and die like a man!" But he remained in that fetal position, wailing into his own crotch. In the end, they had to roll him like an egg up to the paredón to shoot him. Pápi said that his body froze in that position; they couldn't straighten him out after that. His widow, goes the story, had to order a custom oval coffin to bury him in.

Then it was Mámi's turn. She shook herself free of the guards' grip and strode to the paredón of her own accord, not even bothering to step around the patch of ground soaked with the mayor's blood. There she stood, all 5'2" of her, wearing the same practical dress she wore to work every day. She had her hands behind her back like a soldier at ease. She refused a blindfold; instead, she stared down the firing squad, moving from face to boyish face, locking eyes. When a guard offered her a cigarette, she smacked the entire pack out of his hand. The crowd whooped. Here was someone who knew how to die.

On Che's command, the men pointed their guns at her. She raised her chin. Che asked her if she had any last words. He was smiling, Pápi remembered. It was an appreciative smile, warrior to warrior.

Mámi said, "You are all cowards, hiding behind your guns. You know this is wrong. ¿What have I done except work for your benefit all these years? But not one of you had the courage to rise to my defense. There isn't a set of eggs between the legs of any man here. ¡I've bled more eggs out during my period than all the men in Brota Flor have in their pants, combined! And I die today with a thousand eggs inside me that I'll never get to use. What a shame, because I've only given birth to one boy, and Cuba needs brave and honorable men more than ever. This generation is lost."

Che laughed a little, smoked a little. He waited to be sure Mámi had nothing to add. Time held its breath. And then from Che, an afterthought. "Fire."

There were no more executions that day. There were four other men who'd been sentenced, but Mámi's words had shamed the townsfolk, drained them of their bloodlust. Che pardoned the remaining doomed and left quickly.

Among the pardoned were my three uncles. The fourth was Pápi.

My uncles decided to stay in Cuba, though they moved out of town quickly enough. But Pápi had already had enough of Fidel's new order. He hustled me out of Cuba the moment my mother was buried. We came to Miami and he made friends with other expatriated Cubans. He joined the Bay of Pigs invasion, but was part of a unit that was never deployed. Afterwards, he worked as a meatpacker, and remarried, and gave me a typical Cuban-American upbringing: lots of love, lots of hitting, and a steady IV drip of nostalgia for a Cuba that never was.

And Mámi, though dead, lived on. Her speech became legend. Ever since her execution, no one called her by her given name. Instead, they called her "Milhuevos." The woman with a thousand eggs.

~

Our plane wheeled over Havana a good three and three-quarters times before we started our descent, giving those of us with window seats a beautiful establishing shot of the City of Columns.

Havana is beautiful. But in a cemetery kind of way. When you get on the street, there is color, flora, propaganda, joy; but from above, the buildings look short and sun-bleached, and there is almost none of the metal and glass of modern architecture. Fly into Havana sometime, you'll see. It looks like it's three-quarters graveyard.

(And I know what you're thinking: "Oh, you're just one of those comemierda Cuban-American ideologues who can't say a single nice thing about Cuba. Of course you would describe Havana as a necropolis." But I'm no ideologue. I'm a misanthrope. Every society is ruled by the worst people it can generate. We all get exactly the governments we deserve.)

José Martí International Airport was clean, well-maintained, and very orange. We picked up our bags and made our way to customs. It cost me a small fortune, because besides our personal luggage I'd brought four huge suitcases to leave behind for my extended family. One was stuffed to bursting with over-the-counter medicines, bandages, rubbing alcohol, soap, laundry detergent, 25 toothbrushes, toothpaste, and a two-year supply of 100-microgram synthroid for Gusvativo's hypothyroidism. Two suitcases were clothes, especially women's delicates, plus one boy's suit and one girl's dress for First Communion that would be passed between family and friends for the next decade. And one of them was nothing but Café Bustelo, 134 vacuum-sealed bricks of Cuban-style espresso. Gustavito told me there was almost no coffee in Cuba right now. Let me repeat that: almost no coffee in Cuba. It is unthinkable. Unacceptable. Cubans are three things: coffee, sugar, and coño tu madre. I could at least bring the coffee.

I paid a guy dressed like a bellhop from a '30s movie to handle the bags, and we exited the airport. As soon as we walked outside we saw a crowd of Cubans waiting behind a black metal fence to pick up their relatives. Among all the laughing and crying and whooping we were finally able to pick out Gustavito, hands in pockets, rocking on his heels, smiling like Puck.

Next to him was a tall black man in a buttoned-up guayabera and cargo shorts and sandals. The man had a severe case of vitiligo. Really, from what I could see he was only half-black: over his face and arms and legs, continents of white floated atop an ocean of pitch. I have to tell you, that man was beautiful. He looked like some piebald prophet come to carry humanity onto its next evolution.

Oh, and the black/white man had a pert sow sitting next to him. On a leash.

"Welcome to Cuba," Sophie said into my ear.

When we were near enough, Gustavito called out, "¡Fuckee you, mane!" This was our thing; he knows how much I love it when he curses in English. I responded with: "¿Qué tal, culosucio?" which means, "¿How's it going, filthy-ass?" It's better in Spanish.

We embraced, and then he embraced Sophie while apologizing for using profanity in a way that made clear he wasn't at all sorry. Both the black/white man and the pig smiled at us and waited to be introduced. "This is Jesús," Gustavito said. "The historian who is going to help us."

I shook hands with him seriously. "Mucho gusto," I said.

"It's an honor to meet the son of Milhuevos," he said. I didn't see any attempt from him to wear the colors of the saints, and he had a big, quick smile. Cuba's poverty makes it hard to judge people by appearances; people take what they can get, not necessarily what they would choose. But the babalawos I've known spent most of their time trying to look badass and mysterious: wide-eyed, smileless, stentorian, purposefully vague, etc. Jesús, by contrast, came across as a nice guy with an amazing skin condition and a sincere handshake who happened to traffic in the recovery of lost spirits. Interesting.

When I was done staring at him, it was time for Jesús and Sophie to meet. "I'm Sophie," said Sophie. "I'm a journalist. If you don't mind, I've love to ask you a few questions about your work."

"Jesús," said Jesús. "I will gladly answer any question you put to me."

"Great! First question: who's your friend?"

"¿This?" Jesús replied, giving the leash a tug. "¿Fat, isn't she? In a few hours, this will either be Pedro's mother, or tonight's dinner."

The sow looked up at Sophie, smiling widely, as if nothing would please her more than to become either.

~

We drove out of Havana and headed toward Brota Flor. It's a speck on the map between Matanzas and Cienfuegos (i.e., between "The Killing Place" and "Land of a Hundred Fires"). It lay on the way to Santa Clara, where my extended family had lived ever since my uncles had fled town. Our Easter-Island luggage was tied to the roof and back of Gustavito's Tata Nano, a tiny car from India that was only slightly less roomy than a model-railroad prop. Gustavito was "driving": comemierda spent more time looking over his shoulder to joke with Jesús and me than he did keeping us on the road. That left poor Sophie to lean over and try to hold the wheel straight whenever Gustavito remembered a new chiste or chisme to share with me.

The pig sat like a finishing-school valedictorian between Jesús and me, smiling and enjoying the ride. She was surprisingly clean. Fresh from the market was my guess.

Jesús saw me eyeing his pig. "We're going to eat like kings tonight," he said. "That is, if we don't end up using her for the other thing."

I noticed he was touching his left guayabera pocket again. He'd been doing that periodically since we met. And now that we were sitting, I could tell he seemed to have stored something long and hard there. Its outline reminded me of a two-barreled cigar case.

"Feel free to smoke," I said. "My wife and I don't mind."

He looked at me, momentarily confused. Then he stopped touching his pocket and, with a slight, contemplative smile, said, "My wife was killed four years ago."

"Oh. I'm sorry," was all I could muster. ¿The hell did that come from?

"She was murdered by her lover," Jesús continued. "I didn't mind that she had a lover, and I had lovers too—¿who in Cuba doesn't? But her lover was jealous and violent. He wanted her to leave me, to be his alone. When she wouldn't, he knifed her to death."

"It's not easy," said Gustavito. "No es facil" is the island's collective catchphrase. Everyone uses it. Fits pretty much any situation in Cuba.

I asked Jesús, "¿Is that when you became interested in the spirit world? ¿When you learned to contact the other side?"

"Yes," he said simply. Fingering his left breast pocket.

Now we were in Sophie's territory. For the last 25 years she'd worked all over the world as a photojournalist, mostly stories on travel and culture. She practiced no religion but believed in them all; I termed her worldview (when I wanted to piss her off) "sedimentary religion." And now she was ready to add another layer: "How exactly does it work?" she asked Jesús, peeking around her seat to face him. "How do we speak to the dead?"

"We probably won't speak," he answered. "Speaking would require the spirit to enter a living human being, and that is very dangerous. If you want, we could put her in this sow. That's why she's here, in fact. Pigs are very intelligent, so they make good vessels for spirits. They give the spirit a lot of options for communicating with us. But sometimes pigs are driven insane in the process. Sometimes, two souls is too many for one little pig-brain to handle. Then the spirit is just along for the ride as the crazy pig runs itself to death, releasing both souls forever."

"¿We are Legion, eh?" Gustavito quoted, smacking Sophie on the shoulder. He enjoyed fucking with her as much as I did. And just like she would me, she smacked him back twice as hard. He pretended to lose control of the car, she gripped the dashboard and cursed him out, he giggled, and Jesús, softly, told him to drive carefully, or he'd upset the pig, and then she wouldn't be able to serve as my mother's host.

Gustavito sobered up immediately, concentrated on his driving.

"You seemed to imply there was another option besides putting Mámi in the pig," I said to Jesús.

"Yes," said Jesús. "We could place her in a meaningful object. That is in fact what I suggest we do."

"¿What does that mean, a 'meaningful object'?" Sophie called from the front.

"Something important to you to serve as the new home for Milhuevos's soul. It's your attraction to the object that makes the soul interested in it. And then, once the soul decides to stay there, you can hold the object in your hands, press it to your forehead, kiss it, do all sorts of the things to commune with it. But if the soul gets greedy, starts pulling at you, you can put it away for a while. That way, everyone stays safe."

"So it's good to take breaks and maintain a little distance from spirits."

"Absolutely. The past is greedy and gluttonous. It wants nothing more than to consume the present and replace it. And ghosts are living instances of the past. You must always keep them at a safe distance."

"¡Don't be a hypocrite!" Gustavito yelled from the front. In the rearview mirror I could see the mischief in his screwed-up mouth.

"I'm not a hypocrite. I put Gladys in a meaningful object, just like I'm telling them to."

"¡Hypocrite!" Gustavito repeated.

The car went quiet. Then: "He's right," said Jesús finally. "I am a hypocrite. I'm telling you not to do the thing I myself did. But from experience I know how perilous it can be to try to house another soul inside you."

"Enseñale," said Gustavito, his face gibbous in the rearview mirror.

I hugged the pig to get her out of my line of sight. Jesús had already begun to unbutton his shirt. When he finished, he opened it wide, revealing his black and white chest, the map of some alien planet. Sunk vertically into his left pectoral was the thing I had mistaken for a cigar case in his pocket. It was in fact an old knife, its wooden hilt shabby and worn. There was a mouth of scar tissue around the permanent, puckered wound above his nipple, another, smaller one at the bottom of his pec, where about two inches of the well-maintained blade poked out. The knife had worried a crescent-shaped scar into his side, where the point of the blade had scraped his belly for God-knows-how-long.

Jesús carefully pulled the knife free from his chest. The white continents vanished from his body, consumed like sinking islands. He became uniformly black.

Sophie's face, peeking over the seat, was a portrait of wonder. Not good wonder. This-can't-be-happening wonder.

Jesús held the knife aloft, point-down, and said, "This is the knife that killed my wife, Gladys. This was my meaningful object, the vessel I use to ferry her back to me. So long as this knife is in me, she is with me."

Jesús slipped the knife back into his chest. His vitiligo returned, patches emerging from his skin as small, white points, and spreading like drops of watercolor touched to tissue paper.

~

After witnessing Jesús's metamorphosis, both Sophie and I were deranged. For Sophie, who loved myths and legends and local religious practices, what we had seen presented an unprecedented problem: nothing she had ever observed in any of her travels actually challenged her way of understanding the world. When she was writing her human-interest stories, she could always treat the rituals she participated in as curious, anthropologically valuable, but ultimately removed from her way of framing reality. But Jesús has patches of white flesh so long as the knife with his wife's soul was inserted into his body. It was a testable, repeatable, objectively verifiable reality. It was physiology, chemistry, scientific fact. Nothing in her American way of knowing had prepared her to assimilate this into her worldview.

My derangement was of a different order. To me, it marked a return. This was the world I grew up in; this was my native language. The fact is, things like this happen all the time in Cuba. Tell this story to ten Cubans and nine would believe it without blinking. There in the back of that Tato Nano, I embraced the sweet pig and was flooded now with the memory of everything that had been lost in translation for all these years.

And that is exactly what I wanted. That's why I came. I can't say

I believed Gustavito's letter; I'm less a believer than Sophie when it comes to oogie-boogie spirit stuff. But something in my DNA made me come, some part of me I trusted more than my piss-poor, Plato's-cave understanding of reality. We do not know the world. We only know of it what we have known.

~

Gustavito sensed our consternation. So he tried to help the only way he knew how: by telling her funny stories about his most recent crimes. It so happened his most recent crime was stealing the well-behaved pig in the car with us.

Just telling Sophie that was enough to start to ground her, get her laughing. "Really? The pig in the back? Because you had her on a leash."

"I always keep a leash in my car. Put an animal on a leash and people assume you own it. I have collars that will fit any animal: cow, goat, dog, cat, caiman, nutria, and of course pig. I have cages for smaller animals, too, and a nice terrarium for things like snakes and iguanas. I even have tack and harness for horses. ¡I'm like the Cuban Noah!"

"¿But how'd you do it? You can't just walk up to a pig and put a leash on it and say it is yours."

Gustavito rocked his head back and forth as if to say, "Well, actually, yes you can."

"Stealing is like magic," Jesús explained. "The secret is misdirection."

Gustavito honked the horn. "¡Exactly! So before we pick you and Pedrito up, we go to a farmer's market just outside of Havana. I have the leash hidden in my pocket. I send Jesús ahead of me to the pig stall. Because Jesús, he causes a scene wherever he goes. ¡People think he's a leper!"

"He's right. Honestly, it's why I took the job in the museum; so I wouldn't be surrounded by so many ignorant people."

"¡Cuba's the number one country in the world for picking on people with disabilities!" Gustavito added gleefully.

"The pig," Sophie reminded.

"Yes, yes. So I send Jesús ahead of me. People clear a path; it's like the parting of the Red Sea. Rude children are staring and pointing, and their mothers swat their butts to try to get them to stop. Jesús, all smiles, walks up to the pig farmer and tells him he wants to buy a pair of pigs for breeding. The farmer, obviously a racist comemierda, asks to see Jesús's cash first. So Jesús shows him a ball of money. Now the crowd is really interested. ¿How'd this leper get so rich? So then ... you're going to love this, Sophie. The next thing the farmer asks him is, "¿Compañero, are you blanco or negro?"

"No!" said Sophie.

"¡Of course!" said Gustavito. "This isn't the US. Here if you're racist, you don't have to hide it."

Sophie turned to face Jesús: "What did you say?"

"I told him I was 'blanegro.'"

We must have laughed for two solid kilometers.

"They all pissed themselves laughing, too," Gustavito said finally. "The whole crowd, the pig farmer, coño, I think even the pigs were giggling under their breath. Well, that's all the distraction I needed. I mean, fuck, I would have starved to death 20 years ago if I couldn't steal a pig under those circumstances. I put the leash on her and that was that, dicho y hecho."

"¿But how did you know the pig would go along? ¿What if it started squealing and fighting with you?" I asked.

"It's like picking up women at a disco," Gustavito said philosophically. "You have to see which ones are interested. Which ones are scoping you out. But once you notice a woman giving you the eye, you don't wait around eating shit, or some other fulano will get her. You go over and you put the leash on her, but you don't pull. That's the secret. Don't pull, or she'll fight you. Once the leash is on, she's yours. So let her lead. That's the gentleman's way."

"You pick up women at the disco with a leash," I said dryly.

"That's where I learned it. And it works on pigs, too. I have the sow in the back seat to prove it, ¿don't I?"

"But how'd you leave with it?" Sophie asked. "Somebody would have noticed."

"Gustavito is the king of thieves," said Jesús. "He tried to sell the pig to the pig farmer."

"Coño," I said, and meant it.

Gustavito went into full-on gallo fino. "I walk over with the pig on the leash, and she's totally in love with me, trotting alongside me like

I'm the one that raised her, and I say to the pig farmer, '¡Hey! ¡Listen! ¿Are you going to stand here all day talking to this black leper, or are we going to do business? I want to sell you this pig.'

"And he says back, '¿Buy a pig? ¿Are you crazy? I have more pigs than I know what to do with.'

"'But this pig is great,' I said. 'She'll give you a hundred beautiful piglets.'

"'I wouldn't take that pig if you paid me,' he said. 'That mongrel isn't fit to breed or eat.' So you see, he wasn't even really looking at her. Then he said, 'Find someone else to buy that sickly sow. ¡But not around here! I don't want you stealing my business. ¡Get out of here, you son of a whore!'

"So I left."

After an appreciative pause, Sophie said, "You've got balls, Gustavito. My God."

"My aunt was Milhuevos," he said proudly. "She had a thousand eggs. I'd better have at least two."

~

We arrived in what was left of Brota Flor at about 3:00 PM. We wouldn't stay long; my family was waiting for us in Santa Clara. We would just go to the paredón and get Mámi and get out.

It had become one of those almost-dead Cuban towns. Nature was slowly reclaiming it weed by weed. There were no animals: no chickens, no dogs, not even any birds—probably because there were no trees. The big well in the center of town lay in ruins. Not a soul in sight.

Gustavito drove us up to a large wall opposite the town well. Whatever store this wall belonged to had closed a long time ago. On it, someone had painted a caricature of Jesse Helms, complete with Hitler mustache and swastika armband. "¡Heil Helms!" said the speech balloon.

The caricature was faded, damaged. No one'd been by to touch it up for a long time. But despite the ravages of time, some of the artist's original flair still remained. He or she had incorporated the holes in the wall as part of the message. Old Jesse was riddled with bullets. Of course the largest bullet hole was centered on Helms's crotch.

We got out of the car and made for the wall. Gustavito had the pig on a leash, Jesús carried a bottle of aguardiente, and Sophie had her complicated, expensive photojournalist camera hanging from her neck. She raised it occasionally and snapped a few shots.

I ran the modest rosary that had belonged to my mother through my fingers. I had brought it to Cuba with the intention of giving it to my Tía Prieta, but now I figured it would be the perfect "meaningful object" to serve as Mámi's new home.

"¿So what do we do?" I asked. I was suddenly nervous. "Bueno," said Jesús, "I will draw her out of the wall. But then it depends on you."

"¿What do you mean?"

"I didn't put Gladys's soul in an animal because an animal—another body—would be too far away from me. So I moved her into the knife that killed her and stuck the knife in my chest. Now our spirits commingle without the need for words. It's wonderful. It's an actual marriage we have now. I don't need other lovers anymore.

"That rosary in your hands, if Milhuevos goes to live there, will let you feel her presence, bask in the warmth of her existence. You will know a mother's love, a beautiful, meaningful thing. But it will be an inarticulate love, and it will only be as close as your hands can hold a rosary. In some ways, the pig might be a better option for you. Maybe there are things you want to ask your mother. Maybe you want a clearer kind of ... 'interface,' let's call it. If the pig doesn't go crazy, you'll have a more direct way to interact with your mother. Not words, but the kinds of responses an intelligent animal is capable of, which is quite a bit, if you are observant and patient."

He took a swig of aguardiente, then finished. "It's up to you, compañero. Tell me what you want."

I borrowed the aguardiente from Jesús. ¿What did I want? I stared into Helms's eyes—one of his pupils was a bullet hole—and drank and wiped my mouth and sighed. "I was hoping for more, Jesús. Apparently more than rosaries and pigs can give. I'm sorry, but I thought this was going to be like a seance in the movies. I want to ask her about everything. I want to find out who she was. Who Pápi was. What I was like as a little boy."

Another pull from the bottle, then: "I want to know, more than anything, if she's okay with how I turned out. I grew up in the States and lived an American life. I became a meatpacker like my father, then a lectór at the meatpacking plant. I read to the workers day in and day out, sometimes in Spanish, sometimes English, stories of valor and triumph that had nothing to do with the small life I led. I read them the news, too, all the different ways the world is going to hell, and I never did a thing about it except laugh at the terribleness of it all and then turn to the Sports page. I retired early, and all I do now is watch baseball. I don't think I'm doing any harm, but I'm not doing any good, either. If my mother is ashamed of me, I want to know now, while I still have the power to change."

I had no idea all that was in me. ¿Had I always been this broken?

Sophie came up behind me and slipped her arms around my chest and squeezed. "You're okay, mi vida," she whispered. I put a hand on the two she had fastened around me.

Jesús shook his head. "We'd have to put her inside someone for questions that complex. And I won't do that. It's too dangerous. I'm sorry, my friend."

Gustavito came around front and said, sheepishly, "I'm the one who's sorry. I brought you here. I thought this was a good idea."

"You meant well," I said. With this much love coming in from all sides, I couldn't help but feel better.

"Maybe there's a way," Sophie said. She removed her arms from my chest and a few seconds later placed something in Jesús's palm. "Can we use this?"

Jesús's eyes bugged. "¿Is it meaningful to Pedrito as well?" he asked.

"Even more than it is to me."

"¿Is what meaningful?" I asked.

Jesús showed me what Sophie had placed in his hand. It was her fake front tooth.

She'd lost the real one a few years back when we were walking in Miami Beach, both of us dolled up after having seen a terrific production of *Man of La Mancha*. As we headed for the car, some puto ran up and punched her in the face and tried to steal her purse. I grabbed him by the belt before he could get away, and some of the other theater-goers came over, and together we kicked the everliving shit out of him. That hijo de la gran puta was in his twenties and we were a bunch of gray-headed men, but one of the best things about having Cuban blood is that no matter how old you are, you always think you're the baddest motherfucker alive. We had no trouble at all throwing him to the ground and booting him to pieces. We stomped on his balls like we were making wine.

Police came; they took my side; they hauled that knee-knocked loser off to jail, bleeding and crying. But the damage to Sophie was done. Not only had he knocked out her tooth, but we couldn't find it to have it put back in. So she had to get a fake one.

I had failed her as her husband. I know that's old-fashioned to say, but that's how I felt. ¿How could I have let that punk do that to her? But she saw things differently. She called me her hero. Mind you, this is a woman who's worked as a freelance journalist all over the world. She didn't need a man to play gallant; she knew how to take care of herself. But she told me many times afterward that in her hour of need, I didn't hesitate. I turned into a wild animal to protect her. In fact, it was she who had to pull me off the guy so I wouldn't kill him and get charged with murder. She literally had to wrap herself around my leg so I'd stop kicking him in the huevos.

There she was, frightened, bleeding from the mouth, awash in adrenaline, and now clinging to my leg to save me from my own temporary insanity. She had never felt more loved than at that moment, she told me. That's what her fake incisor represented for her. And, over time, she taught me to think of it that way, too. It became the most important thing we owned together.

I turned around to face her. She was 5'2", and her bushy gray-white hair burned like a star's corona. She thought she was overweight, but I thought she had acquired the exact shape of the Forbidden Fruit over the years, and had become exactly that irresistible. "Sophie," I said in English, "you saw Jesús change; we both did. We're not in Kansas. And Jesús said it was dangerous to put another soul inside you. You can't do this."

She smiled that gorgeous, scary-ass gap-toothed smile. "This is your mother we're talking about. The great Milhuevos! She died to save you, Pedrito. She wouldn't hurt me. And anyway, I'm doing it. I decided, and you can't stop—whoa, Pedrito!"

I embraced her, kissed her, licked the socket of her missing tooth until she laughed and pulled away. Then I turned to Jesús and, straightening my shirt, said to him, "That tooth is the most important thing we own."

Gustavito was exultant; his scheme was going to work out after all. But Jesús looked uneasy. "Sophie, this is risky. Too risky. I don't think I can agree to this."

"But I can always take out the tooth," she argued, "just like you can take out your knife. Whenever I feel Milhuevos getting too grabby, I'll pull the tooth. But while she's in my mouth—"

"—she can speak through you," Jesús completed. He smiled at Sophie. "¿Are you sure you aren't a spiritualist yourself?"

"Why? Do you have a job opening?"

We all laughed, Gustavito most of all. He went around me and slapped Sophie on the back. "¡What a woman! You don't deserve her, Pedrito."

"You're right about that," I said.

"Bueno," said Jesús. Without another word, he took the aguardiente from me, swigged some, then slipped the tooth under his tongue and walked to the wall.

Even though by this point I was pretty sure he wasn't a babalawo, I was still expecting some Santeria-like elements to the ceremony. But there was no ceremony to speak of. Jesús just approached each bullet-hole, poured some aguardiente over it (I think just to sanitize it a little), sealed the hole with his mouth, and sucked, hard. He started with Helms's eyeball, then moved to the several holes in his chest, then finished by giving Helms a happy ending. Sophie snuck a picture of that.

He backed away from the wall, slowly turned toward us. He drank more aguardiente, swished it around in his mouth. He sucked on Sophie's tooth like it was candy. After thoroughly churning it in his mouth, he spit the tooth into his palm and bathed it in more alcohol. He held it up to the sun like a prospector assessing a nugget. Then, pleased with his work, he rejoined our little group.

"¿Did you get her?" asked Gustavito.

He nodded, dropped the tooth into Sophie's hand. "Once you put it in your mouth, there's no going back," he said to her.

Sophie jammed the tooth back into place with her thumb. It always took an unsettling amount of force, but now her smile was perfect again.

We watched her.

Watched her.

Watched.

Her.

She shrugged. "I don't feel anything."

"A good sign," said Jesús. "With luck, Milhuevos will always ask your permission before she speaks."

"And I'll be sure to say yes."

"¡And now we'll have a pig-roast for dinner!" said Gustavito, grabbing the pig by her forelegs and dancing with her. "¡Everything is working out perfectly!"

The pig, smiling but put-out, looked at us as if to say, "¿Isn't Gustavito incorrigible?"

The Assimilated Cuban's Guide to Quantum Santeria

We arrived too late at Santa Clara to prepare a full-on puerco asa-do, the kind you cook underground for half a day, so we butchered our sweet pig into chops and chicharones. In fact, I did the butchering, with Gustavito as my sous-butcher and my extended family in attendance. They like to tease me about being a soft overfed American, so expertly deconstructing a pig was one of the quickest ways I could remind them that I was Cubano to the marrow. They were pleased with how good I was at it, and a little stunned. Good. It was nice to stun them for a change.

And thus Sophie and I and my extended family—there must have been thirty of us, spontaneously-generating aunts and uncles and cousins and nietos—began our feast of Cuban pleasures. Because of the farm, my family always had food, but this was the kind of spread these days you only saw at weddings: the aforementioned pork chops and chicharones, but also ropa vieja and Tía Prieta's boliche, complete with a juicy chorizo running through its center; yucca and boñato and other viands, all studded with sea-green garlic; enough rice and black beans and garbanzos to feed all the devils in Hell; and fruit for dessert, guava and mango and mamey and papaya and my favorite, ma-moncillos. They look like mini limes but have a peach-orange pome inside with the consistency of lychee. They're sour and sweet and a little hard to eat because of their large seed; we sucked the fruit off the seeds with our legs spread so the juice wouldn't stain our pant legs, and spit the seeds into a bucket we passed around. We'd roast the seeds tomorrow, and were already looking forward to them.

Then I broke out the suitcase full of Cafe Bustelo so we could have coffee to finish the meal. ¡What a cheer went up from my family! Tía Prieta, who was always wonderful and a bit exagerada, actually wept. "¡Café!" she said over and over.

I distributed gifts from the other three huge suitcases as well. Everybody got something. We spent a long time laughing over all my old-lady tías pressing bras and underwear over their clothes and posing like chulas. When I gave Gustavito the synthroid, he put a hand on my shoulder and said, gravely, "You saved my life, Pedrito." To Jesús, who was staying the night and I hadn't known would be there, I gave my own Kindle. He hugged me and called me his brother.

As we embraced, he whispered, "Watch her closely tonight."

By the time Sophie and I headed to bed we were stuffed and drunk—¿did I forget to mention all the rum?—and overcaffeinated and, most of all, high on family. Every time I came to Cuba I felt the same way. In spite of the poverty and the terrible politics, I never felt more alive, more myself than when I was with my Cuban relatives. Sophie felt it too. We've daydreamed together about moving to Cuba, bringing our American savings to our family here. Maybe one day. Maybe once the Castro brothers die.

We fell asleep somehow, but uneasy dreams opened my eyes. 3:23 AM.

Sophie wasn't next to me anymore. I padded to the bathroom; she wasn't there. So I went to Gustavito's room and, careful not to disturb his wife, woke him. Then together we went to find Jesús.

He was sleeping outside on a hammock, shirtless, the knife in his chest rising and falling. Gustavito did the honors. We gave Jesús a few seconds to let his mind rejoin our shared world. Then I asked, "¿Have you seen Sophie?"

He sat with his legs dangling from the hammock, deep in thought. Then he pointed at the barn. "Someone unbarred the door."

He was right. We walked over and Gustavito pulled one door open.

Sophie sat on a rusted-out kitchen chair. Her hair was streaked with black now, and she had it tied into a bun (a style she abhorred). She faced forward, but her eyes were closed. The horses and chickens were pressed to the barn walls, as far as they could get from her.

Sophie lifted her chin, her eyes still shut. "Mi'jo," she said.

There was none of Sophie's American accent in the way she called me son. Her voice was throaty, coarse, as if from disuse. "¿Mámi?" I asked. I took a step toward Sophie.

A hand gripped my shoulder. I turned to Jesús. His other hand clutched the knife. He shook his head no. Then he exposed his teeth and, releasing his grip on me, tapped one of his incisors.

I turned back to Sophie. Still seated, her eyes still closed, she reached out to me. "Come to me," she said. "Come and embrace your mother, whom you pulled out of time and rescued from death itself."

This time, as she spoke, I saw what Jesús had seen before. Sophie's fake tooth was gone.

I was reeling. Mámi's soul was in the tooth, but the tooth was missing. Yet the woman in front of me was clearly no longer my Sophie.

"Mámi," I said. My voice cracked. "¿Mámi, where's the tooth? ¿How did you get inside Sophie? Please don't hurt her, Mámi. Please give her back." I felt my knees crumpling under the weight of me.

Gusvativo caught me before I fell, hoisted me erect. I had no idea he was still this strong. Once he had me steadied, he said to me, but loud enough for everyone to hear, "That's not Milhuevos."

"¿What?" I asked.

Sophie's eyes opened. Then came the gap-toothed smile, a laugh Sophie's throat could never generate. "Allow me to introduce myself. I am Felicio Alberto Costas y Fernández."

"The executed mayor of Brota Flor," said Gustavito.

Anger grew from the middle of me and reinvigorated my limbs. "¿What did you do to my wife?"

Sophie's shoulders shrugged. "I killed her. That tooth you stuck me in was much too constraining. So, as she slept, I shook the tooth free of her gums and dropped it down her throat. She choked to death quickly. Once she was dead, I was free to move in."

He ran Sophie's hands over her arms and torso, ending on her breasts. "She's a little old for my taste, but I'm not complaining."

"Hijo de puta," Gustavito whispered.

"She's still in there," Jesús said to me. "Her hair is black and white. It's not all black."

"¿Can she fight him?"

"She needs to learn how. That will take time. But we can help her."

"I can tell you about your mother," said Felicio. He stood Sophie up on shaky legs, spread his arms to steady himself. "You obviously don't know a thing about her. A hard worker. Smart. A total prude, though. Pretty boring to be around day after day. A lot of times I look a long lunch just to get away from her.

"How dare you speak of my mother like that," I said.

"Oh, don't get me wrong. She was a great woman. I wouldn't have traded her for five beautiful new secretaries. And even before we were killed, I knew that woman was pure courage. She did not fear death. And then, on the fateful day Che came to town, she died for you, her only son. She chose to die to save you, her husband, her brothers. The very definition of bravery.

"Now I, well, I was a different story. I didn't want to die, I was scared to die, and so I resisted death. I was carried by a bullet out of my body and into the paredón. There I waited, decade after decade, concentrating only on my persistence, raging at the unfairness, refusing to leave life behind. I was too afraid to let my ego go, for if I did, ¿what would happen to me? ¿Hell? ¿Nothingness? I never wanted to find out. I would do anything to live again.

"And that's the difference. ¿Haven't you ever wondered why the only spirits the living ever encounter are either wrecked by sorrow or irredeemably wicked? It's because the ones that are good enough and strong enough would rather die than harm someone else. That's what it takes in this world. Others die so you can live."

"Kill him," said Gustavito. He was still holding on to me; I could feel rage coursing through him, joining with and augmenting my own.

"¿How?" I asked.

"¡I don't know!" he yelled. "¡But get him out of her!"

"Take Gladys," said Jesús. I turned to him. His skin was spotless, uniformly dark; he held his knife-wife out to me handle-first. "She will search out Sophie and guide her back to us."

I took the knife. "Don't stab her anywhere vital," said Gustavito. "Whatever wound you make we'll have to heal."

I nodded, then, knife-first, I made my way toward Felicio.

"¿What are you doing?" he asked. Amazing: already dead, and he was ready to piss himself. Once a coward, I guess.

He lurched away from me like a rusted tin man; he hadn't had a chance to learn to use Sophie's body very well. It was nothing at all to collar him and lay him down face-down on the chair like I was about to spank him.

"¡I'll kill her!" Felicio yelled. "¡I'll kill her, I swear!"

"You would have already if you could have. But you couldn't. And now I am coming for you."

I sat on Sophie's back to immobilize Felicio and kissed the knife-blade. "Go get her, Gladys," I said. Then, wishing I'd never come here but infinitely grateful that I had, and feeling for the first time that I truly understood what Mámi had done for me, what it means to see yourself at the brink of losing everything, not knowing what will happen, yet digging up the courage to make the best move you can, to do the only thing that has a chance of making everything ... not okay, not right, but as right as it can be, I put my faith in everything I did not understand about our world and stabbed my wife in the ass.

Bone of My Bone

1.

It arrived all at once the day after the school closed for the Christmas holiday. At first he thought it was some species of unbridled acne: a hard slippery mountain of red flesh, just above the right eyebrow, that culminated in a white tip typical of your garden-variety pimple. But the white tip felt too sharp and hard to be acne; it felt more like the business end of a tooth.

He thought perhaps time would take care of it, but by Christmas the pimple's base had grown significantly and the white tip extended out by measurable millimeters, defying gravity and, increasingly, identification. His Pre-Med daughter, visiting for the holiday, said in her pre-professional opinion that he should "lance that sucker," and so he tried to, but quickly discovered that he couldn't: the pimple was as hard and insensitive as a pebble, and the white tip completely imperturbable. Worst of all, he had felt no pain during the attempted lancing, though he stabbed at it for close to half an hour. It was as if that little lump of acne was no longer a part of his face.

That worried him. But he didn't want to worry his daughter; Pre-Med is a tough major, after all. He decided to wait until she left—she was going on the 29th to spend New Year's with his estranged wife—before making a doctor's appointment.

By the time she left and he was ready to make the call, however, the white tip had grown to the size of something that could no longer be called a tip; it demanded to be classified as a thing unto itself. Gray-white, striated, solid, pointed, he did not have much trouble trying to name it. It was, unmistakably, the beginnings of a horn.

2.

He could not think of a doctor in the world who would not contact the local news and spread the word about the man who had a horn growing out of his forehead. So he did not contact the doctor after all. Instead, he drank a shitload and went to bed, hoping things would be better in the morning.

When he woke up the next morning, thirsty and woozy, he found that the horn had mercilessly shredded his pillow. The poor old pillow, hemorrhaging polyester pillow-guts, looked like Prometheus's abdomen after Zeus's eagle had done its daily duty.

At least that's what the man thought to himself. He was a high school English teacher who always made sure to cover Greek mythology. He knew other people would think him a pretentious prick for drawing that kind of metaphor from his crusty old pillow, so he never made those kinds of comparisons out loud. But in his head he made them all the time.

After one last forlorn look at his massacred pillow, he got up and looked at himself in the mirror. It was bigger: much bigger. Too big to ignore anymore.

He scrambled through every drawer in his bathroom until he

found what he was looking for: a pair of scissors. Once he had them, he assailed the horn with consequences-be-damned gusto. He tried cutting, sawing, poking, digging, and even, out of frustration, hammering until he was spent. He looked at himself, heaving and sweating, in the mirror.

Neither the horn nor even the scissors seemed noticeably impacted by his efforts. He sighed and made himself a Bloody Mary that was almost all alcohol, almost no tomato juice. He called it a "Hail Mary" and thought it pretty clever.

3.

By the next day, the horn had grown enough to begin to curve upward. It now looked, he thought, like one of the diabolical canine teeth of the fearsome Fenris Wolf, the creature so powerful it was destined to eat Norse father-god Odin.

It was New Year's Eve Day and he had yet to buy champagne. He had thought, before the arrival of his unexpected horn, that he would spend New Year's at a quiet bar near his apartment, where time-ravaged retirees winced down drinks and told blue jokes and performed minute exegeses of last night's game. Now, of course, that was out of the question. But alcohol had saved him; it was the only thing, not medicine or drug or advice or therapy or anything else, that had allowed him to endure his separation from his wife. He doubted he would survive New Year's unless he got so drunk he forgot to die of heartbreak.

So he would have to venture out. But how to cover the horn? It rested too low on his forehead to by hidden by the brim of a hat, but too high to be shielded from sight by wide-brimmed sunglasses. Was there any way for a sane man in this society to reasonably cover his forehead?

He settled on a bandanna. Our man was Mr. Martín Esposito, 51, a balding high school English teacher with the plush-doll physique one expects of a high school English teacher. He no longer owned sneakers, nor jeans, nor even a t-shirt. His bandanna was actually a dishtowel that received a sudden and unexpected promotion. And so our man, in a white long-sleeved shirt and gray dress pants and a belt and black matching shoes and, last of all, a red paisley dishtowel-cum-bandanna, sallied forth in search of New Year's champagne.

4.

As he ran for his car, he felt like every satellite in the sky was trained on him. He fumbled with his keys and used the wrong one twice in a row before finally getting his car door open. He slammed the door shut, took a breath, then looked around the neighborhood. Nobody was out. He took another breath, this time of relief. Probably no one at all had seen him.

The drive was uneventful. He pulled into the parking lot of the liquor store, turned off the car, then checked the bandanna in the rearview mirror. It looked silly, but it remained in place, the horn beneath it only a vague, indeterminate lump that no one would be able to identify. Solidifying his resolve, he exited the car and entered the liquor store.

He and the owner—a craggy, shaggy man whose other job might have been "Ancient Mariner"—were the only two souls in the store. The owner watched him in a distracted way; he was the only thing moving in the small liquor store besides the flies, which the owner had been watching before he came in and would go back to watching once he left.

He made straight for the champagne, picked out a bottle almost without looking at it, walked toward the cash register, realized he had picked out the most expensive champagne in the store, replaced it on the shelf, picked out something in his price range, and, finally, walked to the register, clutching the bottle like a wrung-necked chicken.

The owner asked "That all today?" and he said, "Yes." The owner asked "Need any lottery tickets?" and he said, "No thank you." The owner asked "Got any plans for tonight?" and he pointed to the bottle, and said, "Just that." And they both let out a one-huff laugh.

Then the owner pointed at the bandanna and asked, "What, you lose a bet or something?"

On cue, the bandanna untied itself and fell onto the counter.

They both stood there looking at each other, the owner's eyes locked onto the horn, and Martín watching the owner's reaction. Finally, Martín reached for the bottle, now in a paper bag, and asked, "May I have my champagne now?"

The owner surrendered the champagne, saying as he did, "Your wife must've been screwing around on you for a long time."

He laughed a little then, mostly in surprise that the owner knew of that old legend. And then he stood still for a minute. And then he began to weep the most earnest tears of his life.

"No," he said. "Not her. Me. I cheated on her. With a teacher at school. Who wasn't beautiful or smart or anything. She just showed interest. That's all it took: interest. That's how pathetic I am. And for that I ruined everything."

The owner watched him dispassionately as he cried like Gilgamesh wailing for his lost friend Enkidu; like Isis for Osiris, cut to pieces by his jealous brother Set; like Demeter for Persephone, destined to spend half of every year in Hades with Hades.

Then, knowing no other way to deal with emotion, the owner pulled the bottle of champagne out of the bag and popped the cork. "Let's you and me drink this," said the liquor store owner, "and you can tell me all about it."

5.

He had called his estranged wife's cell phone, but it was his Pre-Med daughter who picked up.

"Hi, Pápi!" she said with alcohol-fueled cheer. He heard outbursts of laughter and the relentless beat of party music behind her. "Happy New Year!"

"Happy New Year, honey. Why do you have your mom's cell?"

"She didn't want to carry it, so I told her I would, so I could call you later, but now you've called me!"

"Right. Well, is your mom around? I wanted to talk to her for a minute."

"Really? Because you know dad," and his daughter's voice became low and conspiratorial, "I think she wants to talk to you too. I think she misses you."

"Did she say that?"

"Kind of. But it's more what she's not saying. She's been having stomach pains for the last few days. I told her we should go see a doctor, but she said, 'I think maybe I'm just missing your father a little.' So see? She misses you. I think things are looking up for you two."

"Don't be so sure, honey. Has your mom told you why we're trying this trial separation?"

"You know, she said people grow apart, and maybe it's not permanent, and mostly just a big load of shit."

"She was protecting me. She didn't want you to hate me. But that's not fair to her." He took a breath, imagined Perseus working up the courage to strike, finally, and behead the Medusa. "I cheated on her. With another woman. That's why we're separated."

He let the silence remain until she was ready to talk again. Finally she said, "I thought that's what happened. If I was with you now, Dad, I would slap you."

"And I'd deserve it. But for right now I just want to do right by your mom for a change. So could you put her on the line? I have some thing I need to tell her. And something of hers I need to return."

"Okay, Pápi. You know I love you, right?"

"I know. And I love you. And even though I messed up our marriage, maybe forever, I love your mámi, too."

"I know. Let me go get her. Happy New Year."

"Happy New Year, honey." And as he waited for his estranged wife to get on the line, he fondled, with melancholy and affection, the bone in his hand that just a while ago had protruded from his forehead. It wasn't a horn after all, once it had run its entire course, there at the liquor store as he drank champagne with the store owner and wept and told him everything: but a human rib, one that was no longer a part of him. The only thing to do was to give it back.

The Magical Properties
of
Unicorn Ivory

Vocations don't grant vacations. I'm supposedly on holiday in London when I get an offer no reporter could refuse: to see a unicorn in the wild.

I'm with my friend Samantha, hanging out at a small pub after a long night's clubbing, still wearing our dance-rumpled party dresses, dying to get out of our heels. Sam's father Will owns the place and tonight he's tending bar, so it's a perfect spot for late-night chips and hair-of-the-dog nightcaps. Plus, most of the clientele are in their 50s. We wouldn't have to spend all evening judo-throwing chirpsers.

Or so we thought. Sam tics with her neck; I look over her shoulder and see a guy sitting alone staring at us over his drink. He could be my dad, if my dad had forgotten to bring a condom to his junior prom. Short, stout, but really fit; looks like a cooper built his torso. The man's never heard of moisturizer. He's wearing a black pinstripe shirt with a skinny leather tie, black pleated pants and black ankle-boots. I am sure some cute sales girl had dressed him—because nobody who cared about him would've let him leave the house looking like dog's dinner.

And now—shit—I scrutinized him too long. He comes over, beer in hand.

"Ladies," he says.

"We're not hookers," says Sam. "I know these dresses might give a gentleman the wrong impression."

"Sorry to disappoint," I add, big smile.

"Right," he says, and turns on his heel.

"Hold on, Gavin," says Will, who's just pulled up with my Moscow Mule. "Don't let these two termagants scare you off. Make a little room for Gavin, Sam, will you?"

Gavin considers us a moment, then pulls up the stool next to Samantha and offers his hand. "Gavin Howard."

"Oh!" says Sam. She's suddenly unironically warm—a rare demeanor for her. "You're the forest ranger. Dad's told me about you. I'm Sam."

I put out my hand. "And I'm Gabby. Gabby Reál."

"A pleasure," he says, then proceeds to purée my knucklebones—one of those insecure guys who has to try to destroy the other person's hand. Charming.

"This man's a national hero," Will says to me. "He's keeping our unicorns safe."

Now <u>that</u> is interesting. Back in the States, we've heard reports of unicorns appearing in forests throughout Great Britain. But in this age of photo manipulation it's hard to get anyone to believe anything anymore.

So I say as much: "Plenty of Americans don't think unicorns are real, you know."

"Oh, they're real, Ms. Reál," says Gavin, pleased with his wit. As if I hadn't heard that one 20 billion times.

"Americans," says Samantha. "You never think anything interesting could possibly be happening anywhere else in the world, do you?"

The Brits share a chuckle. I don't join in.

"We shouldn't insult our visitor," says Will. "I mean, if she were to tell us snaggletoothed pookahs started appearing in California, I suppose I'd want better proof than a picture." He leans to Gavin and adds, "Gabby's a reporter for *The San Francisco Squint*. Her column's called 'Let's Get Reál.' Two million read it every week, don't you know."

Gavin sizes me up. No, it's a deeper, more serious stare: he *appreciates* me, like a squinting jeweler. "I'm all for reality. I have no patience for falsehood. I wish more people would 'get reál.'" His voice gets weirdly sincere.

I lean toward him and say, "Me too. My column's subtitle is 'Truth or Death.'" I smile and sip my Mule.

It's not the first time I've flirted to land an interview. Gavin drinks the rest of his beer but never takes his eyes off me. Neither do Will or the slightly-disgusted Sam, who sees exactly what's happening.

But screw her; a story's a story. Gavin sets down his glass and says the words I am longing to hear: "You know, I'm working the New Forest this weekend. If you'd like, it would be my pleasure to take you with me. You might just see a unicorn for yourself."

I thought this would make a nice fluffy piece for my column. I mean, unicorns!

Gavin—who is completely professional and hands-off, thank God—and I are having a delightful Sunday-morning hike through some less-traveled parts of the New Forest. It's everything an American could want of an English woods: fields of heath; majestic oaks and alders; rivers that run as slow as wisdom itself; and ponies! Thousands of ponies roaming feral and free like a reenactment of my girlhood fantasies.

Of course, that sets my Spidey-sense tingling. Wouldn't it be easy enough for rumors of unicorns to sprout up in a place with so many darling ponies ambling about?

This is what I am thinking when we come across a thick, almost unbroken trail of blood.

"Hornstalkers," Gavin says. And when he sees I'm not following: "Unicorn poachers. Of all the luck."

He calls it in on some last-century transceiver. HQ wants more information. They tell him to send me home and to follow the blood trail with extreme caution. "Do not attempt to apprehend them on your own," says HQ.

"Understood."

"I mean it, Gavin. Don't go showing off in front of your lady- friend."

"I said 'Understood.'" He stows the transceiver and adds: "Wanker." And then to me he says, "Well Gabby, it's poachers. Dangerous people. HQ says I'm supposed to send you home."

"Just try," I reply.

"Atta girl."

We hustle through the wilderness, following a grim trail of blood, snapped branches, hoofprints and bootprints. Gavin jogs ahead, while I do my best to keep up. He's a totally different person out here, absolutely in-tune with the forest. He's half hound, loping with canine abandon through this forest, then stopping suddenly to cock his head to listen, sniff the air.

It's also clear he's used to running with a high-powered rifle in-hand. He told me, as he strapped on its back-holster before we left his truck, that he was bringing it "just in case." So here we are.

He stops suddenly and crouches. I do too. From one of his cargo-pants pockets he pulls a Fey Spy, a top-of-its-class RC flying drone that looks like a green-gold robot hummingbird.

He tosses it into the air and it hovers, awaiting orders; using a controller/display-screen the size of a credit card, he sends the little drone bulleting into the forest.

I peer over Gavin's shoulder at the display and am treated to a fast-forward version of the terrain that awaits us. Gavin's a great pilot. The drone zooms and caroms through the woods with all the finesse of a real hummingbird.

And then we see them: the poachers, two of them. They wear balaclavas and camouflage jumpsuits, the kind sporting-goods stores love to sell to amateurs.

Between them walks a little girl. A little girl on a metal dog leash.

I'd judge her to be eight or nine. She's dressed for summer, tank-top and shorts and flip-flops; she's muddy to her ankles. Her head hangs, and her hair, the colors of late autumn, curtains her face. The collar around her neck is lined with fleece. (To prevent chafing, I presume? How considerate.) The leash seems mostly a formality, however, as it has so much slack that its middle almost dips to the ground.

"What the hell?" I whisper. "What's with the girl?"

Gavin, slowly and evenly, says, "Some hornstalkers believe that unicorns are attracted to virgin girls. So they kidnap one to help them in their hunt."

"What? You can't be serious."

Gavin shrugs. "One too many fairy tales when they were kids, I guess."

~

I can only imagine what is going through that poor girl's head. Kidnapping alone is already more evil than anyone deserves. But as a girl I loved horses, ponies and especially unicorns. If unicorns had existed in our timeline when I was young, they would have dominated my every daydream. I can't imagine how scarred I would have been if I'd been forced by poachers to serve as bait. To watch them murder one right in front of me. Dig the horn out of its skull.

Gavin gives my wrist a fortifying squeeze. Then he hands me the RC controller, takes out his walkie-talkie and, as quietly as he can, reports what he's seen to HQ. I use the Fey Spy to keep an eye on the poachers. The group is moving forward cautiously. The girl's stooped, defeated gait fills me with dread.

Gavin has a conversation with the dispatcher that I can't quite make out. When he's done, he pockets the transceiver and looks at me. Then he holds out his rifle to me with both hands.

"This," he says, "is a Justice CAM-61X 'Apollo' sniper rifle. It has an effective range of 1,700 meters. It's loaded with .50 caliber Zeus rounds. They're less-lethal bullets. Bad guys get hit by these, they lose all muscular control, shit their pants and take a nap. Then we just mosey up and cuff 'em."

I squint. "1,700 meters in a desert, maybe. You'd have to be halfway up their asses to get a clear shot, with all these trees."

He pats the rifle. "Not with these bullets, love. They're more like mini missiles, with onboard targeting computers and everything. They can dodge around obstacles to reach their target. Especially," he emphasizes, "if we can create a virtual map of the forest between us and the target."

Lightbulb. "Which we can make with the Fey Spy."

He nods. "Listen Gabby. That girl's in great peril. We're on the clock here. We can't wait for backup."

As a journalist, my ethics require me to remain disinterested when covering a story. Fuck you, journalistic ethics. "What you need me to do?"

He points at RC display/controller in my hand. "You any good flying one of these?"

"I'm a reporter. I make my living spying on people with drones."

Gavin smiles. Then: "I need you to fly the Fey Spy back to us, slowly and from high up in the canopy, so that it can map the forest between us and the poachers. Then fly it back over to them and keep them in the Fey Spy's field of vision. It'll automatically transmit the map of the forest to my rifle. Once it's done, it's as simple as bang bang bang. Everyone goes down."

I nod in agreement at first, before I realize this: "Wait. Bang bang bang? Three bangs? There are only two poachers."

His face goes green and guilty. "Well, we can't have the girl running scared through the forest. She could hurt herself."

I wait a second for the punchline, because he can't be serious. But of course he is. "Oh my God. Are you insane? You are not shooting the girl!"

"She'll just take a little nap."

"And shit her pants. You said she would shit her pants."

"She's not even wearing pants."

"Gavin!"

Gavin puts his finger to his lips.

"Sorry," I whisper.

"Look, if you've got a better idea, I'm all ears."

"I do," I say. "You shoot the poachers. I'll handle the girl."

Gavin's dubious. "That girl's undergone a severely traumatic sequence of experiences. I'm not sure a team of highly-trained psychologists could handle her right now."

"She'll be even more traumatized if you shoot her. Look, I admit it's not a great option. We just don't have any better ones. As soon as you have a lock on the hornstalkers, you take them out. I'll fly the Fey Spy to the girl and keep her entertained until backup arrives."

He's shaking his head. "What if she runs?"

"I'll go get her myself. She won't get far. She's in flip-flops."

He's about to argue, but decides against it. "Out of time," he sighs. "We do it your way. Don't fuck up."

"Don't miss."

Gavin aims the rifle ahead, looks into the scope with one eye, winks the other. I look back to the Fey Spy display-screen, catch up with my targets. They've barely moved at all. As if they're not sure what to do next. "I don't think these guys are pros," I say to Gavin.

"Unicorn horn is worth a mint," he says, his aim never wavering. "Every imbecile with a gun wants a piece of the action. Start flying the Fey Spy back to us."

I do, slaloming left and right through the forest in large swaths as I fly. It's a little over ten minutes before we make visual contact with our little hummingbird robot.

"Good job," says Gavin, checking his rifle's readout. "We've almost got what we need. Fly the Fey Spy back over to them."

By the time I catch up with the poachers again, they are crouching behind a pair of trees, trying to peer into a hole the wounded unicorn must have punched through the forest as it fled. The girl stands next to the poacher with her leash around his wrist. She's as still as a Degas ballerina.

Within the space of a second Gavin fires two shots, and the two poachers simultaneously suffer seizures. They slap at their necks and fall to the ground, their guns tumbling away from them.

I hover in place; I want to see how the girl reacts.

She doesn't. She just stands above her handler. He is weakly reaching up to her. The leash is looped around his wrist, her neck. Her yellow-orange hair shields her face from me.

The poachers hand finally drops. He's out. It suddenly occurs to me the girl must think he's dead. Jesus Christ: how much worse can we make things for her?

Gavin's already charging ahead to the forest to go truss up the poachers with zip-ties. He'll be there in a minute. All I need to do is keep her entertained until he gets there and make sure she doesn't—

—no! She slips the leash off the poacher's wrist and takes off running.

~

Here's an important safety tips for the kids at home. Do not go tearing as fast as you can through a moderately dense forest while also trying to fly a Fey Spy. You can't run and watch a screen and steer a robot at the same time. After my fourth tumble, I decide to go with the Fey Spy. It can move through the forest much faster than I can, and it will provide me her location via the map of the forest it's been creating this whole time.

It's the right choice. In less than three minutes, I find her. The Fey Spy flies into a small clearing where I witness a scene plagiarized from a medieval tapestry. The girl—the leash still around her neck—is kneeling in front of a horse. Huge and beautiful, chestnut-colored, male. He has folded his legs under him. He can barely keep his dipping head aloft. On his flank a bullet wound yawns; a slow lava-flow of blood gurgles out of the hole. Below it spreads a scabrous beard.

And, spiraling out from the horse's head, is a horn almost a meter long.

~

We have the Large Hadron Collider to thank for unicorns. Once the scientists at the LHC discovered they could make these adorable microscopic black holes, they couldn't resist doing it all the time. "They only last for microseconds," they said. "What harm could they do?" they asked.

How about destabilizing the membrane that keeps other universes from leaking into ours?

Think of our universe as some kid's crayon drawing on a piece of paper. Take that drawing, and place it on top of some other kid's. If nothing else happens, the drawing on top will hide the drawing beneath it. But now, take a spray-bottle and spritz the drawing on top. Don't ruin it or cause the colors to run; just moisten it a little. As the paper gets wet, you'll be able to see hints of the picture that's underneath.

The numberless black holes created at the LHC "moistened" the paper on which our universe is drawn, allowing other universes to come peeking through.

Handwringers have announced the inevitable collapse of our universe but, so far at least, nothing so dramatic has happened. And in fact, a great deal of good has come of the LHC's experiments. Scientists have gained invaluable insights into how parallel universes work.

For instance, we now know that, in at least one alternate timeline, unicorns exist. And a few specimens have found their way into our neck of the multiverse.

~

Even before I entered the clearing, I could hear the girl calling out "Help! Is anybody there? Help us!" Not "Help me." "Help us."

So I enter the clearing slowly. The girl sits with the unicorn's head on her lap, petting its neck. Her face is a tragedy mask.

She asks me, with wounded voice, "Are you a hunter?"

I sit next to her. "My name's Gabrielle Reál. I'm a reporter."

"You're American?"

I nod. "I'm here to help you."

She feels safe enough to start crying in earnest. "Can you call my parents?"

"Help is on the way, sweetheart."

She cries and nods. "Can you help him?"

She means the unicorn. How to reply? I will not compound her future suffering with a lie—truth or death, remember?—but I don't want to compound her present suffering by presenting her with the stark realities of life and death. I finally settle on, "I can't. But I have a friend coming. He's a forest ranger. If anyone can help the unicorn, he can."

She nods, sniffles, redoubles her petting. The unicorns sighs, settles further into her lap. I have to dodge his horn. It's even more amazing up close than any picture I've seen. It's a spiral of silver-gray, pitted and striated, covered with the nicks and flaws that come from a lifetime's use. It doesn't feel as cold as I expect; it's like reaching into a body and touching vital bone.

I should get us away from him, I know. This is a wounded wild animal; he can turn on us at any moment. But the truth is I don't want to move. I don't want this magnificent creature to die without knowing some comfort and love in his passing. It's a girlish, sentimental thought, I know. That doesn't make it any less authentic.

I scratch the unicorn's head. He moves slightly toward my hand, grateful. The girl rests her head on my arm, and together we pet him and weep.

~

Thousands of animals—elephants especially, but also walruses, rhinoceroses, and narwhals—are massacred every year for their horns and tusks. The demand for ivory continues with little abatement in China, Japan, Thailand, Indonesia, the Philippines, and other countries of that region. In spite of the bans and the international efforts to curb the ivory trade, poachers have no trouble finding deep-pocket buyers and government officials on the take.

In fact, the only thing that has seemed to be effective at slowing down the butchering of these animals has been the introduction of an even more desirable source of ivory into our universe. Unicorns.

Unicorn horn is said to possess all sorts of salubrious woo. It can detect and cure disease, anything from nosebleeds to lupus. It's a universal poison antidote. It can impart superhuman strength, speed, and/or intelligence; regenerate lost limbs; restore sight to the blind; recover sexual potency; reverse aging; raise the dead. Slice it, dice it, powder it, or keep it whole and use it as your magic wand—unicorn horn is good for what ails you.

Of course it has no such properties. But what science has learned already about unicorns is almost as wondrous. *Equus ferus hippoceros* seems to fit so well into our timeline's system of classification, there is reason to believe that might actually have existed in our own universe at some point in our past, and that we may someday find indigenous unicorn fossils. Based on the specimens we have found so far, male unicorns seem to be up to 15% larger than the modern horse, females up to 10% percent. Their large skulls somewhat resemble those of large, extinct species from our Eocene era: save, of course, for the horns that spring from their head.

A unicorn horn, much like a narwhal's, is actually a pair of repurposed canines that grow helically from the animal's palate and intertwine as they emerge from the forehead. Scientists believe that when the unicorn's ancestors switched from being omnivores to herbivores, evolution found other uses for its meat-tearing teeth. Defense against predators and mating displays are obvious assumptions, though neither has been observed as yet. They have been observed, however, using their horns as "fruit procurement appliances" (Gavin's words), as well as digging tools with which they unearth tubers and roots. And since the horn is actually two twisted teeth, it is sensitive to touch. Scientists are just beginning to hypothesize the various ways in which unicorns use their horns as sensory organs.

In short, the unicorn is an endlessly fascinating animal, one that not only has enriched our knowledge of our own natural world, but the natural world of at least one other timeline. It's scientifically priceless.

As I sit petting this dying unicorn, I wonder *Why isn't that enough? Why do we have to invent magical bullshit? They just got here, and we're hunting them to extinction based on lies.*

But then I grimly smile. Unicorns are not of our timeline. The few stragglers who have appeared here came by an LHC-induced accident. No matter what we do here, we can't erase them from existence in all universes. Even our folly, thank the gods, has limits.

~

Gavin cautiously enters the clearing. The rifle is holstered. He's walking in smiling, open-armed, crouching, cautious. He reminds me of Caliban.

"There they are," he says merrily. "Glad I finally found you. Now we can get you home safe and sound. So let's get a move on, right?"

Neither I nor the girl move. The girl's eyes are locked on Gavin, assessing. "Is that your friend?" she asks me.

"The forest ranger," I reply. "The bad men who kidnapped you are going to prison for a long time thanks to him."

She doesn't take her eyes off of him. "You said he could save the unicorn."

Gavin shoots me a look.

"I didn't say he could definitely save him," I say. "I said if anyone could, he could. He's going to try."

"He can't just try. It has to work."

"There, now," says Gavin, coming over to us. He's picked up what's transpired between the girl and I and begins playing his part perfectly. Or at least I think he does. He kneels down next to the unicorn and pats the beast's neck and says, "Alright then, let's have a butcher's."

"Gavin!" I yell. I mean, what the hell? He's talking about butchering the poor beast right in front of the girl?

But the girl giggles. "That just means he's having a look," she says, and giggles again.

"Americans," says Gavin, and the little girl smiles at him and trusts him a little more. Yeah, it's another "silly American" joke between Brits, but if it helps us all get through this, I can take it. Mock away.

Gavin turns back to the unicorn and examines it studiously.

"Right," he says finally. "I'm going to have to perform a complicated bit of field surgery on this poor fellow. Gabby, my crew's half a click south of here. You should head toward them with the little lady here."

"Come with me, sweetie," I say to the girl, standing and holding out my hand. "Let's get you back to your parents."

She doesn't look at me. "I want to stay," she says flatly.

"We have to let Mr. Howard do his work," I say. "He's the only chance the unicorn has. You want to help the unicorn, right?"

"Yes."

"The best way for us to help is to get out of the way."

She considers this, pets the horned horse more vigorously to help her think. Then—so, so carefully—she sets the unicorn's head on the ground, scoots her legs out from under. The unicorn is well beyond noticing such subtle gestures. Its black unmoving oculus reflects the clouds.

The girl rises and takes my hand. "Please do what you can, Mr. Ranger," she says to Gavin.

Gavin opens a leather satchel of sharp instruments on the ground. They look a little crude for the fine cuts surgery usually requires. They look like tools for an autopsy: for sawing, hacking, flensing off. But maybe those are the tools field surgery on a unicorn require. How would I know?

"Don't you worry," Gavin says to the girl. "I'll have Mr. Unicorn patched up in no time."

The support team is everything I could want from British rescuers. I'm offered tea and blankets and biscuits and a satellite phone. I call my editor at the *Squint*, Leniquia Yancey, and confess how I blew the story.

"Fuck journalistic ethics!" she says. Love that woman.

The support team does even better with the little girl. They've got her sitting on the tailgate of a pickup, drinking tea from a thermos, wrapped in a blanket she doesn't need. They washed her feet. A comfortingly overzealous Mary Poppins kneels behind her in the bed of the truck and brushes out her hair. The woman chats nonstop the entire time, a stream of solicitous chatter that, like all good white-noise machines, is threatening to put the blanketed girl to sleep.

But the girl wakes up immediately when Gavin rejoins us.

I have exactly one second to gather the truth from his body language. Then Gavin sees the girl scrutinizing him and muscles up a smile. He marches over to her with his elbows out, like he's about to start a musical number. "How are we doing? My people taking good care of you?"

"Yes."

"Did you talk to your mum and dad? I bet they were glad to hear your voice."

"Yes."

"We'll, you'll be back with your family in a few hours."

"Did you save him?"

He had to know that question was coming, but in the moment he still finds himself unprepared to answer. "Well," he says slowly, casting his glance downward, "it wasn't easy." But then, looking at her conspiratorially: "But, yes. I saved him."

"Really?" Her voice is simultaneously dubious and hopeful.

Gavin clears his throat. "We had to pull a bit of a trick to pull it off. You see, unicorns really are magic in their own universe. But when they come here, suddenly they're as normal as any other horse."

"They're magical?"

"Sure they are, in their own time and place. Unicorns don't die or get sick or grow old in their own universe. Once I got him back to his rightful place, he healed up like that." Gavin snaps.

The girl blooms. "You can do that?"

"Sure I can. Can't I, team?"

"Yes. Oh, certainly. Do it all the time," says the team.

The girl is looking from face to face. She seems better. Finally she looks at me. "Is it true, Ms. Reál?"

"If Mr. Howard says so," I say automatically.

"Promise?"

How can I promise? Gavin's lying out of his ass. It's not like there's some handy stargate we can push them through to send unicorns back to their universe. They're the first verifiable case we have of a living creature passing between realities, but that may only be because, since they don't exist in this one, they were easy to identify. Millions of animals may be traveling back and forth between universes, or maybe just unicorns. Who knows? Certainly not us, not yet. We have zero idea how to send them back.

So why am I not telling the girl all this?

Because the truth will gut her afresh. Because she's endured more than enough. Because she can learn the truth later, when she's stronger: maybe even from me, if she happens to read this article. If you're reading this, P—, I'm sorry. As a reporter, I'm supposed to be a steward of the truth. But as unheroic as it sounds, it's <u>way</u> better to lie and stay alive.

I take P—'s hands and look her in the eye and say, "Sweetie, I promise you, that unicorn is as alive as you and me."

American Moat

Hamilton—everyone called him Ham—had fully bought into the bacon-as-fashion fad. That night as he patrolled the Arizona border with Alex, his ensemble featured a bacon wristwatch, bacon suspenders, bacon bolo tie, and bacon boots branded with the image of a pig cutting bacon out of its stomach and eating it raw and loving every lip-licking bite.

Ham's t-shirt was comparatively subtle. It read, "If I Were Muslim, My 2nd Wife'd Be BACON."

This shirt offended Alex. Not because it was anti-Islamist, but because it was poorly written. If you're making a t-shirt about loving bacon and having multiple wives, shouldn't you make bacon the *first* wife? You really want to wear a shirt advertising to the world that you love your wife *more* than bacon? That's not funny. That's half-assed.

And Alex was sick to death of half-assed. That's why he'd volunteered to join MOAT: Maintaining Our American Turf. No pay, no benefits, and it was BYO everything: badge, booze, ammo, porno, everything. But it was a small price to pay to serve your country. Let Mexicans cross over to American soil so they could take American jobs and sponge off American services, all while America foots the bill? Not in his America.

Between the guns and the porno and the camaraderie with other patriots, patrols were the social highpoint of Alex's week. But the watch tonight was uncharacteristically unfun. Ham and Alex reclined on the hood of Alex's blue-and-rust truck—backs against the windshield, rifles on their laps—not speaking. Alex had tried to explain to Ham how half-assed his shirt was, which led Ham to the conclusion that Alex hated freedom.

They might have sat sulking side by side all night long had not Ham seen, from between his bacon boots, two figures in the distance walking blithely toward America.

Ham smacked Alex's arm and said, "Look, Alex! Our first Mexicans! It's go-time! It's show-time! Rock 'n' roll!" etc.

Ham was already hugging his rifle and rolling off the hood of the truck by the time Alex had raised his binoculars. He saw a man and a woman. They looked white, but some Mexicans do. The man wore a tuxedo with a lavender ruffled shirt, and sported pomaded black hair and a mustache so precise he must have trimmed it with a stencil. He was Fred Astaire thin and seemed to have no trouble trekking through desert terrain in tuxedo shoes. The woman was every bit as light on her feet, even though she wore a red flamenco dress and black flamenco heels. She carried a folded fan in one hand and her skirts in the other, and she had a huge red flower tucked behind one ear, burning like a star against her brunette, tightly-bunned hair. The pair did not look like people who'd risk their lives hiking through the desert for days in order to violate American immigration policy. They looked happy, clean, and hydrated, like a rich couple leaving a Spanish-themed costume ball.

They were still a ways off, chatting and laughing amiably, when Ham reentered Alex's field of vision. Ham was chugging toward the couple faster than Alex thought he could possibly move, the bacon suspenders struggling with all their might to keep his buttcrack from showing. A losing battle.

"Ham!" Alex yelled as he mobilized. "Stand down, stand down!"

But Ham had played this scenario out too many times to stand down now. He dropped to one knee and steadied his rifle. Sort of: its aim heaved along with his chest. "Freeze! Mexi! Cans!" he yelled between breaths.

"Oh, we aren't Mexicans, Ham," said the woman. Neither Ham nor Alex should have been able to hear her so clearly from that distance. It was like her voice had emerged from within their own heads. That made Alex jump.

A few seconds later, Ham flinched. His cholesterol-coated reflex arcs took a little longer to react. "The hell you know my name, lady?" he asked finally.

"We are aliens," said the man. He sounded exactly like Ricardo Montalban, may he rest in peace.

"Exactly!" said Ham, straightening his aim. "And we're here to stop aliens from entering this country."

"No, numbnuts," said the woman. "Not Mexican aliens. *Actual* aliens."

"Extraterrestrials," the man added helpfully.

That word, "extraterrestrials," had come from Alex. The man had reached into Alex's brain and borrowed it. Alex could feel it. It felt like the man was a cook searching for a recipe and Alex was his recipe box. It wasn't an unpleasant feeling, exactly. But if you haven't agreed in advance to serve as someone's recipe box, it's a bit of a violation.

Alex, now next to Ham, patted Ham's rifle until it pointed at the ground. He grabbed Ham by his left armpit and lifted him to his feet. Looking at the man and woman, he said to Ham: "You're a slow-witted fuck and these really are aliens. I need to think, so I'm going to buy us some time. Follow my lead."

"Yeah bro," said Ham, his rifle still pointed at his own left boot.

Alex walked over to the aliens until they were in hand-shaking range. "You say you're extraterrestrials? Prove it."

"Sure thing," said the woman. "How?"

"Well, show me something alien. What can your kind do?"

"Oh," said the man with honeydripping Montalbanity, "we can manipulate matter in ways that will seem godlike to you. How about we fulfill some minor wish of yours?"

He squinted at Alex for a moment, and then, smiling broadly at what he'd discovered there, turned Alex's truck into Margaret Thatcher.

The Iron Lady wore one of her classic no-nonsense skirt-suits—this one a flattering powder-blue—and sensible heels. Her hair was a petrified corona of orange dye.

"Couldn't you at least have imagined her in a bikini?" said Ham.

"Show some respect, shithead," said Alex out of the side of his mouth, straightening himself as Thatcher strode toward him and shook his hand.

"Alex. Pleasure to meet you," she said.

"It's truly an honor, Madame Former Prime Minister," said Alex. "You've been a hero of mine ever since I was a kid. I would follow you even unto the gates of Hell."

Thatcher nodded once at him, as if she accepted his fealty and, indeed, might someday call on it. Then she walked over and greeted Ham, then each of the aliens.

"Alex is a big fan of yours," said the Montelban look-alike. "You are literally his dream come true. Ham, by contrast, only vaguely knows who you are. He is currently trying to picture you wearing a bacon bikini."

"What? No," Ham protested, but he could tell no one believed him. So he changed tack: "Just how deep into our heads are you, aliens?"

"I don't know about my friend," said the woman, "but I'm far enough into your brain to serve as your conscience: a position, by the looks of things in here, that's been vacant for a long time. So as my first act as your new conscience, I'm recommending that you seek professional help. Nobody needs that much porno, bro."

"I'm too weak to stop," agreed Ham.

Thatcher crossed her arms and said, "Enough chit-chat. Have you aliens come to invade Earth?"

"Oh," said Alex. Then: "Oh!"

"What?" asked Ham.

"These aliens," said Alex, cottoning on even as he spoke, "are obviously powerful enough to destroy us without breaking a sweat, seeing as they were able to fashion a perfect Margaret Thatcher out of a Chevy. But we're still here, so total annihilation doesn't seem to be what they're after. So maybe invasion is the plan. Is it?"

"No," the man said affably.

"Then what?" pressed Thatcher.

"We are explorers," said the woman, circling the humans, fanning herself. "We seek to befriend all intelligent life in the multiverse. Do you know how the multiverse works?"

Ham and Thatcher shrugged. "I saw a special on the History Channel," said Alex.

"Here you go," said the woman, and inserted into their minds a complete understanding of the multiverse.

"My God," said Thatcher.

"It's so beautiful," said Alex.

"They should have sent a poet," said Ham.

"As you can see, it's all very complicated and very interesting," the woman continued. "So we're making site-visits to all sentient life-forms to learn as much as we can from them."

"But we have rules," added the man. "We always approach a new civilization cautiously, inconspicuously. We wear the local bodies, partake of the local metabolism: you know, try to blend in."

"Dressed like that?" asked Ham.

"Our research indicated that these were appropriate costumes for this location and time. Are they not?"

"Not unless you're an extra in a Zorro movie," said Alex.

"You see?" said the woman. "There's only so much you can learn from afar. That's exactly why we're here."

"We don't make contact with leaders at first," the man picked up. "We don't want to become pawns in the local planet's political maneuverings. Instead, we meet with common folks like you. Get the lay of the land, see if this is a good time to begin a conversation with the species. Only when we're satisfied that all the planet's sentient species are ready to join the greater cosmic community do we share our technology with them."

"Like, how to turn a beat-up 2008 Chevy Silverado into the greatest stateswoman ever to grace world politics?" asked Alex.

"You're too kind, really," blushed Thatcher. Briefly, their eyes met.

"That's nothing," said the she-alien. "We will teach you to manipulate matter in ways that will redefine what it means to be human. Poverty, privation, and scarcity will all be a thing of the past. Economics as you know it will cease to exist, and with it war itself will vanish. You will no longer be bound to Earth and its finite resources. You will travel the stars, like us, and forget all about your petty governments squabbling over pitiful tracts of land or trickles of water. You will become citizens of the Cosmic Interbrane. Our arrival will begin a new evolutionary stage for humanity."

Alex and Ham looked at each other. "That sounds great," Alex said breathlessly.

"We'll be heroes!" said Ham, breathily.

"You shall not pass!" exclaimed The Iron Lady.

"Madame Former Prime Minister?" questioned Alex.

"You'll need to take this up with the American government, Mr. and Mrs. Alien. Otherwise, you will be in violation of U.S. sovereignty."

"Excuse me, truck-woman," said the she-alien, "we've already told you our rules expressly forbid us from beginning our interactions with a new species through a governmental entity." She fanned herself testily.

Thatcher put her hands behind her back and, with a lawyerly air, paced around the aliens as she spoke: "So you're saying that you specifically do not want to deal with any governments before you determine if humanity is ready to accept the gift of your advanced technology. And if you do deem us ready, then your technological gifts will allow us to manipulate matter so effectively that poverty and war will cease to exist, and as a consequence Earth won't need 'local' governments anymore and instead can join whatever ruling body it is that you belong to. Do I have all that right?"

"Yes, that's more or less it," the man said uneasily.

Thatcher turned to Alex and Ham. "This *is* an invasion, plain and simple. If you help these aliens do what they want to do, you will be aiding and abetting in the very destruction of the United States of America as you know it, and indeed, the entire world. Do you want to destroy America, Alex and Hamilton?"

"No!" knee-jerked Ham.

"No," said Alex more slowly, "but this is an unprecedented situation, Madame Former Prime Minister. We're being given a chance to achieve world peace."

"Gentlemen, I believe in duty," said Thatcher. "Did you not promise to protect the Arizona border against aliens trying to enter your country illegally?"

Alex began to lose his patience: "Oh Jesus in a jumpsuit, Maggie, no one was talking about *these* aliens! We were talking about Mexicans."

"Just Mexicans, Alex?"

"No, not just Mexicans," Ham added helpfully. "People from Central and South America and the Caribbean, too. You know, poor people. Who usually speak Spanish. Sometimes French. But not Canadians; they're all right."

But hearing his position in Ham's mouth lent Alex clarity. "Madame Former Prime Minster is right," he said, his voice reluctant but resigned. "An alien is anyone who is not a citizen of the United States. Period. We are not authorized to grant legal alien status to anyone we meet on this border, no matter how many trucks they turn into conservative luminaries. Our sole mandate is to keep unauthorized aliens out. And right now, these two are unauthorized. Illegal."

"You are welcome," Thatcher sniffed at the aliens, "to apply for a visa through the proper channels."

The man nodded with disappointment; the woman fanned herself dejectedly. "Well, so that's that," said the man.

"That is not that!" yelled Ham. "Don't go, aliens! Teach me how to turn trucks into women. I need that power! I give you permission to stay!"

"No you don't, Ham," said Alex. "Not unless you are a hypocrite."

Ham stood looking alternately at the two aliens, Alex, and Margaret Thatcher. He felt strange. If this were any other day in his life, he would have just let his rage guide his actions. But now he was one of the world's leading astrophysicists. He looked up at the star-dappled sky, wonderstruck by its grandeur. Then, unable to suppress his newfound causal-reasoning skills, he heaved a Pontius-Pilate sigh and said, "Mr. and Mrs. Alien, please contact the government of the United States for further instructions as to how you may maintain a legal residency for the duration of your stay."

"You know we can't," said the woman. "What a disappointment."

"All this way for nothing," said the man, tsk-tsking. "Well, I guess we'll be leaving, then."

"You will not just talk to someone else, try to get a different answer?" asked Thatcher. "You will leave, just like that?"

"Your response has made it abundantly clear that Earth isn't ready to join the larger interstellar community. I mean, the U.S. is the largest military and economic power on Earth. It has a history, stretching back to its very founding, of welcoming aliens and enriching its culture through the power of emigration. On paper, you seemed to us like the perfect people for us to contact."

"And you said no," the woman added bitterly. Alex and Ham felt the alien presences leaving their minds. A sudden existential wind coursed through their bodies.

"Aliens?" Ham said meekly.

"Yes, Ham?" responded the woman.

"I'm wondering if you could do me a favor before you go."

"We're not granting any more wishes."

"I don't want you to grant a new wish, I want you to undo the shitty wish you granted Alex, the one that cost us world peace and awesome superpowers. Can you please turn Margaret Thatcher back into a truck?"

"What?" yelled Thatcher. "Now wait just a—"

"Is that what you want too, Alex?" asked the male alien, straightening his mustachios with his pinkie.

Alex looked at Madame Former Prime Minister, his longtime hero, a voice of integrity and resolve at a time when reasonableness and common sense seemed out of vogue. He'd always dreamed of sitting down one-on-one with her and hashing out the planet's problems, shooting them off a picket fence like so many lined-up bottles. The world needed more Margaret Thatchers, that was for sure. And tonight—a miracle!—it had been granted a second one.

But there was sand in Alex's boots. "Well, it's too far to walk home," he said.

"No!" screamed Thatcher, shielding her face, but there was nothing she could do. A moment later she turned back into a rusty Chevy Silverado idling fitfully in the Arizona night.

Fantaisie-Impromptu No. 4 in C#min, Op. 66

This isn't any ordinary piano. This is the infamous Bösendorfer Imperial Concert Grand that Václav Balusek had custom-built for his comeback at Carnegie Hall. One of the first things you'll notice is that it has nine extra keys: five whole-tones and four half-tones beyond the lowest A of an 88-key piano. All the extra keys are black.

I was fascinated by them when I first saw them 15 years ago, and I'm even more fascinated now. They're the bad boys of the piano-key world, the kind of piano keys my dad would never let me date in high school. They whisper to me, in the way only inanimate objects can sweet-talk the insane: "Play us, and you will evoke sounds so forbidden your very soul will thrum."

Like everyone, I want my soul to thrum. I run my long nails over the keys like I'm scratching the back of a lover.

But playing Balusek's piano uninvited would be unforgivably rude. I'm here at the home of the Baluseks in Coral Gables. Consuela, Václav's formidable lawyer wife, is being a proper Cuban host and fetching cafecitos for us, which is how I ended up alone with the piano in the mansion's conservatory. I remind myself that you don't just start playing world class musicians' priceless instruments, especially not without permission. But I'm still sitting on the bench, petting the keys.

The Assimilated Cuban's Guide to Quantum Santeria

Tickling these ebonies, Gabby, I think to myself, *might be more than bad manners. It might be sexual harassment.*

I don't really believe that, but the thought helps me come to my senses. I rise from the bench, take a breath, lift the hair off the back of my neck to let it cool. To remove myself from further temptation I circle the grand piano, taking notes and pictures like a proper reporter should.

God but this piano's a work of art. At first glance it might pass for a traditional grand, lacquered to a gleaming black and oozing old-world, Austro-Hungarian charm. But soon you'll notice the brass-and-glass touches that a generation ago would have been called Steampunk: the scrollwork on the brushed metal hinge of the fallboard; the rectangular portholes in its body, framed by verdigris-veined copper; the gorgeous, Rube Goldbergian system of pulleys, wheels, and hinges that make up the gloriously overengineered pedal lyre.

It's the kind of grand piano some billionaire archgeek would order as a showpiece for a living room, more for the eyes than the ears. It's not the instrument I'd expect a world-class pianist like Balusek to commission. And it's *really* not the vessel I'd expect Balusek to choose as his home for life after death.

Did I forget to mention that? Yeah, in case you've been in a coma for the last decade: Václav Balusek is dead. At least his body is. But true believers like his wife have maintained that his soul lives on in this beautiful, diabolical piano.

Consuela (maiden name Oquendo) returns bearing a silver tray that looks like she lifted it from The Cloisters. It's laden with demitasses of espresso and squares of buttered Cuban bread piled up like a carbohydrate Tower of Babel.

I thank Consuela and pluck myself a demitasse; she rests the tray on the Mondrian coffee table and sits next to me on the parlor's zebra-stripe sofa; apparently she gives zero fucks about matching décor. Their oft-photographed home used to be filled with B-movie bric-a-brac, back when sci-fi enthusiast Václav had a say in matters like these. But even if you believe Václav's still alive inside his piano, Consuela's the only one with eyes anymore. So I guess she gets to make all the interior design choices in their marriage now.

When I don't take any bread, she says, "You have to eat, mi niña! I never would have landed Vaclavito without my curves. Take it from me: men don't like broomsticks."

Ah, the cheerful, feral brusqueness of the Cuban jefa. It's a type I know, and have even sought to emulate in many ways: tireless, cheerful, self-assured women who work 80 hours a week at their jobs, keep their homes impossibly clean, go to church every Sunday, and never, ever let their kids forget who's in charge.

They're great 85% of the time. But they can be a bit, shall we say, peremptory. Like Consuela, they'll tell you to your face you're too skinny. And God help you if they think you're too fat.

"Thank you, Señora Balusek," I say, "but I'm vegetarian. Cuban bread is made with lard."

Now, the typical Cuban jefa would make a passive-aggressive production of "hiding" how much your words have hurt her. Yes, she would take it as a personal attack that you didn't want to eat her store-bought bread.

So I start to strategize how I can get back on her good side when, to my surprise, I see Consuela is embarrassed, apologetic. "Ay, mi niña, I'm so sorry," she says. "It didn't even occur to me to ask, you being Cuban and all."

"Yeah," I joke, to show no harm was done. "Who ever heard of a Cuban vegetarian? What's next, vegan crocodiles?"

She laughs politely and after a moment adds, "I shouldn't have called you a broomstick. Forgive me! You're so beautiful. You must have more boyfriends than you know what to do with."

Since it's required that I return the compliment, I scan her person for inspiration. Consuela's a 48-year-old salt-and-pepper odalisque who's barely as tall as my chin (and I'm 5'3"). Her smile has a practiced guilelessness she probably learned while in law school.

But she's not dressed for court today; today, she's cultivating the Miami MILF look. She wears a tight floral blouse, and a crucified golden Jesus bobs on her cleavage like a castaway on a raft. Her teal pants bell at the bottom, and her ratty house chancletas look like they've been passed down from mother to daughter for five generations. I've seen Cuban women dress like this all my life, and genetics guarantee that someday I, too, will dress exactly like this. Though I'll draw the line at the crucifix.

"Me?" I say. "What about you? You're beautiful, rich, and single. You're one of the most eligible bachelorettes in Miami." I sip a little cafecito and watch for her reaction.

She smiles and gives me an I-see-what-you-did-there look. "I'm still married, mi vida."

"Not according to the law. The court has declared Balusek dead."

"The law is slow to change. It will come around eventually. Who knows how many lawsuits it will take, but eventually the courts will recognize what has happened to Vaclavito and people like him."

"Which is what, exactly?"

There's a little melancholy in the way she tilts her head. Then she says, "He moved."

I let my eyebrows speak before I do. "Moved? As in, out of his own flesh?"

"Exactly. His mind persists. He just 'emigrated' out of his former body and into the eneural."

"Emigrating out of your body sounds to me like a pretty good definition of death."

"Only if you don't have somewhere else to go," she says. And then her gaze guides me to the piano.

After a moment she asks, "Do you believe people have souls, Gabby?"

I never lie during an interview, even when I know my answer may cost me greatly. I suck through my teeth but tell the truth: "No. Sorry."

Consuela smiles, stands, and offers me her hand. "In ten minutes you're going to wish you said, 'Not yet.'"

~

Before we sit on the piano bench, Consuela helps me into a black leather jacket with built-in gloves. It's four sizes too big, but even so, I can feel it's actually an exoskeleton of the "python-rib" variety. A concatenated series of metal rings reside within the jacket's arms and fingers. Consuela fastens me into it from behind and adjusts the arm-length so that it fits me. Kind of.

She can't help but laugh. "Oh, Gabby," she says. "You look so cute! Like a girl playing dress-up in her pápi's biker clothes."

"This is nothing," I reply. "You should see me in a panda suit."

She has no idea what I'm talking about. Probably better that way.

She unceremoniously plants me on the bench. "Right thumb on middle-C, left pinky on the C# an octave lower," she says.

I place my hands on the keys as instructed. The eneural that imaged Balusek's mind and let him keep performing, years after it should have been possible, has been fitted into this piano. It's about to connect wirelessly to this jacket. It's a little freaky.

I keep my hands on the piano keys but turn to face Consuela. She pats my shoulder and says, "This is going to be fun! Relax!" The most unrelaxing thing a person can say.

While I am still looking at Consuela, the exo makes my left thumb and pinkie play a two-note chord, C# and G#. I turn to look at my hands.

"Well hello, Mr. Balusek!" I exclaim. I really do exclaim: embarrassingly, fangirlishly.

The exoskeleton is not nearly as powerful as I thought it would be. I could resist it if I wanted to. The glove holds the chord for a melancholy second, then leaps, the left thumb landing on C#, the pinkie on the G# below it. I watch, amazed, as the left glove start an arpeggio, slowly at first but quickly gaining speed.

A blink later my fingers are moving faster than I can move them myself. The right glove transforms itself into a fairy ballerina who leaps and runs over the keys, leaving a contrail of dulcet music in her wake.

I am not making this music happen, but every time the glove strikes a key, the music shoots up my fingers and passes into my body, just as if I were playing this piece myself. It's so pleasurable and enchanting to feel the music course through me that I forget for a moment to hear it.

So I remind myself to listen as well as feel. The piece reminds me of the ad-hoc soundtracks pianists of yore would play to accompany silent movies. The black-and-white scene the music describes is one of peril, pursuit, combat: a runaway locomotive, a showdown at high-noon, pirates battling for control of a wave-pitched ship. My fingers race down the length of the keys; the music reaches a climax that reminds me of a car tumbling down a hillside. Will Bonnie and Clyde escape the V8 Ford before it explodes?

They do, because the music shifts now to a love story. We see the lovers from behind. They sit on the shore—he wearing a top hat and tailed tuxedo, she in a glistering silver gown and tiara—holding hands and watching waves climb up the shore. There is nothing so beautiful in the world as the oversized moon of a silent movie. It grows a face suddenly and winks at them, but they're too in love to notice. They turn from the ocean and face one another. They lean in, closing the distance between their lips. They almost kiss.

But the music shifts back to the rollicking, riotous fairy-gambols where we started. Again the melody grows ominous; again I am falling right to left down the length of the keyboard: Lucifer cast from heaven and plummeting through the firmament until he finally, with terrible impact, crashes into Hell.

But this time a humble coda rises up, murmuring. One hand mumbles out a pianissimo arpeggio as the other dolefully hearkens us back to the earlier love story. Only this time, love is over, never to return; love is Ophelia drowned, Samson casting one last pleading look at Delilah, Eurydice reaching after Orpheus as she's pulled back into the Underworld. All that remains of that great passion is a memory that is even now fading, fading. Then the music stops and even the memory of love evanesces into nothingness.

The leather jacket goes limp; my arms drop dead and slap against my legs. I didn't do a lick of work—the exo did everything—but I'm exhausted, breathless, tousled. I'm simultaneously euphoric and heartbroken. I finally understand what Aristotle meant by catharsis.

I turn around to face Consuela. She smiles and shrugs and says, "Now you know Vaclavito. Down to his soul."

The piece Václav played was Chopin's Fantaisie-Impromptu #4 in C# minor, Opus 66, a devilishly difficult composition that has become one of Chopin's most-performed works and a kind of rite of passage for piano virtuosos the world over.

But even a player piano could be programmed to play the composition flawlessly, if lifelessly. There was only one way to verify that this wasn't just a robotic recording. Václav would have to play it again, with me still wearing the jacket. And he would have to play it *differently*.

Which he does. The second time around, Václav plays it more athletically, less dolorously. I learn later that this is the way most journeymen play it: it's so challenging to perform that merely getting through it is an accomplishment, and so many pianists end up treating it as a showcase for their technical prowess. Yet, even here, there are millisecond delays and dynamic changes that carry from the first performance to the second. Now that I have lived inside of Václav's style, I can identify some of its qualities, through the way he uses me to apply pressure to the piano keys. I feel I am starting to get to know him. Václav Balusek has shared a bit of his very qualia with me.

That's quite an achievement. Normally, you can't even get inside someone's qualia when they're alive. And Balusek is dead.

And I don't just mean legally dead. You won't catch any of the major eneural manufacturers claiming they can give your mind a new home after your body dies. They never use the term for them the movies and the media throw around: "cyberreliquary."

An eneural, they will tell you, is merely a "cognitive prosthetic" implanted into the brain to help those who have suffered debilitating brain disorders. Like any prosthetic, it's custom-built for the individual. Epileptics get a different eneural than those who've suffered a traumatic brain injury. Those with advanced Alzheimer's get a different one altogether.

There are common elements, of course: there's always, for instance, an AI that, like an eager infant, learns to mimic the patient's brain, synapse by synapse. Over time, the AI's "thinking" acquires an uncanny similarity to the patient's. After a training period that can last for months or even years, the eneural has essentially become an artificial ganglion that provides the patient's brain with supplementary memory recall and cognitive power.

The effects can be positively transformative, as they were for Václav Balusek. I was 14 when Václav Balusek was diagnosed with Parkinson's Disease. His illness was worthy of global sorrow; the world's most beloved living pianist would all too soon lose his ability to play. The media characterized it as a fate worse than death: he would live to see his gift, his life's work, fall to ruins before him day to day.

That was bad enough. But for millions of teenaged girls like me, for whom Balusek was a particular kind of celebrity crush—not muscular, not macho, but artistic, intellectual, and adorably geeky—it was our first taste of life's cruelty.

In the post-diagnosis interviews that followed Václav, holding hands with his wife Consuela (whom I hated back then with unbridled jealousy), vowed to fight the disease. He was a famous proponent of science and futurism; over the years he'd donated millions to the SENS Research Foundation to support a "cure for aging" and was, you will remember, an avid collector of sci-fi movie props. He cheerily described advances in medications and deep brain stimulation that could stave off the ill effects of Parkinson's for years. He made me believe he could win.

By the time I was a sophomore in college, Václav had disappeared from public life. The disease was worsening more quickly than antici-pated and wasn't responding to treatment. He hadn't performed in years, and most assumed he never would again.

And then, back when I was just starting out as a lowly copy editor at *The San Francisco Squint*, Carnegie Hall announced that Balusek would perform there, one night only. Tickets sold out in seconds.

Consuela shares some black and white photos of that performance with me. Picture 1: a steampunk-inspired Bösendorfer Imperial Con-cert Grand (yes, the same one) sits on the stage. The piano choice is curious, but perhaps the most unusual thing about the shot is that there's no bench onstage.

Picture 2: wheelchair-bound Balusek takes the stage, smiling and waving. He's puffy and paunchy; he's aged a thousand years; but most shocking of all is that his hairline is disrupted by a surgery scar as big as a scarecrow's mouth.

Consuela shows me more pictures, but they don't really capture what happened next. Václav rolled up to the piano. He folded his hands in his lap, and never moved them again until the performance was over. He played the grand piano with his mind.

Specifically, he played the grand piano with the eneural he'd had installed and the wireless connection built into the Bösendorfer. His performance consisted of works he had commissioned from promising young composers for this occasion.

Consuela tells me the commissions were her idea, as a way to prove that the performances were really being given by Balusek. Before playing each work, the audience saw a video interview of each composer. The composers spoke of her or his intentions with the piece, the process of composition, the inspiration: but mostly they talked up Balusek as they rehearsed the work at his Coral Gables home.

The audience watched as Balusek, in his wheelchair in front of the Bösendorfer, would play a portion of the piece with his mind, then consult with the properly-awed composer about it, then try again. There was laughing, jokes, and moments of dignified awe as the young composers watched Balusek move the idea he had formed about their music from his mind directly into the piano. My favorite of the composers, Cynthia Gazón, put it this way: "He's fired the middlemen, the hands. He can perform now without having to navigate the cumbersome bureaucracy of the body. It may be the purest music that's ever existed."

~

"That one-night-only engagement at Carnegie Hall turned into a world tour," I say to Consuela. I'm still in the jacket, still on the piano bench. Still catching my breath from my second impromptu fantasy with Václav.

"130 shows in 37 countries," Consuela, sitting in a chair to my left, says wistfully. She's traded the cafecito for a Malbec I can smell from here.

"Playing works no other pianist could play," I prompt.

She smiles. "Vaclavito was no longer limited to two hands and two feet. He could play duets by himself. He commissioned over two dozen works that would be impossible for any other person alive to play. The 97-note smash that ends Gazón's 'Singularity Sonata' is still considered one of the defining moments of 21st century music."

I ask for a little of that fantastic-smelling Malbec. But when she offers to get it for me, I get up, grab a glass from the wine rack, and pour it myself. Then I carry the bottle over to Consuela. As I'm refilling hers, I say, "Lots of people were never convinced. They thought the performances were prerecorded. That this was all a big money-making ploy. A last grab at fame."

Consuela gives me a "you ain't kidding" look. "Because how could you prove it, at the end of the day?" she complains. "We were using the most advanced cybernetic technology in the world. It's not like you could just lift the eneural's 'hood' and let people see for themselves how it worked."

"And then, when Balusek died—"

She stops me short: "He didn't die."

"Sorry! When his physical body could only be sustained through life support, the attacks became more vicious. That's when the media turned on you."

"I could take it. Because I knew the truth." And she completes the thought the way Cubans often do, with an attempt at aphorism: "When you have truth on your side, you fear nothing."

"They called you a ghoul. They said you were using your dead husband to make yourself rich."

Consuela smiles and shakes her head like she's dealing with a child. She contemplates her wine for a moment, then says, "He could still play the piano, there from his hospital bed! All those fancy machines were saying he was dead, but then I would say, 'Vaclavito, would you play "Moonlight Sonata" for me?' And then the Bösendorfer would immediately start to play it.

"There wasn't a doctor or nurse who would pull the plug while he could still play the piano! So it fell to me. But I wasn't going to rush anything. I waited until I was sure his migration was complete. And when it was, I had the life support turned off. And I was right. As you now know, Gabby."

I sit at the bench again. I drink half my wine, then set it down on a side table. I'm still punchy from the aesthetic tidal wave that was Václav performing through me. And the Malbec's making me tipsy in the more traditional way. I'm getting a little loose, a little unprofessional. I exhale with unmastered longing and say, "Yeah. If only everyone could wear this jacket for a little while."

Consuela leans forward. "So you believe me. You know that Vaclavito's still alive."

I tell her the truth. Goddamnit. "No. I think Balusek is dead. I wish I could give you another answer."

There's something leonine in the way Consuela's looking at me. I feel like I'm walking into one of her lawyerly traps, but for the life of me I can't see what it is. And she doesn't tip her hand just yet. Innocent as a telenovela ingenue she asks, "But what about the the music you just played?"

I sigh. "People have been leaving behind huge chunks of themselves after death for eons, Consuela—in their diaries and paintings and the notes in their cookbooks and the stories they tell their children. The eneural is the latest in a long line of media that help us capture some bit of who we were when we were alive, and give it to the future. It's the birth of a new artform. One I already love."

She frowns skeptically. "That's it? My husband is art to you?"

I don't back down. "Art makes life make sense."

"Art is a dead thing trying to tell the living how to live."

There's an edge there. But again, I can't tell if it's real, or just some manufactured anger required for some larger scheme of hers.

Only one way to find out. I pick up my wine again and say, "Look, I know you really believe Balusek's soul resides in the eneural, and I don't want to insult you. But you've gone to court to plead your case and lost. You famously consulted with the Catholic Church on the matter, and Cardinal Bianchi's commission on cognitive protheses was quite clear on the matter: eneurals are wonderful, but they're not human. So the law and the church agree. Whatever Václav's eneural has retained for us, it's not his soul."

The Malbec's almost kicked, but Consuela stops refilling hers to offer me a little. I say no and she tips the rest of her bottle into her glass. "What if they're wrong?" she says to me; it's not really a question. "The state and the church have changed their minds many, many times. What if 300 years from now they decide, 'Actually, yes, eneurals are alive. Sorry for any inconvenience.'"

"Well," I say, "assuming proper maintenance, Václav will still be around to hear that. So that's something."

"Yes, but what? What does it mean if Václav is still here 300 years from now?"

Consuela's urgent, eager. I'm getting increasingly leery of her. "I don't know," I say noncommittally.

She peers at me, smiles a little. Her face decides something. She gets up and leaves the room. When she returns a half-minute later, she has a chrome disc the size of a frisbee in her hand.

"Do you know what this is?" she asks, and when I shake my head: "This is a neodymium rare-earth magnet. Super-strong. I had to get special permission to buy one this big."

I don't say anything. I watch.

"Will you sit on the sofa for a moment?" she says sweetly. I move from the piano bench to the sofa. She puts the magnet on the floor and moves the piano bench out of the way. Then she slips out of her chancletas and gets on her knees and takes the magnet in both hands, like a steering wheel. She knee-walks over to the piano. I can see the magnet is already pulling itself toward the piano; she has to fight it. She hugs the magnet to her chest, lies on her back, and scoots herself under the Bösendorfer.

"What are you doing?" I ask vaguely, wine in hand.

She looks at me. I'd been so busy watching her antics with the magnet that I had neglected her face. Tears stream out of her eyes. "This is why I brought you here," she says. Then she lifts the magnet upwards, and the magnet launches itself into the piano.

The jacket squeezes me so forcefully I gasp. I can't inhale. This is what a python attack must feel like.

I am about to panic when the jacket slowly slackens its grip. Its strength fades, fades. Then it's completely powerless.

Consuela, still on her back under the piano, sobs into her hands. My addled brain slowly assembles a kind of sense of what has just happened. My mouth understands before any other part of me, because before realization has fully dawned in my mind I can hear myself saying, "No. Oh God. No no no no no. Oh God, please no."

~

Almost a month after my interview with Consuela, Leniquia Yancey, my editor at the *Squint*, comes up to my desk with a manila envelope. "Mail call!" she cheerily chimes.

If you're thinking it's weird for an editor to bring a reporter her mail, you're right. Leniquia's been checking in with me several times a day since that interview, because frankly, I've been a wreck: useless at work and experiencing random panic attacks a few times a week. Every night I dream of being crushed to death.

I smile at Leniquia. "You're a good friend. You don't have to bring my mail every day."

Leniquia's constitutionally incapable of pessimism, so whenever her face grows solemn the way it has now, it's cause for worry. "This time I really had to," she says. "It's from Consuela Balusek."

The *Squint*'s mostly a wall-less workspace where snoopy reporter types spend all day overhearing each other's shit. I look around and, yes, everyone's pretending not to look. "Can we do this in your office?" I ask Leniquia.

A minute later, we're in her office. "You open it," I say to her.

She grabs a letter opener and starts slicing open the envelope. "It's clean, by the way," she says. "I had our guys check it."

I make a wtf face. "Consuela wouldn't try to kill us."

She stops opening the letter to look at me incredulously. "After what that crazy bitch did? Erasing her husband right in front of you?"

"She thought she was freeing his soul."

Her affect flattens. "That is pure bullshit. She didn't think his soul was really in there. She just wanted the publicity. Think about how famous she is now. This was all part of her big plan."

This is an old fight between Leniquia and me. I take my traditional tack: mocking her. "You've been in San Francisco too long amongst the godless liberals. You've forgotten that there are radically different worldviews out there. Consuela's actions are totally consistent."

They are. My therapist and I have been over it several times. If you believe in a human soul, and in a Catholic heaven, and that your husband's soul resides in an eneural, then, QED, you have prevented your husband from entering into an afterlife of bliss, for your own mortal, selfish reasons. After much soul-searching, she decided she had to erase Balusek publicly—in front of a reporter—to show the world the pitfalls of that thinking: immortals never get to go to heaven. They're destined to an eternal Hell on Earth.

"There is no way a woman of her intelligence and education could possibly believe that," Leniquia insists, arms crossed.

All I would need is a week with Leniquia in Miami to prove to her how wrong she was. But for now we've reached our traditional impasse. "Are you going to open the letter?" I ask her.

She smiles and shakes her head clear. "Almost forgot!"

She finishes cutting through the top and blows open the envelope. From it she extracts a picture and a note.

We look at the picture together. It's a photograph of Consuela and Guy Sauveterre, Chair of the Board of Regents for the Smithsonian Institution. They're wearing expensive suits and are sitting on a piano bench, hands on knees. Behind them is a 97-key Bösendorfer Imperial Concert Grand.

I grab the note. "Dear Gabby," I read aloud, "I've had Vaclavito's backup eneural installed in the Bösendorfer and donated it to the Smithsonian. You'll be receiving an invitation for its debut. I hope by then you will have forgiven me. Please come. Que Dios te bendiga y proteja. Consuela."

Leniquia's mouth hangs open for a good five seconds. Finally all she can manage is, "Bitch had a backup?!"

But I understand completely. I can't get over the validity of her logic: so perfectly consistent! A soul can't be mechanically reproduced, goes Consuela's thinking. By definition, a soul is singular. So when they made the backup copy of the eneural, they didn't copy Václav's soul: just his mind. In her eyes, she sent her husband to heaven by destroying his original eneural. In the meantime, she's donated the soulless backup to the Smithsonian, thus preserving his art on Earth forever.

"Eneural ex machina," I say to the piece of paper in my hands. And breathe.

The Assimilated Cuban's Guide to Quantum Santeria

I was heading toward Parking Lot Four on the east side of campus, mentally reviewing the interview I'd just had with NPR's *All Things Considered* about my new book, when I almost kicked a pigeon.

I'm a physics professor at CalTech specializing in unspeakable information, and my new book is called *The Grid of Time*. The idea is this: what if time, instead of being a single dimension, itself contains multiple dimensions? Well, my book contends, it would unify a lot of disparate theories: if only it were true. The book is the kind of speculative, sweeping thought-experiment that all the cool physicists are writing these days. I am probably wrong about almost everything. But I hope I'm wrong in the ways that will someday lead us to science. That's exactly what I said to my kid-gloves NPR interviewer, and she seemed, in her throaty, sleepy, liberal-media way, duly impressed.

And then I almost kicked a pigeon. Though I was too distracted to see it at the time, in hindsight I can describe exactly what happened: the pigeon stood in place as I approached, as inert as an abandoned football, watching me approach with one curious eye. Only at the last moment did its little birdbrain realize that I was about to kick it, and, once kicked, there would be no turning back on this XY point on time's Cartesian grid, and the pain and consequences of the kick would forever be a part of its history. It therefore decided to get out of the way, with a commotion of wings that startled me back to our shared dream of the world.

There on the sidewalk, surrounded by the cool of an autumn night in Pasadena, I got down on one knee and said to the pigeon, who was now eyeing me gravely, "Sorry little fella. Didn't see you there."

All was forgiven. It immediately came ambling up to me, eager for a handout. I laughed. And when I find something funny, I often switch to Spanish. "¡Ay, pero niño!" I chastised. "¡No debas ser tan confiado! ¿No sabes que cuando yo era un niño, maté a puñaladas una paloma ...."

I fell quiet. To the pigeon, who stared at me with one curious eye, it must have looked as if I had suddenly shut down, like an unplugged robot. And in body I had. But my mind, like a ghostly projector that had started itself, began playing the reel of the time I killed a pigeon in the kitchen sink of my boyhood home.

I had to. The heart of a pigeon was the last ingredient I needed for the Santeria ritual I was performing so that Pápi could find love again.

~

Mámi died the summer before third grade. Doctors were removing a benign tumor from her uterus when ... well, we weren't allowed to know exactly what had happened. One of the conditions of the settlement was that all documents relating to the case remain sealed. The official cause of death on her death certificate is "cardiac arrest," but her heart was doing just fine prior to surgery. They must've done something to her.

Once the settlement came through, Pápi didn't work full-time anymore. He had been teaching senior math at Samuel Adams High School in Handcock, Connecticut, since before I was born, and substitute teaches there to this day. At Samuel Adams they call him "The Professor," partly because he has a Ph.D., but mostly because he *is* a Professor, capital P.

You know the type: the kind of man who has to bite down on a pipe (or in his case, a puro) to remind himself that he has a body as well as a mind, whose eyes are always looking past you and into a reality that is somehow less substantial and more consequential than the one you exist in. It's one thing when these professor-types are tall, bearded, tie-choked, corduroy-jacket-wearing sages who are as white as the faces on Mount Rushmore. Then they're easy to spot. But on the outside, Pápi is as Cuban as they come: 5'5", fat as a top and just as agile, with a nose like a head of cauliflower and Wolfman hair growing off his ears—and always, always wearing a pastel guayabera, even in the ice-age middle of a Connecticut winter. He looks like a guajiro who just needs to pick up his machete to be ready for a full day of cutting cane. But then, just as people start feeling superior to him, he starts talking mathematics—in virtuoso English that will send responsible listeners scrabbling for their dictionaries. It just takes one meeting. After that they call him "Professor."

We were the only Cubans in town. Therefore, the Connecticut

Yankees of Handcock thought all Cubans were like Pápi. So did I. Using a kind of commutative-property logic, I reasoned that, since Pápi was Cuban, all Cubans were Pápi: intellectual, distracted, blunt, cheerful, apolitical, and immune to neurosis of any kind. Kind of like Mr. Spock, but with a better sense of humor. And a *lot* more body hair.

I got to hear from other kids how much better Cubans were than other Latinos, who sent their kids to American schools even though they were illegal. They were poor because they were lazy, and the only reason they couldn't speak English was because they didn't try hard enough. You speak English, Salvador, why can't they? Stick those stupid spics in Special Ed with the other retards.

I agreed with them completely. You see, while they were insulting those other Latinos, they were complimenting me.

I forgot at those moments that, as hard as she tried, even after years of study at the Vo Tech, Mámi still struggled with English, that whenever we went shopping without Pápi she always sent me to talk to Customer Service. But at night I would remember. When I spoke to Mámi then—surrounded by a darkness so complete I wasn't sure I still had a body—and asked her why she left Pápi and me alone, and when she was coming back, I spoke to her in halting, failing Spanish.

~

When I was eight, it was dinosaurs. When I was nine, it was magic. And when I was ten, I got into Santeria.

Not even a month after starting third grade, I got in a fight with

a kid at school because he said Mámi didn't die, she'd been deport-
ed, because eventually that's what happens to all spics. I was Latino
small, so the kid, Timmy Andersen, thought I was an easy mark. Big
mistake. I rushed him, but instead of taking a swing, I yanked down
his pants. And his underwear, perhaps understanding the justness of
my cause, slid down like they'd been buttered. I will never forget the
sight of his tiny white penis: it looked like one of those miniature
rosettes adorning the edge of a wedding cake. Little Timmy screamed
and tried to pull his pants up, while I, almost leisurely, pushed him to
the ground, grabbed his hair in two fists, and bashed his head into the
playground loam. It's the third happiest moment of my childhood.

Because little Timmy was more embarrassed than hurt—his forehead was red and plenty dirty, but no lump emerged—the principal
took it easy on me. He just sent me home for the day with a note for
Pápi to sign. Because it was too early to take the bus, Mrs. Dravlin,
one of the assistant principals, drove me home. She and I were buds;
I had known her since I was in Kindergarten and had always been one
of her favorites. She wasn't as pretty as Mámi or as chubby as Mámi or
as vivacious as Mámi, and she didn't know any more Spanish than you
need to get licensed as a teacher in Connecticut. But she smiled as big
as Mámi, a huge, scary, dental-exam smile, as if she wanted you to be
able to count her teeth.

I loved her teeth.

She wasn't smiling then, though; she had to watch traffic as she
drove, but she kept sneaking fretful, motherly looks at me and saying

things like, "Salvador, you're too smart to get in fights," and "I want you to apologize to Tim tomorrow," and "Maybe you should have your dad call me."

I wasn't at all sorry about pounding stupid Timmy's head into the ground, but Pápi had taught me to respect teachers, even when they're wrong. So I agreed with everything she said, and, once she had parked in my driveway, I said to her, "I'm sorry I was bad, Mrs. Dravlin."

Something in the way I said it? She cried exactly three tears. The first two tumbled out of her eyes like the boulders of a surprise avalanche. I was a little scared; I'd never seen an assistant principal cry before. As she erased the tears from her cheeks with the back of her hand, a third skittered down her face without her knowing and hung pendulously from her chin. It refused to let go of her face as she spoke. "Listen to me, Salvador. You are not bad. You're a very, very, very good boy." Then she leaned over to the passenger side and hugged me. The tear on her chin sank through my t-shirt. Long after it must have evaporated, I felt its warmth and wetness on my shoulder.

I waved goodbye to Mrs. Dravlin, who was waiting to make sure I could get in the house, and "snuck" past Pápi. After the settlement came, he was always home. He sat in the living room with his chin in his hand, studying a Rithomachy board on the coffee table; I could've brought a dead cat into the house and he wouldn't have noticed me. To prove it, when I was nine I actually did bring a dead cat into the house, but I'll tell you about that later. For now, I went to my room.

On the bed lay an illustrated encyclopedia of dinosaurs. It was the biggest book I'd ever seen, even bigger than Mámi's Bible. The inscription inside read, in Pápi's plain and serious script, "The best way to honor Mámi is to better ourselves."

At the end of that school year I became the youngest winner ever of the school's Science Fair for my project "How the Dinosaurs Really Died," where I explained, based on the exciting new research of this wicked-smart Latino named Walter Alvarez, that the dinosaurs had actually been killed by a huge chondritic asteroid with the cool name of Chicxulub that had blasted the Yucatan Peninsula about 65 million years ago. The judges must've known Pápi wrote it, gathered the research, made the graphs—this was stuff even the science teachers hadn't heard about yet. But, in my defense, I *memorized* every last bit of it. I won because it's cute to hear an eight-year-old say phrases like "unusually high concentrations of iridium" and "nemesis parabolic impactors."

~

To celebrate, Dad bought us tickets to go see locally famous prestidigitator Gary Starr make a giraffe disappear. But Pápi was unimpressed by Gary Starr; he told me after the show, "That guy couldn't even fool his own giraffe." But after seeing with my own eyes a full-grown camelopard disappear off the stage and reappear in the theater's parking lot, where it was waiting for us, next to a Gary Starr flunky selling Gary Starr t-shirts and Gary Starr prepackaged magic tricks, I was hooked. Pápi wouldn't buy me any Gary Starr tschochkes, of course, but he would gladly take me to the library. I checked out the fattest magic books they had.

By the time I was nine, I had become a not-too-shabby magician and could even fool adults right in front of their faces. You know the trick where you cut the rope into pieces, only to pull on both ends and—tada!—it's back together again? I did that one for show-and-tell and pissed off my fourth grade teacher, Mr. Liss, when he couldn't figure out how I did it. And of course I wouldn't tell him. Magician's code.

But my best trick of all was a bit I did with the help of Roadkill the Magic Dead Cat. Roadkill wasn't a stuffed animal. Roadkill was a dead black cat, stuffed and mounted and made—why?—into a piggybank. The taxidermist had done a good, if clichéd, job with her: she had a permanent arch in her back, an eternal horripilation of the hair along her spine, and a look in her glass eyes that said "I am three-quarters demon." I got her for ten bucks from Mr. Strauss at the magic shop I frequented after school because he was getting remarried and his wife hated it, had threatened to call off the wedding if he didn't get rid of it. I think he made up that story just to get a sale, but who cares. A dead-cat bank for ten bucks?

Here's how the trick went down, as per the performance I gave to Mr. Liss's class. I went to the front of the room and put Roadkill on Mr. Liss's desk. Everyone said "Ooh!" One girl, Jenny Chalder, said, "That's gross."

I said, "Ladies and Gentlemen, allow me to introduce you to Roadkill the Magic Dead Cat!" I pulled out a phone book and handed it to Mr. Liss. Then I turned back to the class. "My dad's a math teacher, and he's always saying that math lets you do magic, but I didn't believe him until I got Roadkill. Roadkill's going to predict what name we pick out of a phone book, using math."

Jenny Chalder said, "Cats can't do math."

I pulled a slip of paper and a new, sharpened pencil out of my bag. "First, we have to give Roadkill stuff so she can write her answer down." I stuck the piece of paper in Roadkill's mouth, then used the eraser-end of the pencil like a ramrod to jam it down her throat.

Jenny Chalder said "Don't hurt her!"

And I said, "You think that hurts, watch this!" Then I took the pencil and strugglingly pushed it all the way in Roadkill's mouth. Kids squealed and laughed, in that order.

"Okay," I said, "Roadkill has paper and pencil. She's ready to predict which name we pick out of the phone book. So now we have to pick the name. Mr. Liss, call on someone."

"Why?" asked Mr. Liss. His brain was working overtime, trying with all its might to figure out the trick.

"So everyone will know I'm not cheating. Everyone knows you would never help me."

"You got that right." He scanned the room, then villainously smiled. "Okay. Jenny Chalder."

Everyone oohed. Perfect choice.

"Okay. Jenny, say a three-digit number."

She scrunched her face at me. "What's a three-whatever number?"

"Pick a number between 100 and 999, Jenny," Mr. Liss explained.

She scrunched her face again and said, "I don't know. 1-2-3."

I said, "Okay, one-hundred and twenty-three. Mr. Liss, can you go to the board to do some math for us?"

Still suspicious, he asked, "Why don't you have a student do it?"

"Because kids are always messing up math, and the trick won't work if the math is wrong."

He went to the board. I said, "Okay, please write 123 on the board." He did. "Okay, now reverse it and write down that number." He wrote 321. "Okay, subtract 123 from 321." That gave us 198. "Okay, reverse that number." He did; 891. "Okay, what's 198 plus 891?" He did the math: 1089.

"Okay," I said. "That means we go to page 108 in the phone book and go down to the ninth name. Can you find that, Mr. Liss? Don't tell us what it is. Just find it."

Mr. Liss went to the phone book, opened it to page 108, and dragged his finger until he got to the ninth name. "Got it," he said.

I picked up Roadkill and said, "Okay. Roadkill's going to give us the answer now." I put Roadkill over my shoulder like I was burping a baby and patted her on the back. "Okay, she's got it!" I said, and brought her over to Jenny Chalder's desk. "Okay, Jenny, reach in to Roadkill's mouth and pull out the answer she wrote down."

She flared her nostrils. "I ain't putting my finger in no dead cat's mouth."

Instantly, the class exploded in yells and boos. Two cannonballs of paper bounced off Jenny's head. Our resident bully, Willie Toomer, got up from his desk and made like he was going to whale on her right there, but Mr. Liss made him sit down again.

Jenny was so intimidated she said, "This thing better not bite me," stuck her finger in Roadkill's mouth, and hooked out a slip of paper. "Okay. Read what the paper says to the class, Jenny," I said.

Jenny was having trouble with the last name; she practiced a few times to herself, mouthing the syllables like a dying fish gasping for air. Finally she said: "Rosa Ber-to-li-ni."

"That's impossible!" said Mr. Liss, charging for Jenny Chalder's desk. When he got there he said "Let me see that," and snatched the piece of paper out of her hands. He read it over several times, flipped it over, rubbed it between his fingers, even smelled it.

The whole class waited for his judgment. One kid fell out of his desk he was leaning forward so far. Finally, quietly, he said, "It's not even your handwriting, Salvador." And then he smiled. "The cat got it right, children! The name in the phonebook is Rosa Bertolini!"

Children shot out of their desks and formed two circles: one around Mr. Liss and the phone book, where he happily showed them Rosa Bertolini's name, and another around me and Roadkill. They asked me over and over if she was really a magic cat. Over and over I said, "Yes."

That moment remains my second best childhood memory. I walked from the bus stop with Roadkill under my arm, thinking that maybe I would be a magician when I grew up. But, as I walked up the driveway to my house, I could feel that something wasn't right. My chest suddenly felt like I had swallowed a beehive. As I got closer, I thought I saw the house ... waver. Like a mirage. And then, like any good mirage, it became solid again, reasserted its reality.

There were voices coming from the house. One was Pápi's. He was shouting. Pápi never raised his voice about anything anymore. And there was someone else in the house shouting at him. In Spanish. A woman.

I walked in. There was Pápi, in the living room. "It's just a stuffed cat ..." he was saying.

But Mámi interrupted him. "¡No te atrevas hablarme en inglés!" she screamed.

Then they both saw me. They went quiet, just like they always used to when I caught them fighting.

I looked from Mámi, to Pápi, to Mámi, to Pápi. He shot me a look that said, *She's in one of her moods. Don't say anything to make her angry.*

Mámi came over to me, knelt so we were eye level, hugged and kissed me. "Ay, mi hijito," she said. "¿Cómo te fue la escuela?"

Her eyes were less green than I remembered. They were more of a hazel that went green the closer the irises got to the pupils. "Good," I said. "I did magic today."

She laughed. "Do no' tal' to jour Mámi en inglés," she said. "Tal' to her en español. ¿Hiciste magia hoy?"

"Sí."

"¿Y te fue bien?"

"Sí."

"Qué bueno," she said, and impressed another kiss on my forehead. "Pero tenemos que hablar seriamente de algo."

I didn't quite follow. My Spanish was rusty. Pápi said. "She wants to talk to you."

Mámi shot him a look that said, *I know how to talk to my own son.* Pápi put his hands up, took a step back. Mámi looked at me again, sweetly. "¿Sal, por qué estás andando con ese gato negro?"

I understood "cat" and "black" and deduced she meant Roadkill. "It's for ..." I started, but then, catching the look on her face, tried Spanish: "Es ... por ... magia."

She patted my head. "'Para.' Es *para* la magia," she corrected. "¿Pero por qué tienes que usar un gato negro? ¿No sabes que ése es símbolo del Diablo?"

I couldn't follow her. I couldn't understand my mother. I said in English "I don't know." And I added, *sotto voce,* "I can't understand you."

She looked at Pápi. This time she wasn't angry; she looked worried. "¿Qué le pasa?"

"Nada más que necesita un poco de práctica con el español, mi vida," said Pápi.

"¿Práctica?" said Mámi. She looked more confused than I did. "¿Mi hijo necesita práctica en español? Yo le hablé esta mañana, y le dije que dejara ese maldito gato aquí en la casa, y él me dijo, 'Sí Mámi' como un niño bueno, y me entendió perfectamente."

She was getting pissed again. She stood up to face Pápi, looking glorious and powerful and unmistakably alive. "Pero me desobedeció, por qué *tú* le diste permiso a traer ese gato endiablado para hacer magia negra. ¿Y ahora tú me vas a decir en cara que él no me puede entender?"

Pápi stumbled out the beginnings of a response, but she cut him off: "¡No quiero la magia negra en esta casa!"

She charged for the door to the house, then turned one more time to Pápi. "Voy a dar una vuelta por el barrio. ¡Cuando yo regreso, si ese gato no está en la basura, se va a formar el titingó!" Then she looked at me. Her face was both soft and stern; she pointed at me and said, tenderly, "El titingó." Then she walked out of the door.

The beehive in my chest stopped buzzing. I turned back to Pápi. "Pápi?" I asked.

He knelt so we were eye to eye and put a hand on my shoulder. "I don't know, Sal," he said. Then he looked past me, at the door, and started carpet-bombing the carpet with his tears. "We'll just have to wait and see."

We stood for a long time, hands on each other's shoulders, watching the door. But she never came home.

~

"Salvador, is your father okay?" asked Mrs. Dravlin. I mean, Ms.

Anbow. She had gotten divorced last year, much to the delight of the fifth-grade boys who were just coming into their first erections.

Pápi wasn't okay. The day Mámi came home for a few hours cut a permanent, diner-sized pie-slice out of his will to live. It was bad enough that Mámi's return was illogical, impossible, and, for all that, irrefutable. It was that they had fought. They had spent that last precious coda of their marriage fighting over a stupid dead cat. *My* stupid dead cat.

But I wasn't going to tell Ms. Anbow any of that. I just said to her "He's okay."

She looked at me askance. "I called to tell him that we're awarding you the Science Student of the Year Award. Again. Most parents would've been thrilled. Do you know what your father said to me?"

"No."

"He said, 'Science is just the lie of the moment. Like religion. Or astrology. Or alchemy. Right now it's science.'"

I just waited for her to continue. "Your dad has a reputation for being one of the smartest teachers in Connecticut, Sal. But this ... well, I don't know him very well, but that didn't ... that's not the sort of thing I would expect him to say." She gripped her nose, shook her head. "I'm sorry. I'm not making any sense."

I just kicked my legs and looked at her.

She came around her desk and to the chair I was sitting in, kneeling down to look at me eye to eye. Her blouse bagged; she had on a practical tan bra. "Sal, I want you to let me know if you need anything.

Sometimes it takes years to work through the grief of losing someone you love, like a mom, or a wife. Hey," she said kindly, pushing my chin up with a single finger so I would look at her eyes. "You're doing great. Your dad, too. But everyone needs a little help sometimes. I want you to let me know if there's anything you want to talk about. I know I am your principal, but I am also a trained psychologist. I can help you, if you want me to. I just want to help. Okay?"

When I went home that day, I said to Pápi, "Ms. Anbow is worried about you."

He sat on the floor, in front of his shrine to Elegua. He had set it up in the living room a few weeks after Mámi had come back—had gone—and hadn't much moved from it since. It was decorated with a red and black runner and candles and rum shots and hard brilliant candies and old fruit collapsing in on itself and a big coconut with shells for eyes and mouth. And Mámi's wedding picture, dead center.

Pápi sat in a half-lotus in front of it, dressed all in white, except for a necklace of red and black beads. He had shaved his head, his beard. He looked thinner and younger. But older too, because though he had lost weight, he still had all the skin that had bagged his fat for so many years. Now it hung off his skeleton like the wrinkly hide of a shar pei. Without turning to me, he said, "Let her worry."

I walked up behind him. There was a new addition to the shrine, next to the coconut: a painting of a young boy. Bright colors, almost psychedelic. The boy looked like he came from a couple hundred years ago. He had on a cloak and a hat with a feather in it, and he carried an empty basket and a staff with a gourd hanging off the tip. Putti flew around his head and smiled down on him.

"Who's that?" I asked.

"That's Elegua."

I pointed at the coconut. "I thought that was Elegua."

"That's Elegua too. See, when the Africans were enslaved and taken from their home countries and brought to the Caribbean to work the fields, they weren't allowed to practice Yoruba, their own religion. But they were allowed to be Christians; they could have all the Christian icons they wanted. So they practiced Yoruba by using Christian saints. All of their gods got assigned one: Chango got Santa Barbara, Oshun got Our Lady of Charity, and Elegua got that little fella: El Santo Niño de Atocha."

"So Elegua is a little boy?"

"Kind of. He is an old man with a little boy's face. That's because he is eternally young and playful. But wise, too; he is the pathfinder god, the guide to travelers. He helps you find your way when you are lost and takes care of you along the journey."

"Really? He can do that?"

Pápi looked away from the shrine, at me. Some of the old irony came back into his face and made him seem more himself. "I don't know," he said finally. "I don't know anything. Before I met your mother, back when we were in Cuba, I was a Santero. A cabeza of Elegua. But I gave it up for her. She was a Catholic and thought Santeria was all black magic. It really scared her. She equated it with witchcraft, and the Bible says witchcraft will get you a one-way ticket to hell, and then she would spend all eternity without me." He laughed. "That woman. She was so sure she was going to heaven! Well, long story short, she cried and cried until I finally gave up my religion and became a Catholic."

"We used to be Catholic," I said. I had forgotten.

He stood and went to the shrine and picked up a shot of rum and dumped it down his throat. He looked at the coconut and said, "Don't worry, I'll get you a refill."

Then he turned back to me. "When your mámi died, I thought God was dead, too. But then your mámi came back. We both saw her. She kissed us both that day, you on the forehead and me on the lips." He got on his knees in front of me, locked our eyes. "And that ruined everything. Because it's impossible. Your mámi is dead. But there she was, in our living room, kissing and fighting with us like she had never gone. It's like there's a parallel universe out there where she and you and I are still a family, with small arguments and small problems—" he was crying now "—and all the unspoken love. And only God brings people back from the dead. Only God can do magic."

"I do magic," I said quietly.

Pápi didn't hear. He took a second shot glass from the altar, but this time he poured a trickle of rum on the coconut. "Okay?" he said to the squinting Elegua. "¡Pare jodiendo entonces!" He drank the rest, and breathed through his teeth for a second, and then, still looking at the coconut, said, "I don't know what to believe anymore. So I'm going back to the start. This is where I started, as a child of Elegua. So this is where I'll begin again."

He laughed without joy. "I've forgotten almost everything I used to know about Santeria. I can't find the things I need to perform the few rituals I remember. Connecticut isn't exactly a Santeria Mecca, you know. Where the hell do you get aguardiente in Handcock? But Santeria was born of adaptation. I will do the best I can with the materials at hand. If Elegua wants to hear me, he will hear me."

We stood quietly and together studied the altar for a while. And then, pointing at El Santo Niño de Atocha, I said, "He kind of looks like me."

Pápi looked at the picture, then at me. "I guess he does, a little. Hey, you're going to be ten soon. You want me to get you an outfit like his for your birthday?"

"No!" I yelled, and laughed; Pápi laughed too, which made me feel better. That's when I knew I was on the right track. That I needed to learn everything I could about Santeria.

~

Pápi was right; Connecticut in the '80s was no Santeria Mecca. My library didn't have a single book on Santeria. They did, however, have lots of books on psychology. I found a book on grief written for the parents of grieving kids called *Child of Mourning*. It featured chapter titles like "The Maze of Grief: The Child's Journey through Suffering"; "Voicing Pain: Giving Your Child the Words He Needs to Grieve"; and, my favorite, "Telling Time: How to Align Your Adult Internal Clock with Your Child's." You see, adults think of time as linear, a one-way street with a consistent speed-limit. But not children. They think time can go forward, backward, sideways, and loop like a Hot Wheels race-car track. You need to understand how children see time to help them understand that the dead stay dead forever.

Unless the dead show up one day to tell you to get rid of your stuffed black cat.

One chapter toward the end of the book I did find useful. It was called: "Love Again: How to Bring a New Member into the Family without Destroying your Child's Trust." Apparently, it's very natural to fall in love again after your husband or wife has been dead for a long time. It's nothing to be ashamed of. Your departed loved one would want you to be happy, would want your child to grow up in a household with both a mommy and a daddy. But your child—young, ignorant animal that it is—may not understand that it's okay for you to love again, may feel that you are betraying the memory of the deceased parent. So here are several steps you can take to prepare your child to welcome a new member into the family.

But I didn't need to read the steps; I got the message. Pápi needed to fall in love again. It was natural. It was good. It would help him find his way.

Now, who would make a good wife for Pápi? A good mom to me?

Ms. Anbow handed me a thin book with a heavy green cover; on the inside flap was stamped "Property of the University of Connecticut Library System." Printed in gold lettering on the spine was *The Ebos of Santeria*. It was a typewritten manuscript that had been the Master's thesis of a student named Ines Guanagao. Recently, in a fit of nostalgia, I tried interlibrary-loaning it, but it seems to have gone missing in this timeline. I'm jealous of the Many Worlds that still have a copy. I would've loved to have Proustianly perused it again as an adult.

"It's the only thing I've been able to find so far," Ms. Anbow said back then. "The librarian from my Alma Mater said she'd keep looking for more, but she said 'Don't hold your breath.'"

"Thank you," I said. "Did you read it?"

"I flipped through it." She studied me for a moment, then asked, "Santeria is a religion?"

"Yes. It's my dad's religion."

"Okay." She seemed unconvinced. "It's just that this book looks like ... well, like a spellbook." She smiled. "You're not going to cast any bad spells on me, are you?"

I smiled back—Pápi would've known I was lying—and said, "Magic isn't real, Mrs. Dravlin."

"Ms. Anbow, Sweetheart. I'm divorced, remember?"

"Oh yeah," I said, tucking the book in my bag. "I keep forgetting."

An Ebo to Remove Evil Spirits from your House. An Ebo to Bind Good Luck to You. An Ebo to Sharpen Your Mind. An Ebo to Bring Ruin Upon Your Enemy. An Ebo to Discover Hidden Money. An Ebo to Ward Against the Evil Eye. An Ebo to Win a Case in Court. An Ebo to Make a Man Infertile. Getting closer. An Ebo to Destroy a Marriage. An Ebo to Stop a Husband from Cheating. An Ebo ... there it was. An Ebo to Attract a Lover.

Whoever Ines Guanagao was, she wrote one hell of a thesis. As a Master's student, her job wasn't to write an exhaustive book on Santeria, but it was her introduction to the thesis that gave me a functional understanding of my father's religion. Oh, so that's why Pápi wore a necklace—sorry, an ileke—of black and red beads: those were the colors of Elegua, whose name can also be spelled Elegguá or Elegba. Oh, that's why he called himself a cabeza of Elegua—when the spirit "mounted" him he became the "talking head" of the god. Aha! So that's why Mámi's picture was dead center in the altar: she was Pápi's main eggun, the pantheon of protector ancestors who basically hang out all day waiting for you to call and ask for help.

Pápi was trying to commune with Mámi, but he wasn't doing it right: at least not according to Guanagao. He shouldn't have a single altar for both Elegua and his eggun. Your eggun should have a dedicated bóveda, with a white runner, and nine glasses of cool water, and flowers, preferably white, and, sitting on the floor in front of the bóveda, a shot glass with a little clear rum and a cigar in it, and next to it a cup of black coffee, in case you poured too much rum and they get drunk and need to sober up fast.

Mámi never drank when she was alive. Had she started after death? Nothing left to lose?

There were lots of ebos for making people fall in love with you. Most of them were disgusting—even to a ten-year-old boy. Every single one in Guanagao's thesis required some mix of pubic hair or urine or poop or blood or head hair or nail clippings or some other body part from the person you wanted, and sometimes you had to throw in your own pubic hair or urine or etc. as well. And since I wouldn't be performing the ebo for myself, but on behalf of Pápi, that meant I'd have to gather gross stuff from *two* people: him and Ms. Anbow. Wasn't gonna happen. Plus, most of the ebos required other weird stuff I wasn't going to be able to find. Pápi had complained about not being able to find aguardiente, but that was nothing. Where was I supposed to get sea turtle eggs, preferably powdered, or whale oil, or smoked jutia, or amasa guapo, whatever the heck that was?

There wasn't a single love ebo in the thesis I could—or would—follow all the way through. But there were ingredients of different love ebos that I didn't mind, like cinnamon sticks and wine and hard candies and incense and Borax. So why couldn't I combine those to make my own ebo? Pápi said that Santeria was born of adaptation; if the orishas wanted to help me, they would. I just had to prove I was serious. Willing to sacrifice for the sake of my desire.

Sacrifice. According to Ines Guanagao, the orishas needed food. Blood. The sacrifice of animals is vital to the rituals of Santeria. As life leaves the sacrificed animal, it radiates outward, bathing the participants in the mystery of life, carrying them out of the bounds of normal reality and into the realm of the spirit. Minds grow sharper, senses keener. Souls awaken from their quotidian slumber and stand ready to receive the wisdom of the gods.

Guanagao's rhetoric, fantastic and sincere, utterly convinced me. My soul definitely needed to awaken from its quotidian slumber and hear the wisdom of the gods. I needed a sacrifice.

In several of the love ebos, one consistent sacrifice was the heart of a "paloma." Guanagao left the word "paloma" untranslated, so I looked it up in our Spanish/English dictionary. I found two main definitions: 1) a dove; 2) a pigeon. At first I thought the ebos probably called for dove hearts. Doves are beautiful and beloved and are symbols of peace and hope. And "dove" rhymes with "love": game, set, and match, right? But then I read in the thesis that Olodumare, the father/creator of all the orishas, didn't like animal sacrifices of any kind, and he was symbolized by a dove. You can't possibly be allowed to symbolically sacrifice the creator of the universe, right? So the paloma hearts in the ebos *must* be referring to pigeons. That made me feel better: there were always a few doves in cages in the magic store, so I had formed a bit of an attachment to them. I didn't think I could kill one, even in the name of love.

But nobody liked pigeons.

Nobody, that is, except for Handcock's resident crazy lady, whom we affectionately called Miss Pigeon. And even she only liked to eat them.

Miss Pigeon was the most efficient can-collector in town. Her shopping cart bulged with can-stuffed garbage bags so full, they made that homely cart look like a steampunk flying machine. She had further customized the cart, housing it with what looked like a pantry cupboard that had been ripped out of some country-kitsch kitchen. In it—all the kids in town had been dared at one time or another to sneak a peek—she kept a small electric deep-fryer; some staples, like corn oil and Veg-All and potted meat; extra yellow kitchen gloves (she always wore a pair, which made her look kind of like a superhero); a huge jug of Clorox; a lunchbox, square and gray; and a Cabbage Patch Doll so mangled someone should've called Children Services to put it in foster care. For her lunch she always went to the park that surrounded City Hall, where she would douse a park bench with Clorox, take a seat, and, still wearing her kitchen gloves, daintily pick at what looked like deep-fried chicken, but what any local would tell you was deep-fried pigeon.

Everybody in Handcock, CT, had received an involuntary education on how to catch, prepare, and eat a pigeon. Most members of polite society would pretend to avert their eyes, but even the most squeamish among us would pause to watch her nab one. She was a master. Her favorite hunting ground was the park, where stood the remains of a wall where, it is said, Generals Washington and Rochambeau debated the merits of attacking the English in New York.

Pigeons had since "whitewashed" that wall with their droppings. Miss Pigeon'd sidle up to the wall, where the birds stood packed together like targets at a shooting gallery. They'd hop and flap and caper in pigeony fashion as she approached, delighted to see her. She would lean against the wall, wait for just a second or two and, in one elegant motion, swipe at the wall with her Grendel-like arm, dragging whatever she caught into a sack she kept just for that purpose. Sometimes she'd catch two; most of the time she got one; every once in a while she missed. Whatever the result, afterwards she threw some bits of bread at the pigeons. They exploded into an ecstatic battle for those crusts. Then she slung the rice sack over her shoulder and headed back to her cart.

Nobody talked to her, interacted with her, or, by the way, tried to stop her. We just watched from a distance and tittered and judged. So imagine her surprise when one day, a ten-year-old boy who didn't quite look all-the-way American came up to her and asked, "What's your name?"

She stopped dead. She looked at him as if through a fog. She squinted, cogitated. And then she said, "Maggie."

"Thank you," said the little boy. Miss Pigeon immediately turned back to her cart and started pushing. The little boy ran home. He was happy. Excited. He now had the last ingredient he needed for his ebo. One that would compel Miss Pigeon to help him. One he made up himself, though it was based on many others he has read. "An Ebo to

Make Someone Help You," he would call it. He wondered if it would end up in a book someday.

An Ebo to Make Someone Help You

One iron nail

One coconut

Black, red, and yellow ribbon

Rum (aguardiente is preferred, but if you live in

    Connecticut, rum will do)

Wash the coconut with a sponge dipped in rum, asking Elegua to assist you. Heat a nail over a flame (a gas stovetop works perfectly). Drive it into the coconut, then yank it out. Pour some rum into the small hole (but not so much that your Pápi will notice you stole his rum). Tie black, red, and yellow ribbons to the nail. Push it back into the same hole in the coconut you made before. As you do, repeat seven times the name of the person you want to help you. Sleep with the coconut in your arms that night. The person will be willing to help you the following day.

Miss Pigeon—Maggie—didn't recognize me the following day. I caught up with her as she approached the pigeon wall, yelling, "Miss Maggie, Miss Maggie!" She slowly turned around and stared at me, squinting and straining her memory to figure out how this little boy had come to know her name. "Hello?" she said cautiously.

"Hello, Miss Maggie. I'm the little boy from yesterday."

"I don't remember anything," she said.

"That's okay."

She laughed. "Says you."

I held out an empty 100-pound rice sack. (Pápi always had some lying around.) "I was hoping you would do me a favor."

She stared at the rice sack and said nothing.

"I was hoping you would catch a pigeon for me."

Instantly she said, "Okay."

"Thank you. It means a lot."

"Okay."

We stood there looking at each other. Stood. There. Looking.

I said, "So should we go now?"

"Okay," said Miss Pigeon, and took the rice sack out of my hand. She trundled over to the wall, took her customary place. The pigeons danced for her. She threw her patented left hook and swept one into my bag; the pigeon pecked ineffectually at her yellow kitchen glove as it went in. For a few seconds it looked like grenades were going off in the rice sack, but soon the pigeon stopped rioting. Miss Pigeon took a crust of bread out of a pocket and threw it to the other pigeons on the wall, who fell upon it in a catastrophe of wings. Then she trundled back over to me, the sack held before in modest triumph.

"Here you go," she said, handing me the sack. After a second, she added, "You gonna eat it?"

The pigeon came to life again in the bag, but I held on firmly. "Yes. Santeros always eat their sacrifices, unless they're using it to remove a curse or an evil spirit from themselves. Then they can't eat them. But most of the time they do."

She understood nothing of what I had said, I could plainly see. Still, she said, "If you're going to eat it, make sure you deep-fry it."

"Why?"

"Because pigeons are filthy. Full of lice and disease. You got to kill the germs, okay?"

"Okay," I said. After a moment's thought, I asked, "Miss Maggie, if pigeons are so gross, why do you eat them?"

"'Cause they're free, okay? That's a whole wall of free food over there. And they taste good, once you kill the germs." Then she gave me a look that I think was meant to be motherly and said, "You're a boy. You're young. You want me to kill the pigeon for you, okay?"

"No thank you, ma'am," I said. "I have to perform the sacrifice myself, or Elegua won't help me."

Though again she didn't understand me, she said, "You're a good boy, okay? Remember to kill the germs." Without another word she turned and headed back to the wall to catch herself tomorrow's lunch. The pigeons cavorted with joy.

~

On some of the points mapped on time's grid, at least a few of the

Salvadors, marching beside me on my right and left like my reflection in a pair of opposed mirrors, must have felt a little trepidation about killing the pigeon I had in the bag. But not this Salvador. I was excited. My test ebo had worked perfectly: Miss Pigeon agreed to help me so quickly that she must have been enchanted. And that meant, even though I had no idea what I was doing, even though I had never been initiated into Santeria, the gods were on my side. They wanted to help me, had accepted the ebo I had made up on my own. Maybe Mámi, my main eggun, had helped convince them. And that led to one evitable conclusion: if the gods and my mom were willing to help me, that meant they thought I was on the right track.

Pápi was almost always home: except that day, he was running an SAT-prep seminar at Samuel Adams after school. This was my one chance to kill, eviscerate, cook, eat, and dispose of the pigeon without Pápi ever knowing. I had even bookmarked a recipe for deep-frying a pigeon in *The Joy of Cooking.* (Actually, it was a recipe for squab, but close enough: I wasn't eating it to delight my palette.) Pápi had the 1962 edition, which begins with an epigram from Goethe's *Faust* that reads: "That which thy fathers have bequeathed to thee, earn it anew if thou wouldst possess it." Yet another clear sign from the gods.

All the way home, the pigeon insisted on reminding me it was alive. It batted its wings and tossed itself around the bag and, during periods of rest, cooed plaintively. I didn't feel bad for it, exactly. But all the way home I wondered if its primitive bird brain had figured out it was going to die. That would be just like Elegua, trickster that he was—to whisper into the pigeon's ear the fate that was about to befall it, inspire fear in it, make my job that much harder.

I opened the front door, shed my bookbag in the entranceway, and trotted, the rice sack still struggling for its freedom, to the kitchen. I switched the sack to my left hand and got to work: emptied the sink of the breakfast cereal bowls; brought out the cutting board; took out Pápi's Cutco French Chef knife; decided it was too small and went to the garage and got his machete; slowly, one-handedly, washed the machete in the sink; got a bowl for the blood and the entrails and the heart; another, bigger one for the feathers. Okay. Everything was ready.

Now then. How to get the bird out of the sack. Hadn't thought of that.

Suddenly, I was terrified that it would fly out of the bag and perch somewhere where I wouldn't be able to get it. Pápi would come home and hear the pigeon cooing and then look up and see the pigeon and it was obviously my fault that it was there and how would I explain it?

I gripped the sack in both hands. With all my strength I heaved it in the air, and brought it crashing to the floor. The pigeon cried, flapped, fought for its life. I heaved it again. Again. Four, five, six times. It stopped fighting after the third, crying after the fifth. I had to be sure. Seven. Eight. Nine.

Ten.

I bent over, huffing. I hadn't noticed I'd started crying. I wanted to wipe the tears off my face, but I was afraid to release my two-handed chokehold on the neck of the sack. So I just let them fall. They beaded on the rice sack before scurrying off.

I looked at the kitchen clock—it was one of those weirdo Kit-Kat clocks with the moving eyes and tail—and watched it for two full minutes. All the while I listened. No sound came from the sack. No movement.

Slowly, cautiously, I grabbed the lips of the sack and opened its mouth a little, ready to squeeze it shut if the bird tried to escape, and peered in.

The pigeon blinked. It was alive. But it lay crumpled at the bottom of the sack. Awkwardly angled: living Cubism. I'd broken the one wing I could see and a lot of bones I couldn't. Blood pooled behind its blinking eye.

"I'm sorry," I said. I opened the sack as wide as it could go. "I'm sorry," I said, and cautiously reached into the bag. The bird seemed to watch me, but I thought with all the blood filling its eye it was probably blind. "I'm sorry," I said, and gently grasped the pigeon in both my hands. It should not have felt that soft, that cartilaginous. It did not resist. I lifted it up; the head swung loosely on its shoulder. It opened its beak in surrender, but then, slowly, willfully, closed it. "I'm sorry," I said, and carried it to the sink.

I placed it in the sink on its side as gently as I could. There was no risk of it flying away now. I put the bowl for the blood and innards in the sink next to it, brought the feather bowl a little closer to my work area. Guess I wouldn't need the cutting board after all. Or the machete.

I took a breath. *It's okay*, I thought. *Just stay calm and work fast.*

I clutched the knife in my right hand, held the pigeon steady in my left. Should I cut off its head first, put it out of its misery? I was afraid I would do it wrong, that I would cut indecisively and have to hack at the neck, torturing the bird even more. I was desperate to kill it mercifully, quickly. With my left hand I lifted its useless wing. With my right I guided the knifepoint to where I thought its heart was. "I'm sorry," I said. "I honor your sacrifice. Thank you." Then as hard as I could I pushed the knife all the way through the bird. My brain burst into a swarm of bees. The knifepoint gouged the sink's porcelain.

The front door opened. Pápi. Home early. The pigeon lay dead in the sink, transfixed by the knife still in my hand. I looked around wildly, sought any means of escape, but it was as if my fingers were glued to the knife. I couldn't let go.

Wait. No. I could let go. I just didn't want to. I wanted to be punished for what I had done. I took a breath and faced the kitchen's swinging doors.

Mámi shouldered her way into the kitchen, struggling with three paper bags overflowing with groceries. She couldn't see me over the bags. "Sal, I'm home!" she yelled, loud enough for me to hear her in any room of the house. In English.

"Hi, Mámi?" I asked.

"¡Oh! ¿Jou're in here?" She laughed. "¡Bueno, no te queda parado cómo un bobo! Come hel' jour Mámi with these bags." But she was already putting them down on the kitchen table. "¡Tonigh' we're goin' to have a feas'! I goin' to ma'e jour favorite. ¡Boliche! I was at the estore, and I saw ... ¿Qué te pasa?"

She stopped dead, stared at me, her eyes following my arm, to the hand, to the knifegrip. I stared back. Then I started to cry.

"¿Qué te pasa?" she repeated, terrified, running over. She looked in the sink.

Covered her mouth. Screamed into her hands.

"¿Qué hiciste?, Sal?" She yelled. She started crying too. "Bendito sea Dios. ¿Qué hiciste?"

I started to respond through my bawling, but Mámi slapped me. I instantly tasted blood, stopped crying. She slapped me again. "¡Dime que diablera hiciste aquí!"

Oh yeah. I'd forgotten Mámi was a hitter. She took off a sneaker and proceeded to give me the walloping of my life.

It was the happiest moment of my childhood.

~

When Mámi disappeared again, slipped off the tightrope of my timeline and tumbled into another, I knew I had to look for conclusive evidence to prove to Pápi she had returned. And of course I found none: time retroactively righted itself the moment she vanished. The only thing it left were the marks she left on me. Shoe-welts on my back and legs. The cut she slapped into my lip.

Nevertheless, when Pápi got home, I told him everything: I showed him *The Ebos of Santeria* and described my encounter with Ms. Pigeon and showed him the pigeon I sacrificed, still in the sink, and pointed to my lip. "Mámi did this," I said.

"Did you get in a fight at school?" he asked.

"No. I told you what happened."

He picked up The Ebos of Santeria. "This book told you to kill a pigeon?"

"No. Not exactly. I made up my own ebo. But I used it as a guide."

"Where'd you get it?"

"Ms. Anbow."

"Your assistant principal?"

"Yes."

Pápi called information and got her number and even paid the extra 25 cents to put him through immediately. "Ms. Anbow? This is Augustín Vedón, Salvador Vidón's father. I'm sorry to bother you at home, but we need to talk. Now. In person. Would you mind if we went to your house?" He looked at the sink. "I'd invite you here, but my house is a little messy right now."

~

I don't know exactly how long I spent kneeling on that Cal Tech sidewalk speaking cooingly to the pigeon I'd almost punted. I didn't stop until my cell interrupted my reverie. Caller ID showed the number. Home.

I flipped it open and said "Hi, Mom and/or Dad."

"It's both of us," said Mrs. Dravlin. I mean Ms. Anbow. I mean Mom.

"We heard you on the radio," said Pápi, his voice younger than it had been for the span of years when he'd been unmarried.

"How'd I sound?" I asked. Fishing for compliments like a ten-year-old.

As always, Mom obliged. "Like a genius," she said.

And, as always, Pápi said, "Well...." He made that word four syllables long.

"Oh, don't start, Auggie. He sounded brilliant, and you know it."

"Of course he did. But that NPR reporter: what an idiot! Couldn't they find someone who at least knew the first thing about quantum physics?"

"No, they couldn't, because nobody knows the first thing about quantum physics. Except maybe Elegua." Suddenly inspired, Mom added, "Hey Sal, you know what would make this moment perfect?"

"What?"

"Your mámi."

"Don't say that," I kneejerked. "You're my mother."

"Oh, don't be so sentimental. I know that. I'm just saying it'd be nice if Alma were here to see this. Don't you think, Auggie?"

Pápi went quiet; we listened to him think. Then he said, "Well, sure. If only that were possible."

"You know what," Mom said, startlingly chipper. "I forgot I need to pick up some things for dinner tonight. I need to run out of the store."

And then, her voice devoid of connotation, the way only psychologists master, she said, "You boys be good."

"Love you Mom," I said. I heard her smile before she hung up.

Pápi and I waited until she shut the front door behind her. Then Pápi said, "Now all we need is a pigeon."

"No worries, Pápi." I held out my hand, and the pigeon I'd almost kicked trundled toward it happily, as if it were as pleased by this serendipity as I was. "I've got one right here."

Ashé O.

Acknowledgements

I recently read an article that called for the end of acknowledgement pages. They all say the same thing, we don't know any of the people the author's referring to, it's masturbatory modestbragging, etc.

What a bunch of comemierdura. It's not only ungracious, but straight-up inaccurate. Writers gleefully steal from the people they know, the art they love, the ideas that life decides to thrust in their way. They foist their raw, flawful pages onto their beta readers, believing—utterly deluded, every time!—that every word is perfect as-is. They choose what to use and what to scuttle, finally, and there's an art to that, sure: but at the end of the day fiction is a debate that the writer chooses to end prematurely. The hope is there's enough left in the prose to be interesting.

Let us begin, then, as writers always should: with their publishers. Bill Campbell, publisher of Rosarium, Milhuevos ain't got nothing on you, brother. Your whole press is about speaking truth to power with a smile on your face. Thank you for your work, and thank you for my book.

Bizhan Khodabandeh created the amazing cover for the book, which I love with a relentless passion.

Without my family I have no stories, no language, no desire to speak. Mámi, Pápi, Maria and Holmes, Jesse, Bárbii, abuelos y abuelas, tíos, tías, sobrinos/as y todos: thank you for my me.

I was a member of the SFF writers' group Tabula Rasa for two years, and in that time, Barbara Krasnoff, Robert Howe, Terrence Taylor, Richard Bowes, Daniel José Older, and Jon Armstrong tumbled and polished many of these stories and helped professionalize me. I want to go forward giving to other writers as generously as you have given to me.

To the Clarks—Gloria, Rick, Emily, Alanna, Maria and Isaac—you were a second family and supported me in every way a writer could ask for. Thank you forever. To Liz Clark I especially owe a debt I can never repay.

Cynthia Hawkins and Margaret Hiebert have read every word of every story I've written, often on unforgivably short notice. I have never laughed so hard while getting my ass kicked. Whatever I have is yours, my heart-friends.

Delia Sherman and Christopher Barzak published the title story of this collection in *Interfictions II*; that story is ground zero for more or less all the good fortune I have had as a writer (and a person) since. And Delia and her wife, the inimitable Ellen Kushner, have become both aspirational ideals of how to be an artist in the world and two of my closest friends. I am your most obedient servant.

The long list of intelligent and generous folks who critiqued stories and/or provided invaluable support for the writing of these stories include: Joe Bisz, Ava Chin, Kelly Cogswell, Sarah Cortez, Andy Cox, Amanda DeBonis, Joshua DeBonis, Jeffrey Ford, Jim Freund,

Matthew David Goodwin, Kay Holt, Chris Kreuter, Bart Leib, Richie Narvaez, Ekaterina Sedia, Diane Simmons, Sergio Troncoso, and Erin Underwood. I've spent a lovely, heartening time recalling just how many artistically astute people have helped save my stories from me. My thanks always.

Toward the end of putting together the final manuscript, C. S. E. Cooney read or heard aloud every word and caught errors and infelicities I seemed hellbent on including. What an ideal audience you were, Claire. Are.

To all of you, and to anyone I have overlooked: everything I have to offer is better for your intervention. My endless, endless gratitude.

About the Author

Carlos Hernandez is the author of over 30 works of fiction, poetry, prose, and drama. By day, he is an Associate Professor at the City University of New York, where he teaches English courses at BMCC and is a member of the doctoral faculty at The CUNY Graduate Center. Carlos is also a game designer, currently serving as lead writer on *Meriwether*, a CRPG about the Lewis and Clark expedition. He lives in Queens, which is most famous for not being Brooklyn.

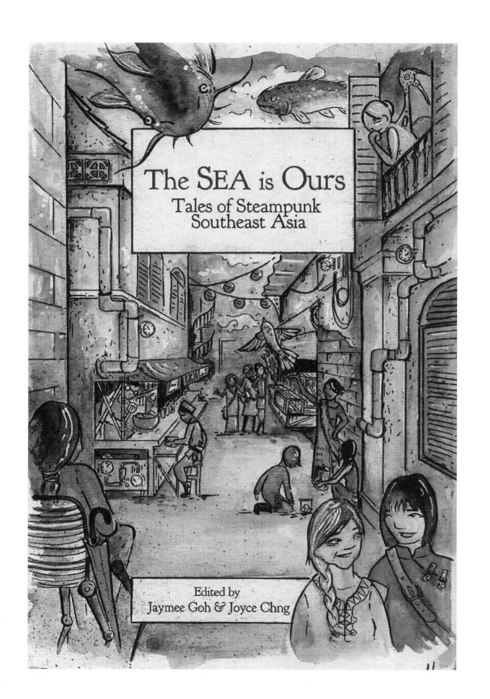

The SEA is Ours

Tales of Steampunk
Southeast Asia

Edited by
Jaymee Goh & Joyce Chng

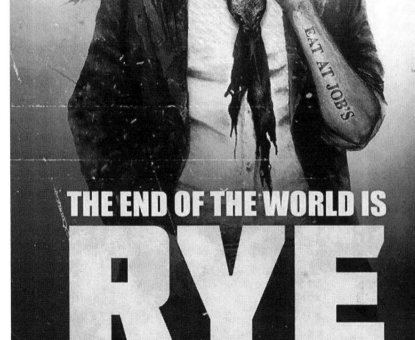

THE END OF THE WORLD IS
RYE

BRETT COTTRELL

Coming Soon ...